Medieval Runaway Wives
Song of the Heart
A Promise of Tomorrow
Destined for Love

Knights of Honor Series
Word of Honor
Marked by Honor
Code of Honor
Journey to Honor
Heart of Honor
Bold in Honor
Love and Honor
Gift of Honor
Path to Honor
Return to Honor

DISCOURAGING THE DUKE

Dukes Done Wrong
Book 1

Alexa Aston

ARE YOU SIGNED UP FOR DRAGONBLADE'S BLOG?

You'll get the latest news and information on exclusive giveaways, exclusive excerpts, coming releases, sales, free books, cover reveals and more.

Check out our complete list of authors, too!

No spam, no junk. That's a promise!

Sign Up Here

www.dragonbladepublishing.com

Dearest Reader;

Thank you for your support of a small press. At Dragonblade Publishing, we strive to bring you the highest quality Historical Romance from the some of the best authors in the business. Without your support, there is no 'us', so we sincerely hope you adore these stories and find some new favorite authors along the way.

Happy Reading!

CEO, Dragonblade Publishing

CHAPTER ONE

Wildwood, Kent—August 1796

MILES NOTLEY AWOKE and immediately grinned.

Today, he was ten years of age. He would be in double digits the rest of his life, unless he made it to the ripe old age of one hundred years. He didn't know anyone who had ever lived that long. Not anyone of his acquaintance, much less any figure mentioned in the history books he loved. Maybe he would do the impossible and live to be in triple digits.

His grinned widened. That would irritate Ralph to no end. One of Miles' favorite things in life was annoying his older brother, who never let anyone forget that he was the heir apparent in the family. Ralph constantly mentioned how he would one day be the Duke of Winslow and his two younger brothers would be no ones. It didn't bother Miles in the least. He didn't want to be a duke. Especially if it meant being anything like his father. Winslow barely acknowledged Miles' presence. Sometimes, he thought his father hadn't a clue as to what his two younger sons were called. The duke was all about his heir and didn't hide his favoritism.

It hurt Tony. He was only six and sensitive to criticism. Miles had made it his mission in life to protect Tony from Ralph, who could be cruel in both actions and words. Ralph would do something careless and blame the outcome on Miles or Tony, knowing they would be punished for his misdeed. Miles had taken many a thrashing which he didn't deserve, all to protect the youngest Notley.

It didn't matter. Neither of them cared for Ralph and tried to have as little as possible to do with the current marquess and future duke. If they weren't family, Miles knew he would never wish to be friends with Ralph, who was lazy and spiteful. When Miles had gone away to school, it was expected that Ralph would look out for his younger brother, who had been sent to the same school all Notley boys attended.

The opposite had happened.

Miles had been bullied by several older boys, all at Ralph's urging. He had learned to take whatever was doled out to him that first year. By the next school year—thanks to a painful growth spurt—Miles stood as tall as Ralph, who was three years his senior. He had laid a bully flat the first day of that second year and since then, Ralph and his crowd had given Miles a large berth. With Tony turning seven in two weeks, he would also go off to school with his older brothers. Miles intended to see his baby brother protected from Ralph and anyone else who might do Tony harm.

He rose and went to the window. The lawn of Wildwood looked like a magnificent green carpet rolled out as far as the eye could see. He wondered how he would spend his birthday. Probably riding with Tony. They could also go swimming in the nearby lake this afternoon. He knew not to expect any presents, however. Neither parent ever remembered his birthday. He told himself it didn't matter when he knew that it did. When he was grown up and had children, he promised to always remember their birthdays. He would lavish gifts upon them, toy soldiers for the boys and dolls for the girls. He would take them somewhere special on that day and tell them how much he loved them.

And he would never let his parents see them. Ever. Miles swore never to expose them to his father's cruelty and his mother's indifference. He hoped the woman he wed would have nice parents. They would be his children's grandparents, not the Duke and Duchess of Winslow. As far as Miles was concerned, the two of them could fawn over Ralph as much as they wanted. He and Tony would make separate lives, far away from the pair.

Leaving the window, he washed and changed into his clothes for the day. Heading to the schoolroom, he found Tony already there. A maid entered, bringing in a tray, and the boys breakfasted in peace, thanks to Ralph dining downstairs with their father. That had started a few weeks ago when Ralph turned thirteen. The duke had said Ralph was becoming a man and would take all his meals downstairs. Ralph had taunted his younger brothers, laughing at how privileged he now was. Miles and Tony had merely shrugged and proceeded to enjoy their meals for the first time in their lives, without Ralph's constant taunting and badgering.

"Are you going to have a cake?" Tony asked. "For your birthday?"

"Yes. Cook is making a special one for me," he shared with his little brother. "She remembers every year."

Left unsaid was how their parents would ignore Miles' special day.

Tony looked at Miles with undisguised devotion. "Do you feel older, being ten? That's such a long way off," he said forlornly.

"I don't feel a bit different than when I was nine. But I plan to act as if I do."

Tony's eyes widened. "Do you mean to say that to Ralph?" he asked anxiously.

"I may," he said.

"You know he doesn't like you, Miles. Or me," Tony said mournfully.

"Well, we don't like him either, do we?"

"No," Tony said resolutely. "We don't. He's mean to us. He broke a vase yesterday and told a maid I did it."

"Were you punished?" Miles asked quickly. "Why didn't you

tell me about it?"

Tony shrugged. "You always stand up for me. I wanted to take the punishment."

"You shouldn't do that, especially when you hadn't done anything wrong."

"I wasn't punished," his brother said. "Once Ralph left, the maid swept up the pieces and told me she would throw them away. She promised not to tell anyone." Tony bit his lip. "I think she knew I hadn't broken it."

Miles was certain the servants knew exactly what Ralph was like and appreciated that Tony hadn't been blamed for the broken vase. He only hoped Ralph wouldn't discover what had occurred. If he did, his brother would seek the maid out and blame her for the breakage and demand that she lose her position. It had happened before.

"Rub your bottom when you next see Ralph," he suggested. "Wince a little as if you're in pain. Make him think you're so sore you can't sit down"

Tony's eyes lit up. "You want me to act as if I were punished?"

"Yes. Can you do that?"

His brother nodded solemnly.

"Good. Finish your breakfast. We'll go riding after if you'd like."

Tony shoved the rest of his food into his mouth and chewed quickly. Miles knew how much Tony enjoyed riding because he also enjoyed it more than any other activity. Being on a horse meant freedom. Being away from the house. Away from Ralph, who only tolerated riding and rarely chose to climb atop a horse.

The boys went to the stables, where a groom saddled ponies for both of them and then accompanied them across the estate. They rode for almost two hours, waving at tenants and taking a break to walk their horses through the forest so they could water them at a nearby stream.

When they returned to the house, Ralph was waiting for

them, his arms crossed over his chest and a surly look upon his face. He seemed to resent any fun his brothers had, especially if they did so together, even though he never chose to spend time with them himself.

"Father wants to see you in his study," he told them.

"Why?" asked a panic-stricken Tony, who looked to Miles for reassurance.

Miles couldn't help but wonder if this was in regard to the broken vase. When Tony started to speak, Miles shook his head subtly, causing his brother to clamp his lips together.

"Come with me," Ralph insisted, leading the way through the kitchens.

As they passed Cook, she gave him a conspiratorial smile and pointed. His eyes flicked to the tall cake, already iced and sitting on a nearby table. His mouth watered at its sight. He grinned at her and hurried to catch up with Ralph, Tony trailing behind him.

When they reached the study, Ralph ushered them inside and closed the door, throwing the lock. The duke wasn't present. A sick feeling coursed through Miles. If Winslow had been waiting and grew tired, whatever punishment that would be administered would be horrible.

He turned to Tony and whispered, "Rub your arse."

Tony, whose mouth trembled, did as he was told. Miles saw the gleam of pleasure light Ralph's eyes.

"Sore today, little brother?" Ralph taunted, rushing over and slapping Tony's arse hard, so hard the boy cried out.

Miles pushed Ralph away. "Leave him alone," he said, staring directly into Ralph's eyes.

The two held their gazes and then Ralph looked away. He shuffled off but Miles knew Ralph wouldn't stay intimidated for long.

Ralph went to the desk and opened the bottom drawer on the right side. He lifted a pistol and aimed it at Miles.

"What are you doing?" he hissed at his older brother, his insides going cold at the sight of a weapon being pointed at him.

"Just playing," Ralph said, moving his hand and pointing it at Tony.

Immediately, Tony teared up. Fat tears coursed down his cheeks.

"You're such a baby," Ralph taunted. "You better be ready when you get to school next month. The boys will really have it out for you."

"Leave him alone," Miles warned as Tony began to visibly shake.

"Or what?" Ralph said, pointing the pistol back at Miles. "What will you do about it?"

"I will protect him—as you should. He's your brother, Ralph. You shouldn't bully him or have your friends do so. Like they did to me," he added.

Ralph puffed up with importance. "I am a marquess. I will be the Duke of Winslow someday. You can't tell me what to do."

He shook his head. "Don't you ever get tired of saying that? We know you are the heir to the dukedom, Ralph. Tony and I don't care. It's yours and we don't want it."

"Of course you do. Everyone wants to be a duke. Only those good enough get to be one," Ralph said smugly.

"If being good is what is required, then you will never be Winslow," Miles declared, his temper flaring. "A duke is one of the highest peers in the land. He has great responsibility to his family and his tenants. You are a selfish dolt who can barely ride a horse. You are cruel and wicked. You should be glad you are the firstborn Notley and will inherit everything because if you truly had to be good to become the Duke of Winslow, you never would."

"How dare you!" Ralph shouted. "You are a conceited, arrogant little nobody. You'll never be anyone. I'll see to that."

"No, you won't," Miles said, reining in his anger. "I am a second son. I will go into the army and fight for king and country. If I am lucky, I will be sent halfway across the world to India. Then I'll never have to lay eyes on you again. Ever."

Ralph's face grew red with rage and Miles figured his brother had never thought that both his brothers wouldn't be around to be kicked like stray dogs once they reached manhood.

"You'll go into the army if I say you can," Ralph said stubbornly.

Miles shook his head. "That's not how it works. Second sons are meant for the military. Third sons become clergymen."

"I'll be a vicar?" Tony piped up.

He looked to Tony. "Yes, if you'd like to do so."

His little brother nodded enthusiastically. "I would, Miles. I like the smell of a church. And I would get to marry people and christen babies. That would be fun."

"You will be good at," Miles said. "I know you would take good care of your parishioners."

"No," Ralph growled. "I won't allow it. Father won't allow it. When I am Winslow, you will work for me. You will be a steward at Wildwood and do everything I say, Miles."

He smirked. "I will be doing whatever my commanding officer says, Ralph. You won't have any part in my life. You won't have me to blame when you are reckless or thoughtless. You will have to stand on your own two feet. Yes, people will fawn over you and tell you what you want to hear, merely because you are a duke.

"But I won't be one of them."

"I hate you!" declared Ralph. "The both of you."

"Hate us all you like," Miles said casually. "We are indifferent to you. You think we are nobodies?" He snorted. "Well, you are no one to us."

Ralph's nostrils flared. "I will make Tony's life miserable once we're at school. You won't always be around to protect him. I will see that he becomes a blubbering mess."

Hate reared within Miles. "Don't threaten him," he warned. "Tony is your brother. He is young and innocent."

Ralph smiled triumphantly. "I can get to you through him."

"I'll tell Father," Miles blurted out, instantly regretting his words. "He won't let you be cruel to Tony."

"Will you? Would he even believe you?" Ralph asked softly. "Father only loves me. He doesn't care one whit about the two of you. I am his heir. I am the marquess."

"You are so full of yourself," he said. "You are a terrible person, Ralph, and you'll make for a terrible duke. No one will like you. They will smile to your face and laugh at you behind your back—the way all the boys at school do now."

"They do not!" roared Ralph. "Take it back."

"I will not. Because it's true."

Ralph swung the pistol up and aimed it at Miles. He froze. The murderous look in his brother's eyes told him that Ralph was going to pull the trigger.

Then courage flooded him. "Go ahead," he said. "I dare you."

"They won't send a marquess to the gallows. I am your better and always will be."

As Miles stood defiantly, he steeled himself for the bullet. As Ralph fired, a blur went past him. He heard a grunt.

And then Tony fell to the ground before him.

He dropped to his knees. "No," he whispered.

Miles scooped up his brother's shoulders and placed Tony's head in his lap. Blood bubbled from the young boy's lips as a crimson stain spread across his thin chest.

He glanced to Ralph. "Get help. Now."

Looking back to Tony, he cooed, "You'll be fine, little brother."

Tony swallowed hard. "I . . . wanted to . . . save you."

"You did," he assured Tony. "You were very brave."

"It hurts."

"I know it does," he murmured, brushing Tony's hair from his brow. "Not for long. The doctor will come. He'll make it feel better."

Tony's eyes grew glassy. Miles heard a pounding and someone shouting for the door to be opened.

"*You* must take the blame," Ralph said, coming close and

staring down as the life ebbed from the youngest Notley. "I am going to be the duke. You're just a second son."

Miles watched as the light faded from Tony's eyes. His shudders ceased. He kissed his little brother's brow as the pounded continued.

Calmly, he looked up at Ralph. "I won't. For once, you will have to live with the consequences."

Ralph's mouth trembled as he turned and numbly walked to the door, the muffled shouts growing in volume as fists beat against it. Miles focused his attention on the dead brother cradled in his arms. He thought quickly. He could tell on Ralph, ruining his life, but would Tony want that? His sweet brother had given his life to protect Miles. His gut told him Tony wouldn't want Ralph to suffer. Tony had always been more forgiving, which is why he would have made for an excellent vicar. As it was, Ralph would always have to live with the fact that he had shot his brother.

No, he would tell them it was an accident. Spare Ralph from the world knowing that he shot and killed his own brother.

He glanced to the door and saw Ralph unlock it. It was immediately pushed back. The Duke of Winslow stormed into the room.

"What in God's name . . ." His voice trailed off as he caught sight of Miles holding an unmoving Tony.

Their mother rushed in and came to a halt at the sight. Her piercing shrieks nearly burst Miles' eardrums.

"It was an accident," he said as Winslow slowly approached.

Before he could say another word, Ralph shouted, "Miles shot Tony!"

His eyes cut to his surviving brother. "No, I didn't. You shot him. You know you did. But it was an accident," he said calmly.

By now, the duchess had fallen to her knees. She yanked Tony from Miles' embrace and held him to her chest, blood smearing her pearl gray gown.

"My boy. My sweet, sweet boy," she moaned, rocking back

and forth with the dead boy as she sobbed.

Tony had always been her favorite of the three of them, just as Ralph had always been favored by the duke, leaving Miles out in the cold.

His father strode across the room and jerked Miles to his feet. "How could you?" he asked harshly. "Blame your brother for . . . *this.*"

Anger flared within him. "I didn't kill Tony," he said.

Winslow released him, only to backhand him so hard that it knocked Miles to the ground. His cheek screamed in pain. He lifted his hand to it and felt warm blood, realizing his father's signet ring had sliced open his flesh. Instantly, he knew the injury would leave a scar—a reminder of the day his brother died.

"I didn't shoot Tony," he said stubbornly.

Winslow struck him again, this time with his fist. Blood spurted from Miles' nose as he stumbled backward, bumping into a chair.

The duke grabbed him by the shoulders, his fingers digging into Miles' flesh.

"You did this," he insisted. "You killed my son. The least you could do is be a man and accept the blame."

Ralph stepped close. "No, Father, I am the one to blame."

Relief swept through him. Finally, Ralph would straighten things out.

"I shouldn't have taken the pistol," Ralph continued. "If I hadn't, then Miles never would have grabbed it from my hand." He hung his head, his gaze falling to the ground. "I am the one responsible for Tony's death."

The duke shoved Miles away and put comforting arms about his heir. "No, my dear boy. You aren't responsible for this reprehensible act. I won't hear of it."

Shock filled him. Ralph wasn't owning up to his actions. Nothing had changed. Only this time, Miles would be blamed for the death of his beloved brother.

"I did not kill my brother," he insisted.

Winslow glared at him, hate filling his dark eyes. "Deny it all you want. You are a monster. You have killed my boy and tried to blame my heir for your carelessness."

The duchess wailed loudly and collapsed. Her maid and a footman helped her to her feet and led her from the room.

The butler stepped forward. "What shall I do, Your Grace? Send for the authorities? The doctor?"

"Her Grace certainly needs a physician. As for the magistrate?" The duke gave Miles a withering look. "Ask him to come at once, Sevill." He looked at the remaining servants hovering in the doorway. "This was an accident. Miles was playing with my gun and it went off, tragically killing Anthony. Is that understood?"

The servants nodded collectively and quickly vanished. Only the butler remained.

"Send for both men now."

"Of course, Your Grace."

Winslow turned to Miles. "As for you? You are to be locked in your room and remain there until I see fit for you to leave." He glanced to the butler. "Escort the boy there now. Place a footman outside so he doesn't attempt to leave. Bread and water only. Once a day."

"Yes, Your Grace."

Sevill's eyes narrowed. "Come along, Lord Miles," he ordered brusquely.

He ignored the instructions and went to Tony's body. Pulling his brother up, he kissed his brow and then lowered him to the ground again.

As he passed Ralph, he noted the look of triumph the marquess wore. He brushed past Ralph, slamming his shoulder into Ralph, who hissed as a snake.

"Murderer," his brother said, so softly that no one else heard.

Miles stormed from the room and raced up the stairs, running down the corridor and slamming his door. He threw himself onto his bed and began to sob.

Tony was gone. He was never coming back.

And the world would think Miles had killed him.

CHAPTER TWO

September

M ILES STARED MOROSELY out the window. He had been banished to his room for the past three weeks. The only time he had been allowed to leave had been to attend Tony's funeral. Surprisingly, his brother had fought for him to do so, according to the duke. Winslow had come to Miles' room and told him that Ralph had insisted Miles come to the service and burial. That Ralph wanted people to see how contrite Miles was for his careless action that ended a life.

He swallowed hard, thinking of the coffin standing at the front of the church and Tony inside it. Sweet, happy Tony. He would never go away to school. Make friends. Attend university. Become a vicar. Have a family. All that had ended with his brother's brave, foolish leap, an act of love and protection. Miles knew he should have been the one laid to rest, buried six feet under in the graveyard standing beside the church.

Of course, he had been aware of the whispers inside the church. The looks as he stood at Tony's grave. For the rest of his life, Miles would be blamed for the death of his beloved younger brother. Perhaps that was why Ralph had wanted him to be present at the funeral, to put the focus on the one who supposedly killed Tony.

Miles couldn't imagine the guilt Ralph now lived with, every morning opening his eyes and remembering he was the one who had shot and killed his own brother. Knowing Ralph, though, Miles supposed that his surviving brother had convinced himself that it was Miles who had pulled the trigger that day. Ralph had spent no time at all with Tony and probably didn't even miss the boy.

Miles missed his baby brother every day.

He had kept track of the days while he remained in solitary. Once a day, a footman unlocked the door and delivered a tray with bread and water on it and collected Miles' chamber pot. After a few days, the tray came with a cloth draped atop it. Once removed, he had found more than bread and water. Sometimes, a cold, roasted chicken came. Other times, a few vegetables or a fruit tart. He suspected it was Cook who prepared the tray and handed it off to a footman, deliberately hiding its contents. Gratitude filled Miles every time the tray arrived. He had never been so hungry in his life, receiving only bread early each morning during those early days. He worried that Cook might be found out and lose her position and prayed each night that wouldn't occur.

Hearing footsteps outside his door, he turned from the window. Their butler entered without knocking, motioning to servants as he ushered them inside. Two men carried a copper tub, which they placed in the center of the room. Other servants followed with buckets of steaming water, pouring them into the tub. The housekeeper appeared carrying a bath sheet and soap. She set them down, giving him a sympathetic look.

"I'm to gather up your clothing, Lord Miles," she said. "I will see that it is laundered for you."

"Everything's over here," he told her.

He had changed clothes daily but had run out of fresh ones and started repeating the outfits. He spread them out each day to air, not having had any way to wash them.

Sevill frowned at him. "You are to scrub yourself from head to toe. I will return in an hour and take you to see His Grace and the marquess."

"His lordship will need fresh clothes in order to meet with His Grace," the housekeeper pointed out to the butler.

"Bring him something Lord Ralph has outgrown," the man sniffed. With that, Sevill left the room.

The housekeeper gathered up Miles' things. "I'll be back soon with something you can change into, my lord."

"Thank you," he said, his voice breaking at the simple show of kindness.

Quickly, Miles stripped off his clothes once the door closed. He sank into the water, sighing. He swore to never avoid a bath again as he dunked his head under the water and then lathered it up.

A footman came in, bearing fresh clothes. He placed them on the bed.

"Thank you, Thomas," Miles said.

The servant quietly said, "We all know you ain't done nothing wrong, Lord Miles. It's that other one that causes all the mischief."

His eyes widened. "Don't say that aloud," he warned. "You don't want to be booted from Wildwood without references."

Thomas grinned cheekily. "Bide your time, my lord. You'll get what you deserve. We're all for you." He exited the bedchamber.

The footman had no way of knowing just how much Miles needed to hear those words of encouragement. His spirits bolstered, he finished bathing and rinsed himself, drying off and dressing in clothes slightly too small for him. Ralph's hand-me-downs made it obvious Miles had passed him physically. The trousers struck just above his ankles. The shirt's sleeves were a tad short, exposing his wrists. He tried shrugging into the coat but it was impossible, its shoulders far too narrow. At least the clothing was clean. He was finally clean. As he combed through his wet hair, smoothing it down, he steeled himself for the encounter with the duke and Ralph.

As expected, Sevill arrived and silently escorted Miles to the library. He wondered if the duke would ever enter his study again after what had occurred there.

When he entered the room, his father and brother were seated side by side. The duke gestured to the chair opposite them. As he sat, Miles thought how much the two were alike. Their posture. Their facial features. Their disapproving looks.

"We are here to discuss your education," Winslow began.

Miles knew in two days he and Ralph should be leaving for school. Suddenly, apprehension filled him. He wondered what Ralph would tell his friends about Tony's death. Officially, it had been ruled an accident by the local magistrate but he knew his brother would insinuate otherwise. He could see a year of brawling ahead of him as he fought off the boys Ralph would set upon him. Because of that, the boys his own age would probably avoid him, not wishing to be caught in the middle of the trouble.

"You won't be returning to school with me," Ralph added, a smug look upon his face.

Surprise filled him. "What?"

"I can't have you anywhere near your brother," the duke said pompously. "It would reflect poorly upon Ralph. As my heir and the future Duke of Winslow, it won't do to have you taint his reputation in any way."

"Where am I to go?" Miles asked, stunned by this revelation.

"Father has found just the place for you," Ralph said. "A school just outside of Westerham, on the border of Surrey and Kent. Turner Academy. It is for troubled youth who are sons of the *ton*. You will be with others like you. An odd mix of fellows who for one reason or another don't fit into their families anymore."

His fists balled and he forced himself to relax them. He kept a bland look on his face. He didn't want to go to this place—but he most certainly didn't want his brother to know this.

"When do I leave?"

"In the morning," his father said. "This is goodbye, Miles.

Ralph and I will be preparing for his departure the day after."

"Mother doesn't want to see you," Ralph added, a sly grin on his face. "You know Tony was always her favorite. She despises you, you know. Never wants to see you again."

"It will be hard for her to avoid me during holidays. Unless I am to remain in my room the entire time."

"You will spend your holidays and breaks at your new school," Winslow said smoothly.

Stunned, he asked, "For . . . how long?"

"Permanently," the duke snapped. He rose and hovered over Miles. "As far as I am concerned, you are no longer a part of this family. I will do my duty and see you educated but this is the last time we will ever speak in person. I cannot have you influencing your brother with your wicked ways."

"I am to never return?" he asked, feeling tears fill his eyes as his father took a seat again.

"That's right," Ralph said, superiority oozing from him. "You will reside at Turner Academy until you graduate."

"And then?" he asked, helplessness washing over him at the thought of never returning to his home. Never riding his horse again. Never visiting Tony's grave.

The duke frowned, as if he hadn't thought that far ahead. "I suppose I will send you to university. I can't have my peers think less of me. There will be enough gossip as it is about you and the family." He paused, mulling it over. "Yes, you will go to university and then into the army as planned. My solicitor will purchase the commission for you. The discipline the military brings will be good for you."

Ralph looked alarmed by the turn of events. "Shouldn't Miles come home after university, Father?"

He remembered how badly Ralph wanted to have him under his thumb and decided to speak up, knowing he could never serve under his brother.

"No, Father is right. I should enter the army. A lifetime in the military, away from England and our family, is what I deserve. I will do my penance and serve king and country at the same time." Miles looked to the duke. "Thank you, Father. You are right to keep me away from Wildwood."

"Good," the duke said, nodding sagely. "Perhaps there is hope for you after all." He rose. "Come along, my boy. Your mother is waiting for us. We're to call upon Lord Hamilton."

Without a backward glance, the two exited the room.

Miles glanced around, knowing he would never see this—or any room—at Wildwood after his departure tomorrow. He was being sent into exile.

Standing, he crossed the room and plucked his favorite book from a shelf. No one would miss it. His father barely skimmed the newspapers and Ralph never picked up a book. Miles knew it would bring him comfort in the days and weeks ahead. The one familiar thing from home.

With a heavy heart, he returned to his room and spent his last night in his bed.

MILES TAMPED DOWN the trepidation inside him as the carriage pulled up to the imposing stone edifice. No sign marked that the building was, in fact, a school for troublemakers. He had no idea what class of boys he might encounter and doubted the curriculum would be as rigorous as what he was used to. The boys in attendance at Turner Academy might very well have committed heinous crimes. Murder. Arson. As sons of the nobility, though, they were above the law. He wondered if this was the only place difficult boys were sent or if other schools such as this existed. While Miles wanted to believe he could take care of himself, he had no idea who he would encounter behind these doors.

The carriage slowed and came to a halt. No one from Wildwood had accompanied him. He had been sent with only a driver, who gave him a pitying look as he exited the vehicle. He mustered a smile and waved to the driver as someone came out the front door of the academy.

"Greetings!" he proclaimed. "I am Mr. Smythe. Who might you be, young man?"

He cleared his throat. "Lord Miles Notley."

"I see. Well, my lord, titles aren't recognized here at Turner Academy. You will be Mr. Miles to me and your instructors."

He nodded, not knowing how to respond. He had been Lord Miles his entire life, the son of a duke. Despite not being the firstborn son, he had been made aware of his rank in society at a young age. Obviously, the school had put into place certain rules and there was nothing he could do about it. He grinned, thinking how put out Ralph would have been not to be acknowledged as a marquess by the staff and servants. The thought put him more at ease.

"Driver, can you help me bring down Mr. Miles' trunk?" called Mr. Smythe. "Thank you."

Once the trunk was on the ground, the driver looked to Miles.

"I'll be fine," he told the servant. "Go on. Tell Cook I will miss her fine meals."

"Aye, my lord. I will do so," the driver said. "Good luck to you. All the Wildwood servants wish you the best."

He waved farewell as Mr. Smythe easily lifted the heavy trunk and tossed it upon one shoulder.

"That's a good sign," the servant said. "For you to have the respect of your family's staff."

"They have always been kind to me. More so than my own family," Miles admitted.

The man studied him a moment. "I know you wonder what you are getting into here. Let me tell you that there are some boys who are sent here, ones who truly are a bad seed. The Turner brothers—Mr. Nehemiah and Mr. Josiah—do their best to help them live up to their full potential and put their difficulties behind them. Others are sent here because they were an inconvenience to their families or they were accused of something that they wouldn't have done."

"Like me," he muttered.

Smythe nodded. "Like you," he agreed. "Whatever happened is in your past, Mr. Miles. You start with a clean slate at Turner Academy. Come along."

They entered the school and as they journeyed up the stairs, the servant said, "You'll be with four new boys. We have anywhere from eight to twenty students at any given time. Some stay a short while and leave for other schools. Others are with us until they finish their education."

"I've been told I will stay. Until university. Holidays and all," Miles said glumly.

"That's a good thing because you'll be wanted here," Smythe said good-naturedly. "You'll make friends. Good ones, I believe."

They went down a corridor, passing several boys who greeted the servant, before stopping at a door at the end of the hallway.

"This is yours, Mr. Miles. Your home for the upcoming years. Three boys have already arrived."

He rapped on the door and opened it, breezing in and placing the trunk at the foot of a bed. Above the bed was a placard with his name. It was a good omen to Miles. At his other school, spots were never assigned. It sometimes turned into a bloodbath as to where a boy might bunk. This way, no arguments would ensue regarding who had what bed.

"Assemble in the ballroom in half an hour," Mr. Smythe said. "Don't be late. The Turners can't abide tardiness."

"Thank you," he told the servant, who departed quickly.

Miles looked around at the three boys present. One sat on his bed, his forearms braced on his legs, his hands gripping his knees. His gaze was focused on the floor so Miles couldn't really see anything but a head of blond hair. He didn't bother looking up or acknowledging that a new boy had arrived, causing Miles to grow wary of him.

He glanced at the other two, who had ceased their conversation and eyed him with interest. One was tall and lanky, with chocolate brown hair and hazel eyes. The other had dark chestnut hair and gazed at Miles with sapphire eyes. He was lean and lithe. Both looked as if they would be good athletes.

They came toward him and he stiffened until the first held out his hand.

"I'm Wyatt. Wyatt Stanton. They say I burned down our stables and killed all our horses. I didn't. It was my idiot brother's fault."

Miles took the offered hand, surprised by the open declaration from the boy but deciding to return the favor. "I appreciate you being frank. My older brother shot and killed my younger brother. He's a marquess and my father's favorite. Ralph blamed me—and no one dared to question his version of the events."

He wouldn't have thought within minutes of arriving at his new school that he would share such a confession but it felt good getting it off his chest.

The second boy also stuck out his hand and Miles shook it.

"I'm Aaron Hartfield. My friends call me Hart." He looked at Miles. "I hope we can be friends."

"I hope so, as well," he replied. "Why are you here?"

Hart snorted. "It seems we three have something in common. My older brother, Reginald, pushed my baby brother into the water. Percy was scared. Always hated the water. Reg thought he'd force Percy to finally conquer his fear. Instead, Percy somehow landed wrong and broke his neck. Guess who got the blame?" Hart shrugged. "It doesn't matter. I hate the lot of them anyway."

"Do they want you back?" he asked, looking from Hart to Wyatt.

"You mean are we allowed to go home?" Hart asked, immediately understanding Miles' question. "Not me. My father, the Duke of Mansfield, washed his hands of me. He hasn't spoken a word to me since Percy died. His solicitor is the one who told me

I would be attending school with a bunch of wayward, wicked boys. And that I am not welcomed at Deerfield ever again."

Wyatt sighed. "Thank God. I thought I was the only one who had been banished for good. I live—lived—at Amberwood, about ten miles southeast of Maidstone. Our family butler delivered me here. My parents have disowned me." He paused, his voice becoming deep and gruff. "Oh, I'll do my duty to you, you worthless piece of scum. Polite Society would frown upon me if I abandoned you. You'll be educated. You just won't be allowed home. Ever," he emphasized.

"I suppose that you're imitating your father," Miles stated.

"Yes. The mighty Duke of Amesbury. May he rot in Hell someday." Wyatt turned and spat on the ground for good measure.

He looked to the blond boy sitting on his bed. "Does he talk?" he asked quietly.

"Not yet," Hart said.

The door opened and Smythe entered again, carrying another trunk with a different boy in tow.

"Back again," he said cheerfully. "This is Mr. Donovan Martin," he informed them as he placed the trunk down. "Take good care of him. He's the last of those you'll share the room with."

Once the servant left, the three introduced themselves and quickly told why they'd been sent to Turner Academy.

"So, what did you do—or not do?" Miles asked.

Donovan shrugged. "Nothing."

"No one is sent here without doing something," Wyatt pointed out.

A pained expressed crossed Donovan's face and Miles said, "You don't have to say anything. If you're ever ready, we're here to listen."

He went and opened his trunk, shuffling items around.

Donovan said, "It was my mother."

Miles stilled and rose from bended knee. He went to Donovan. "Did something happen to your mother?"

The dark-haired boy nodded, tears filling his piercing, blue eyes.

"We loved to talk and walk. We were cutting through the forest to return home and she accidentally stepped in a trap."

All three boys winced.

"I ran for help and they got it off her but it was horrible. Her skin jagged and ripped. Blood everywhere. The doctor said he would need to remove the limb." Donovan's mouth set stubbornly. "But my father wouldn't let him take it."

A sick feeling filled Miles. "What happened?" he asked.

"Infection set in. She ran a high fever for days. She was delirious. And then she died," Donovan said dully. "Father can't stand the sight of me because I look just like her. She always favored me over my older brother, who will be Duke of Haverhill someday. That's why I'm here." He looked about defiantly, mopping the tears from his face. "I loved her so much I hate my father. And my brother. I don't care if I ever see them again."

Hart placed a hand on Donovan's shoulder. "We're here for you," he said solemnly. "We've all been done wrong. We may not have our families anymore—but we have each other."

The four boys regarded one another solemnly and nodded.

Then Miles glanced to where the fifth boy sat mute.

"Won't you join us?" he asked.

The boy raised his head and he saw the pain filling the bright, blue eyes. Slowly, he came to his feet and moved toward their circle. Wyatt stepped back, allowing the newcomer to join in. They faced him.

"I'm Finch," he finally said. "William Finchley. And I don't give a damn about what any of you did or didn't do." Sullenly, he met the gaze of each boy within the circle. "I sure as hell won't ever tell you why I was sent here."

"You don't need to," Donovan said. "You're here. And you're with us. That's all that matters. We're all new here. That's what Mr. Smythe told me. I think we could all use a few friends."

Miles saw Finch was still filled with tension. "Donovan's

right," he asserted. "Whether you did anything or not, you're a part of us. We're all stuck here together. We might as well make the best of it." He glanced around the circle. "Agreed?"

"Agreed," chimed in the other four.

He stuck out a hand. Wyatt placed his on top. Hart, then Donovan, and finally Finch added theirs to it.

"To the Turner Terrors," Miles declared.

"The Turner Terrors," the four echoed.

"We should make our way to the ballroom," he told them.

As the five boys left their room, Miles hoped that he had a future here.

With these boys. His new friends.

CHAPTER THREE

Wildwood—April 1810

E MERY JENSON AWAKENED after a brief sleep. She rose and changed out of her gown, which she had fallen asleep in when she came home last night. She had spent every waking hour at the Duke of Winslow's bedside for the past three weeks. The duchess was in London for the start of the Season and had been informed of her husband's ill health.

She had chosen not to return home.

The couple had never been close. Or at least not ever since Emery arrived in Kent with her parents, who came to work as steward and housekeeper at Wildwood ten years ago. The duchess spent a majority of her time in London or traveling to see friends. Emery could count on one hand the times Her Grace had come to stay at the country estate. The duke rarely left Wildwood unless it was to go visit one of his other numerous properties.

They must have been close at one time. At least enough to make two sons together. The marquess, Winslow's older son, came to Wildwood even less than his mother. When Emery and her parents arrived to work on the estate, the marquess was away at school. He had returned for a couple of weeks before leaving for university. He spent holidays in the city with his mother or visiting school chums, making only the occasional visit to

Wildwood. It hurt her to see how much the duke loved the boy and how his heir apparent treated His Grace as if his father were rubbish.

There had been a younger son. The only reason Emery knew of him was from running across his grave in the churchyard. She had a keen interest in history and found a great deal could be learned about a place and its people from reading headstones. It was there she stumbled across the Notley family plot and found the grave of young Anthony Notley, who had died a few months before his seventh birthday. Neither the duke nor any of the staff ever spoke of the boy. She supposed his youthful death had been a painful experience for all and curbed her natural curiosity, vowing never to ask anyone about the boy.

She repaired her hair, removing a few pins and smoothing the locks before sliding the pins back into place. That would have to do. She needed to get Papa his breakfast and then head back to the main house, where her mother would have arrived a few hours ago to supervise the servants starting their day.

Emery boiled water for tea and then poached an egg for her father, the only thing he would eat for breakfast. Worry filled her. Papa had seemed different lately. She couldn't put her finger on it but something troubled him. She was loath to speak to her mother about it. Mama already had so much responsibility running Wildwood. Usually, Emery helped with some of those tasks, just as she aided her father with estate business. Lately, though, she had spent the bulk of her time nursing the duke.

"Good morning, my dear."

She glanced up. "Hello, Papa. Your breakfast is almost ready. I'll let the tea steep a minute longer."

He seated himself and tapped on his egg as she studied him. He seemed his usual self today. Even in good spirits, judging by his smile.

She poured his tea and added the two lumps of sugar which he insisted made it drinkable. Passing the cup and saucer to him, he took it and rested it on the table.

"I need to go to the house now," she informed him.

"Will you be with His Grace all day?"

"Most likely."

"Any improvement?"

She sighed. "None. He has grown progressively weaker. Mama asked Mr. Sevill to write to Her Grace and the marquess and implore them to return home."

Concern filled his face. "It is that serious?"

"Yes, Papa. I don't think His Grace has long to live."

Emery leaned down and kissed the top of his head. "I am sorry I have abandoned you lately in order to tend to His Grace. I miss working with you."

"That is quite all right, my dear. I can manage on my own. You caring for the duke allows your mama to run the household, knowing His Grace is in good hands. If not for you, she would need to be by his side since his family is not in residence."

"Is everything going well on the estate, Papa?"

He looked perplexed by her question. "Of course. Why do you ask?"

She shrugged. "No reason. I suppose I miss having a hand in things. That's all."

"I will see you later," he said, lifting his cup and sipping from it.

"Goodbye," she called as she went out the door.

As she left the cottage they lived in, a perk of Papa being the estate's manager, she hoped her misgivings would be proven wrong. Her father had always been in excellent health. He was fifteen years older than her mother, waiting to wed until he was forty. She supposed since he was now in his mid-sixties, it was only natural that he slowed a little bit, both physically and mentally. She still planned to keep an eye out for him, though. If he needed her to take on more of the estate's business, she was more than willing. She enjoyed the work and especially liked dealing with the tenants, many of whom felt like family to her.

Emery arrived at the house and cut through the kitchens,

waving to Cook. She passed her mother, who was in conversation with Mr. Sevill, the butler. She had never seen a servant more loyal to his master than Sevill was to the duke.

Nodding to them as she passed, she hurried up the back stairs to His Grace's rooms. Thomas, the head footman, sat by the bed.

"How is he?" she asked softly.

"A bit restless, Miss Jenson. He slept but kept thrashing about. I don't know how much rest he truly got."

"Thank you, Thomas. Go get yourself something to eat and then sleep a few hours."

He smiled gratefully. "Thank you, Miss Jenson."

She took his place in the chair next to the bed and studied the man lying there. The Duke of Winslow had turned seventy his last birthday and up until then had been in excellent health. Shortly after his birthday, he had come down with a nasty cold which he hadn't been able to shake. From there, it seemed his health went downhill. Now, he had been bedridden the past few weeks, his breathing labored, and he possessed no appetite. The village doctor had been called in and had bled His Grace, which had done nothing to improve his condition and only seemed to weaken him instead.

He groaned and opened his rheumy eyes, blinking as he looked around. Then a coughing fit seized him. She helped him to sit up, firmly patting his back before easing him back onto the pillows.

"Some broth, Your Grace?" she asked.

He shook his head. "Tea," he rasped.

A pot sat on a table next to the bed. Though it wouldn't be hot, she poured it anyway. Emery had him sit up so she could fluff his pillows and then gave him the cup, bringing her hands around his to guide it to his parched lips. He took a few sips and then pushed it away.

"So . . . tired," he managed to say.

"I know you are, Your Grace. Try and get some rest. I will be here if you need anything."

He did as she instructed and Emery sat for another two hours, thinking about the spring planting and summer harvest.

"I want . . . it."

She came out of her woolgathering to see the duke had awakened.

"What would you like me to fetch, Your Grace?"

"The portrait. Sevill . . . will know . . . which one."

"I will see to it now, Your Grace."

Emery rang for a maid and Addy appeared.

"Stay with His Grace for a few minutes. I will be back soon."

The maid traded places with her and Emery went to find the butler. He was supervising two footmen polishing the silverware. To her dismay, she saw Thomas was one of them. She started to speak up and tell Sevill that Thomas had kept watch over His Grace and deserved a few hours of sleep but the footman shook his head, warning her off.

She understood. No one wanted to be on Sevill's bad side. If she pointed out that Thomas needed rest, Sevill would deliberately keep Thomas up another twenty-four hours, assigning the footman meaningless tasks simply because he could do so without anyone questioning his authority. Her mother and the butler had been at war for years. Mama loved her position at Wildwood—except for having to work with the cantankerous butler.

"Mr. Sevill, might I have a private word with you?"

He gazed upon her with disdain. "Now is not a good time, Miss Jenson. These footmen need constant supervision in order for their tasks to be completed correctly."

"It involves a request from His Grace," she said, knowing that would do the trick.

Immediately, Sevill strode from the room, waiting for her just outside the doors.

"What can I do for His Grace?" the butler asked eagerly.

"He wants you to retrieve a portrait. He didn't say which one. Only that you would know the one he spoke of."

Surprise flickered across the butler's face. "He asked for it?"

"He did," she confirmed. "I have no idea which portrait or where it is located. Can you retrieve it for me?"

"Wait here," he commanded.

The butler disappeared and was gone a good quarter-hour. When he returned, she saw the item he carried was covered with a cloth.

"Are you certain he wanted this?" Sevill asked, doubt in his voice.

"All I know is that His Grace asked for it and knew you were the one who could locate it."

"It is just that . . . well, it is of his boys."

Understanding dawned within her. Though no one ever spoke of young Anthony, the duke must have wanted to once more see a picture of the child he had lost so long ago before he passed.

"I will take it to him," she said. "Thank you for bringing it, Mr. Sevill. His Grace will be most appreciative, I am sure."

Emery returned to the duke's rooms, the covered painting in hand. She dismissed Addy and returned to the duke's side.

"Your Grace, I have what you asked for. Mr. Sevill located it."

"Good." His voice, usually so strong, sounded feeble and faint.

She withdrew the cloth from the frame and sat, placing the picture in her lap so the old man could view it at eye level. A smile crossed the duke's face as he gazed upon it. Though curious, she knew she could look upon it after he did.

"My . . . boys," he rasped, reaching out a hand, his fingers touching the canvas.

She sensed another presence and saw that Sevill had slipped into the room. He came to stand on the other side of the bed, his gaze turning to the picture.

"Send for my boy," the duke said, his voice quavering with emotion.

"I have sent for him, Your Grace. A week ago," Sevill said,

unable to mask the sadness in his eyes.

"Then go for him in person," His Grace said, a tear rolling down his cheek. "I need Ralph here."

"Of course, Your Grace. And Her Grace?" Sevill asked.

"She can go to Hell."

The vehemence in the duke's words struck Emery, almost if he had landed a blow to her belly. She wondered what had passed between the pair that had left them so estranged. Then the duke began coughing again. She propped the portrait against the wall, once again helping Winslow. Sevill stayed, too, and finally the fit finished. The duke collapsed against the pillows, exhausted.

"Do as he said," she told the butler. "Leave for London immediately. I fear the end is near. His heir should be here. Don't come back unless he accompanies you," she said sternly.

For once, the butler didn't argue. He nodded solemnly and left the room.

Emery watched her patient for a few minutes and when she was convinced he was sleeping deeply, she rose and moved to view the portrait. Turning it so that it faced her, she sucked in a sharp breath.

Three boys were pictured together. Not the two she had expected.

She recognized the marquess immediately. His face hadn't changed much since the artist had completed his work years ago. The youngest of the three looked to be about six, meaning this portrait had been commissioned shortly before Anthony Notley's untimely death.

Her eyes were drawn to the unknown boy, who had to be ten or eleven. He had golden brown hair that seemed kissed by a summer sun. His sky blue eyes were those of his mother's. He looked as though he had been told to take the portrait sitting seriously, yet a glint of mischief shone in his eyes.

Who was this boy—a son no one ever spoke of?

She had come to Wildwood ten years ago. This Notley boy would have been a couple of years older than she was if she was right about the timeframe of the painting. Had he been at school? Had some terrible tragedy also befallen him? How awful for His Grace to lose not one but two sons. Perhaps that is why the duchess avoided Wildwood, not wanting any memories of the two boys she had lost.

Yet if this boy was a Notley—and dead—then wouldn't he be buried in the family plot, next to Anthony?

Her curiosity grew, wondering if Winslow had called for the painting in order to see the sons he had lost and would soon be joining. She could understand the portrait being hidden, especially if it caused the duke and duchess so much hurt to view it.

Placing it against the wall again, she remained by the duke's side another hour. A low moan came from him and he opened his eyes. They were filled with pain—and something else she couldn't identify.

"I couldn't help but look at your sons, Your Grace. They were handsome boys."

His face softened. "Ralph," he said softly. "My heir."

"Yes, I saw the marquess. A very distinguished lad. As were the others."

The duke frowned. "Anthony. Gone . . . so many years now."

She placed a hand over his. "I have seen his grave in the churchyard. I know you must miss him." Emery hesitated and then said, "And your other son. The middle one. He, too, was quite handsome."

The duke's eyes narrowed. "He is dead to me. He ruined everything."

Suddenly, Winslow clawed at his chest, wheezing. His face grew a bright red. Emery pulled the cord and a footman rushed into the room after two minutes. By then, it was too late for a doctor to help. The Duke of Winslow had taken his last breath and was finally at peace.

"Bring my mother," she told the servant. "His Grace has passed. Arrangements will need to be made. Summon the doctor and the vicar."

"Yes, Miss Jenson," the footman said, quickly exiting.

Emery glanced back at the still body on the bed and then her gaze turned to the portrait of three young Notleys.

Who was the middle boy—and what had happened to him?

CHAPTER FOUR

E MERY COULDN'T STAND the new Duke of Winslow.
And he'd only been at Wildwood a week.

She grit her teeth thinking about how arrogant and overbearing Ralph Notley could be. He had shown up with his mother in tow. She was as unpleasant as Emery remembered, finding fault with everything from the temperature of her tea to how far the curtains had been drawn. The next day, a party of five rowdy gentlemen showed up, all friends of the new Duke of Winslow. They had accompanied the new duke to the funeral, where the former duke was buried next to his son, Anthony, and then the guests had stayed for a week, drinking and carousing far into the night. Emery did her best to avoid them, knowing what they would have on their minds. She had never been kissed and wasn't about to experience her first kiss forced upon her by a drunken lord.

Today, she and Papa had an appointment with Winslow. His friends had left yesterday and she supposed he was ready to settle down and see about the business of the estate. Fortunately, she had come across her father going over the books, a dazed look on his face. He told her he was trying to balance accounts.

And didn't remember how.

Tamping down her fear, Emery had sent him back to their cottage, telling him he looked tired and was probably in need of a nap. That the numbers would make sense to him once he had gotten some rest. Then she had spent the rest of that afternoon and all the next day sorting through the mess he had made, reworking columns of numbers and adding things correctly. She left the pages she corrected inside the ledger, merely drawing a large X through them and initialing beside it. She didn't want His Grace to think she had tampered with the books in any way. She doubted he would take the time to study them. He seemed more the type to skim them. If that.

Fortunately, she was the one who paid the bills at the estate and so no merchants had gone without their funds. Emery worried, though, about her father's rapid decline. That was why she would sit in on his meeting today with the new duke. Hopefully, she could cover for Papa and answer the His Grace's questions. If the duke suspected Papa's mind had grown weak, he would sack him immediately. That would mean losing the cottage, which was attached to the position of steward. She prayed that wouldn't come to pass and that her mother would also be able to retain her position as housekeeper.

Entering the office, she found her father seated behind the desk, staring into space as he often did these days. Emery's heart went out to him. Papa had always been such an intelligent man, well versed in a good number of topics. As a viscount's son, he had received an excellent education. Being a fourth son, however, he had to make his way in the world the best he could. He had attained the position of steward for the Earl of Raydon just before he turned forty. Having secure employment, he had then married the local doctor's daughter. Emery arrived a few years later and when she was twelve, Papa had accepted the position as steward at Wildwood, a far larger estate. When the duke's housekeeper had passed away unexpectedly a short time after their arrival, Papa had suggested Mama for the position. Winslow had agreed, having come to trust his estate manager implicitly.

These had been good years at Wildwood. The estate had become home to Emery. Leaving it would be difficult. It would be up to her to help hide Papa's deficiencies and answer the duke's questions. She had already overheard Winslow tell the duchess that he didn't plan to stay in the country with the London Season in full swing so Emery knew today's appointment might be the only time the duke spoke with Papa.

She watched her father a moment. He did not recognize her presence. It pained her to see how he had seemingly grown old overnight. His graying hair now had an abundance of white in it. His lined face continually looked weary. His posture, once tall and proud, now was slumped.

"Papa," she called softly.

He turned and smiled. "Hello, Emery. Have you balanced the ledgers?"

"Yes, I have, Papa. Do you remember His Grace is coming to meet with us regarding the estate?"

He frowned. "I thought he was very ill."

She swallowed. He had already forgotten the old duke had recently died.

"Remember, Papa, that His Grace passed away. We went to his funeral last week," she reminded gently.

"Oh. Oh, that is quite right. His Grace is dead. The son is here. I remember now." Papa frowned. "His friends are quite ill-mannered."

She chuckled. "They are, indeed. You should keep that to yourself, though."

"Of course. I would never say that to His Grace. It is not my place to judge his companions or their behavior."

They waited a quarter-hour. After half an hour passed and still no duke, Emery rang for a footman.

When Thomas appeared, she asked, "Do you know where His Grace is? He was to discuss estate business with my father and has not kept his appointment."

Thomas' mouth twitched. "His Grace only awakened a few minutes ago, Miss Jenson. He called for hot water. It could be some time before he remembers this meeting."

"I see. Thomas, would you let His Grace's valet know to send

His Grace our way when he is presentable?"

The footman bit back a smile. "Yes, Miss Jenson."

She got to work, allowing her father to flip through the pages of a book as she did. After another hour, the door opened.

The Duke of Winslow staggered in, a bottle in one hand and a brandy snifter in the other.

Her gut tightened. He may have bathed but he still looked disheveled. While dressed in the manner of a city gentleman more than a country one, his cravat was askew. His face sported yesterday's whiskers. His hair stuck up in the air.

And he reeked of the brandy.

He weaved his way across the office, falling into a chair. Tilting the glass to his lips, he drained it and poured another.

"Good afternoon, Your Grace," she said and Papa echoed her words.

Emery wanted to slap the man for a litany of things but kept her face neutral.

"What can we do for you today, Your Grace?" Papa asked politely.

The duke flicked his eyes to her. "Why are you here? Who are you?"

She steeled herself. "I am Miss Jenson. My father is your estate manager and my mother is your housekeeper. I aid them both in their work."

His eyes looked her slowly up and down, causing her cheeks to heat in embarrassment. If he was a servant, she would slap him and give him a piece of her mind. Instead, because he was a peer and her parents' employer, she sat mute.

"Tell me about the estate," the duke said, his eyes still raking over her.

Papa began to speak and Winslow cut him off. "I want *her* to tell me. Let's see what a female actually knows."

Emery thought this a blessing in disguise. It would save Papa from stumbling through any explanation and show His Grace that she did pull her weight at Wildwood.

She began talking about the upcoming planting and harvest and watched as his eyes glazed over. He emptied his glass and refilled it from the bottle he still held.

Finally, he interrupted her. "This is boring. Tell me how much Wildwood makes each year. And how much I receive from the other estates—if you know."

"Certainly, Your Grace."

Emery threw numbers at him. Numbers were her friends and she knew them backward and forward. When she finished, the duke grunted.

And poured himself a final glass of brandy.

The bottle now empty, he let it drop to the floor and said, "You do know quite a bit."

It was probably the closest she would ever come to a compliment from him. She bowed her head slightly, not trusting her tongue, which wished to dress him down for being drunk at two o'clock in the afternoon.

"I don't plan to spend much time here," he said, his words slurring. "I suppose I should see something of the place before I leave for town."

"Did you grow up here, Your Grace?" she asked politely.

"I did. I never liked it here. Take me out now."

"Take you . . . where, Your Grace?"

He frowned at her. "I said I wanted to see the estate. You do ride, don't you, Miss Jenson?"

"I do. Perhaps you might wish to ride the estate when you can get an earlier start," she smoothly suggested, knowing he had no business being on a horse in his inebriated condition.

His eyes narrowed. "I want to see it *now*." He stood, letting the tumbler fall from his fingers. It landed on the carpet with a soft thunk.

"Very well," she said, marching briskly out of the room and straight to the stables. She had a riding habit but knew this man didn't have the patience to allow her time to change into it. She would have to make do. As it was, she doubted they would be out for long. If he made it a quarter-mile from the house without falling off his horse, it would be a miracle.

Mr. Harris, the head groom, met her, glancing over her shoulder. "You wish to ride, Miss Jenson?"

The duke arrived. "She does. We do. Fetch horses for us both."

The groom looked at her uncertainly. Emery nodded slightly.

"Would you like Zeus, Miss?" he asked, knowing the mount was her favorite in the stables.

"Zeus?" the duke asked.

"Yes, Your Grace. The horses are all named after Greek gods. Zeus is the most spirited and hardest to control. He likes no one but Miss Jenson on his back."

"He will prefer me," Winslow proclaimed. "Saddle him. Give her something else."

Worry creased the groom's face. "Yes, Your Grace." Harris hurried away.

"Zeus can be a handful, Your Grace," she cautioned.

He glared at her. "If you can handle him, so can I. I can ride any beast and bring it to heel." He paused and leered at her. "I would like to ride you."

Her face flamed at his crass comment. Although two and twenty, she had little idea what went on between a man and a woman and sensed he knew that. What she did know was that a gentleman would never speak to her this way.

Winslow was definitely no gentleman, despite the title he now claimed.

"We can have fun together, Miss Jenson. I can show you things. Many things."

"I am not interested in fun, Your Grace," she said primly.

He roared with laughter.

Thankfully, their horses arrived. As usual, Zeus snorted and huffed. She stepped to the horse, his nostrils flaring and murmured to him softly as she stroked his neck, calming him.

The duke stepped toward her and said, "Would you like to

stroke me that way, Miss Jenson?"

Horrified, she stepped back and quickly went to Ares, a groom helping her to mount. She took up the reins as she tried to gather her wits about her. She had drawn the duke's attention in a terrible way and had no idea how to stop his advances. Fortunately, he had said he wouldn't remain at Wildwood for long. If she could avoid him for a day or two, he would be gone and forget about her. Thank goodness she lived away from the house in the cottage with her parents. If she'd had a room in the main house, she knew she wouldn't be safe from this lecherous drunk.

Turning, she saw Winslow had been helped into the saddle and asked, "Where would you like to see first, Your Grace?"

He grunted.

"I will show you the fields then."

Emery nudged her horse and Ares responded, taking off at a slow trot. The duke joined her, riding by her side. She could tell, though, that he struggled to keep Zeus under control. She wondered if she could suggest they trade mounts but couldn't think of any reason why they should that Winslow would accept.

She showed the duke the fields where various crops had been planted and then took him by the rows of his tenants' cottages.

"I remember a bluff," he said. "It overlooked a good deal of land."

"I know where that is," she replied. "Follow me."

She kept Ares at a steady canter, knowing if she sped up that Zeus might think the duke was giving the horse his head and take off at a raging gallop.

They reached the area and Winslow dismounted. He looked at her expectantly and she slid from the saddle, worried about how she would get up again without assistance, especially in the gown she wore. She didn't want him having any excuse to put his hands on her. The thought of that made her uncomfortable and might give him a reason to try and take liberties with her.

He stepped forward unsteadily and gazed across the land below.

"It is finally all mine," he said, satisfaction evident in his voice. "I've waited long enough."

It angered her that this man seemed to hold no feelings for his father. While the previous duke might not have been the best of men, he didn't deserve such disrespect from his heir.

"Where is the mill?" he asked.

Emery pointed. "Over there."

Before she could lower her arm, he latched on to her wrist and jerked her toward him. Panic raced through her.

"Please, let me go," she said, her voice quavering.

"No," he said, a slow smile crossing his face. "I don't think I will."

His fingers tightened on her wrist. She thought the bones might shatter. His other hand went to her breast, squeezing it painfully. She gasped in outrage.

"We are going to have fun, Miss Jenson. What is your first name?" he asked, his eyes glowing with his newfound power.

"That is none of your business," she snapped at him.

His hands dropped, surprising her. She started to turn, only to find he grabbed her upper arms, his fingers digging into her tender flesh. He yanked her to him.

"*You* are my business," he said boldly. "You are my property. Just as Wildwood is. I will do with you what I want. I thought to bring you to my bed but I think I will take you right here."

Fear paralyzed her for a moment. His mouth slammed down on hers, bruising it as her arms would also be bruised. She opened her mouth to protest and he forced his tongue into her mouth. Disgust filled her. She had hoped one day to be kissed. To find a man who respected her and wanted to marry her. This was no kiss. This was some vile act by a horrid man drunk on his newfound power.

She remembered hearing one maid tell another what to do if a groom or footman grew frisky. Without thinking of the consequences, Emery slammed her knee into Winslow's groin.

Immediately, he roared, his mouth disengaging from hers as

she pushed hard against his chest. He tumbled to the ground. She looked at him, horrified at what she had done but having had no other way to stop him.

Then she ran to her horse and, somehow, the blood racing through her, she threw herself into the saddle and took off. As she rode away, she heard him loudly cursing her.

Emery didn't dare look back.

When she reached the stables, Harris met her, helping her from Ares.

"Where is His Grace?"

"He decided . . . to continue the ride. He said he didn't need me anymore."

The groom looked at her with sympathy. "Are you all right, Miss Jenson?"

She imagined she looked as white as a ghost and a bit disheveled. "I am. Thank you for asking."

More than anything, she wanted Mama.

Emery hurried to the house and found her mother, who took one look at her and said, "Come with me."

They retreated to her mother's office. Both Wildwood's housekeeper and butler had a room of their own to manage the household. Mama used hers to work on the accounts and plan menus with Cook. She also retreated for a few minutes every afternoon for a cup of tea to fortify her. She prepared tea for them now, not asking anything until they had mugs before them.

"What happened? I know you went riding with His Grace and that he had downed an entire bottle of brandy."

Her mother always had been well informed of events within the household.

Her fingers tightening on her skirts, she briefly told Mama what had happened.

"Oh, Emery. This is very bad."

"I know. You and Papa might very well lose your positions and be dismissed without references."

Mama shook her head. "That will be the least of it. You have assaulted a peer of the realm. You could go to prison. Even be transported to Australia."

The knowledge of what she did now slammed into her and she began weeping. Her mother stroked her hair.

"You need to leave," Mama insisted. "Go now and pack. If you are gone—if they cannot find you—then you will be safe."

"But I would be on the run for the rest of my life, Mama," she protested. "That is not the right thing to do."

Her mother, always sage when dispensing advice, said, "You did the right thing as a woman. In a society where laws are passed by men of privilege, you are held to a different standard."

She took Emery's hands in hers. "I would rather you live in England, under an assumed name, never seeing you again, than have you convicted and sent halfway around the world to a penal colony. Or you can sail to America. Perhaps that would be best."

Mama came to her feet and embraced Emery. "Go," she whispered. "Pack just a few things. Look in the trunk at the foot of my bed. Inside a small chest, I have a pearl necklace you can sell. No, do not protest, my sweet. Also in the chest is an old reticule. It has money in it. Take it, as well."

Her eyes welled with tears. "Mama. I love you."

"I love you, too, my dearest child." She released Emery and handed her a handkerchief. "Dry your tears. Avoid talking to any servants."

"Yes, Mama."

Emery slipped from the room, knowing she would never see her parents again. She had no idea where she might go. London, she supposed. It would be best to lose herself in the large city. She could take time to figure out her future and if she should cross the ocean to America.

She reached the cottage and opened the door, thankful that she hadn't seen anyone on her way home. Going to the trunk, she found the necklace and savings her mother spoke of. She left half of the coins, knowing Mama and Papa would need them since they, too, would be leaving Wildwood. The new duke was an angry, spiteful man. He would boot them from the estate without a second thought.

She looked under their bed for the lone valise and then decided to leave that for them, as well. In her room, she donned a second gown over the one she wore and wrapped her favorite shawl around her. She rarely carried a reticule since she hardly ever left the estate, but she withdrew hers and stuffed the necklace, money, a night rail, and an extra chemise into it. She glanced around the bedchamber she had spent so many years in and swallowed the lump in her throat.

When she emerged from the room, her father came shuffling in, his eyes downcast. She uttered a quick prayer of thanks that she was able to see him once more.

"I don't feel well," he said as he glanced at her. Then he crumbled to the ground.

"Papa!" she cried, racing to him.

Emery managed to get him on his feet and had him lean against her as she led him to his bed. She slipped his shoes off and loosened his cravat, removing it and tossing it aside.

"What's wrong, Papa?" she asked, trying to keep the urgency from her voice, wanting to soothe him instead.

"I . . . don't know. I feel . . . I feel odd."

"I will send for the doctor."

Knowing she was wasting time—time that should be spent fleeing—Emery ran back in the direction of the house and veered toward the stables. Finding a groom, she told him to fetch the doctor at once and have him come to the Jenson cottage. She returned and sat on the bed, holding Papa's hand.

Doctor Collier arrived at the same time Mama did. Her mother's eyes widened when she saw Emery still here. Briefly, she told the physician what Papa had said and Collier went into the bedchamber.

Once he was gone, she said, "I couldn't leave Papa. I just couldn't. And I won't go now. Not until I know what is wrong."

"I understand."

She saw the sorrow in her mother's eyes. Emery wondered if she would regret her actions but decided Papa's health was more important.

The physician called them into the room. She saw Papa was asleep.

"I think Mr. Jenson has suffered a mild case of apoplexy," Doctor Collier said. "He told me he has numbness along his right side and he had trouble moving his right arm when I asked him to do so. His speech seems unimpaired. That is a good thing."

"He has been forgetful of late, Doctor," Emery said. "More so than one would expect in the elderly. He has forgotten how to do things he has done all his life."

Dr. Collier nodded. "It could be connected to this episode. However it could be dementia."

"What is that?" Mama asked, frowning.

"It is a new term which describes a progressive condition. It affects one's memory and can impair behavior. How old is Mr. Jenson?"

"Sixty-five," Mama said.

"It might be best if he retired from his position at Wildwood. With a new duke in residence, you could suggest to His Grace that he might want his own man in the position," Dr. Collier suggested.

The physician gave them a few instructions on how to care for their patient and left, promising to call again tomorrow morning.

The moment the door closed, Mama said, "You must leave, Emery. I cannot believe His Grace hasn't already sent for us all."

A strong knock sounded at the door. Both women froze.

"No matter what happens, we love you," Mama said.

"Even if I have cost you your livelihood?" she asked sadly.

Emery opened the door and found Thomas standing there.

"You're needed at the house, Miss Jenson," he said solemnly.

"I understand."

She pulled her shawl tightly around her, hoping to disguise

that she wore two sets of clothes and had been about to flee. She would leave her reticule. No sense in taking it now.

"Goodbye, Mama," she said softly, not having the courage to glance at her mother a final time.

As she and Thomas left the cottage, he said, "His Grace is dead."

She halted in her tracks. "What?"

"Zeus must have thrown him. Mr. Oldham discovered the body and brought it back to Wildwood. By then, Zeus had already returned to the stables. Come along, Sir William is here and wishes to speak with you since you were the last one to see the duke alive."

Sir William Grant served as the area's magistrate. Numbly, Emery accompanied Thomas back to the house and to the drawing room, where Mr. Sevill and Sir William awaited. She also saw the duke's London valet present, along with Mr. Harris.

"Ah, welcome, Miss Jenson," Sir William said. "Please, have a seat." He turned to the three men. "You are dismissed."

Emery watched them leave. She clutched her hands in her lap, forcing herself not to wring them.

"Miss Jenson, I have already spoken with the others regarding the duke's . . . delicate condition. You accompanied His Grace out on the estate this afternoon?"

She swallowed. "Yes, Sir William. I did not think it wise for him to ride but His Grace insisted that he wanted to ride the estate once before he returned to London."

"Mr. Harris said it seemed as if His Grace had a bit to drink."

Emery nodded, knowing Sir William carefully watched her as she spoke.

"Yes. He met with Father and me before our tour. His Grace arrived at the meeting smelling of brandy and brought a bottle with him. He consumed three or four glasses during this time, finishing the bottle."

"I see." Sir William hesitated and then said, "Mr. Harris said His Grace was insistent upon riding a horse that is unmanageable."

"Yes, Mr. Harris is correct. Zeus is a difficult horse for a sober rider to handle." She swallowed. "I assume His Grace fell from the horse?"

"That is what I wished to ask you about. You returned to the stables without His Grace."

"Yes," she said, nerves rushing through her as she prepared herself to tell a white lie. "His Grace wished to continue surveying Wildwood on his own. I had shown him the crops and the cottages where his tenants live. I had things to do, helping Papa, and His Grace—against my advice—decided to continue on his own."

Emery took a deep breath and looked the magistrate in the eyes. "It was not my place to tell His Grace what he could and couldn't do. We parted ways and I returned to the stables."

Sir William nodded. "I understand, Miss Jenson. Mr. Harris said much the same thing. That he would have advised His Grace not to take Zeus out under any circumstances. But especially under these."

He rose and she followed suit. "I will be ruling His Grace's death as accidental. You and I both know that it should be death by misadventure since His Grace voluntarily took the risk and rode out on an unfamiliar, highly-spirited mount when he was soused. I think it best for all concerned, though, to say there was no unreasonable willful risk involved. It would be better for the family."

She thought of the duchess, first losing her husband and now her son. That led her to wonder who would now inherit the dukedom. She recalled the words the previous duke had spoken to her just before he died.

He is dead to me.

Would the son no one ever spoke of—and who might very well be alive—now become the Duke of Winslow?

CHAPTER FIVE

Portugal—May 1810

CAPTAIN MILES NOTLEY drew close to his destination just as dawn broke. Though his belly growled, he knew Wellesley would want him to report immediately. For the lieutenant-general in command of the Peninsular War troops, everything was secondary to the war. Miles understood this because, like Wellesley, he was confident, motivated, and responsible. Even a bit stubborn at times. His loyalty to his friends, his men, and his country would never be called into question. The army was his life.

As he rode, he reflected on the few hours he had spent with Wyatt, who served as a scout and sometime spy for Wellesley. Wyatt had inserted himself into a group of men with French sympathies and was building a case against them. Miles couldn't help but admire his friend's ability to court danger with no fear. Wyatt took risks no other man would but he achieved the necessary results, which was all Wellesley was interested in. Miles now carried a dispatch from Wyatt to the commander. He only hoped that Wyatt would stay alive in these trying times.

He reached the edge of camp and though dressed in civilian clothes, a soldier greeted him by name.

"Good morning, Captain Notley," the private said. "Lieutenant-General Wellesley said to direct you to his tent when you arrived."

Miles dismounted and handed his reins to the soldiers. "Thank you."

As he made his way through the camp as it began to stir, Hart fell into step with him.

"Did you see Wyatt? How is he?"

"I did. He's fit."

"And the men he's spying upon?" Hart asked worriedly.

He shrugged. "You know Wyatt."

"That's the problem. I do. He can be reckless at times."

"I agree," Miles said. "But we are not to smother him. If he needs help, he will ask for it."

Left unsaid was how both Miles and Hart were so independent that they would never seek help from others.

"Wyatt has developed his own network of spies. If he finds himself in trouble, they will get him out," Miles continued.

"Are you on your way to the viscount?" Hart asked.

"I am. I was informed he is eager to see me." His belly rumbled noisily.

Hart laughed. "Tell you what. You go have your meeting with Wellesley and I will be waiting outside his tent with your breakfast. I cannot promise it will be tasty. Only that there will be plenty of it."

By now, they had reached the commander's tent and Miles said, "Thank you. It's been over two days since I've eaten."

"Good luck," Hart said with a wink.

Miles approached the tent. No soldier stood on sentry duty. Instead, Beckerman, a German who was partly a soldier and sometimes a servant to Wellesley, greeted him.

"Captain Notley. Let me announce you."

Beckerman disappeared and reappeared moments later. "You may go inside." He held the tent flap open.

Miles stepped through and found Wellesley standing beside a large table that held a map of the area from Torres Vedras to Lisbon. As usual, Wellesley wore civilian clothes, immaculate in their cut and flattering to his trim figure. Why he chose to eschew wearing a uniform when he commanded the entire British army in Portugal was one of the great mysteries of the war. He raised his gaze from the map he studied and focused on Miles, his brilliant, blue eyes almost seeing through Miles as he saluted the commander.

"You look parched, Captain Notley," he said, motioning for his valet, who immediately filled a glass with wine and brought it to Miles.

Wellesley was known for his limited diet but the man did enjoy his wine. Being in a region that specialized in wines made their availability a benefit to being stationed in Portugal.

He took a long pull of the rich, red liquid and then lowered the glass, setting it on a nearby table. The British lieutenant-general was notoriously impatient and Miles didn't want to test him. Withdrawing a thick letter from the pouch he wore, he handed over the dispatch.

"From Captain Stanton," he said.

Anticipation filled Wellesley's face but he took the letter and set it on his desk.

"I will read this once you have made your report, Captain. Tell me, how are my lines?"

Miles had been sent to observe construction on the Lines of Torres Vedras, a secret project commissioned by Wellesley. Even the British government had not been made aware of the vast construction, conducted by Sir Richard Fletcher, an esteemed army engineer. Work on a set of four lines running from the town of Torres Vedras to Lisbon had begun the previous autumn.

"They are six months into the project and Sir Richard believes it can be completed in another six—or less."

Wellesley nodded, his expression pleased. "Tell me what you observed, Notley."

Miles had been sent not only to speak directly with Fletcher but explore the countryside and see to the actual construction. Though it seemed as if Wellesley had complete faith in Fletcher, the lieutenant-general was a careful man. He wanted the full picture and not what others would want him to hear.

Briefly, Miles described the defenses, a series of interlocking fortifications, knowing he served as Wellesley's eyes for this project. From redoubts to escarpments to dams, the Portuguese laboring under Fletcher's direction had done a remarkable job, incorporating features of the landscape into the actual fortifications.

Once more, he withdrew something from the leather pouch and handed over a sheaf of papers. The lieutenant-general spread these out on a table and studied them.

"Describe everything."

Miles went page by page, detailing the sketches he had made of various portions of the four different lines. While not a gifted artist like Finch, the drawings were decent and visually supplemented his report.

"And the roads?"

He knew the lieutenant-general spoke of the roads being constructed during the same time.

"Our troops will be able to move rapidly on them, Lieutenant-General."

"And any leaks?"

Part of Miles' mission had been to talk to citizens in the surrounding countryside. He, like his friend Hart, had an affinity for languages. The boys had learned both French and Spanish, along with Latin and Greek, at Turner Academy. Portuguese, another romance language, had been easy for Miles to pick up. Though he didn't have the accent of a native, he could easily be understood.

"I believe the integrity of the project is intact," he stated. "The French and Spanish haven't a clue as to what is truly being built. It will serve the British army well. From those I spoke with, I also feel no news of the lines will reach home."

Wellesley nodded in agreement. "You seem a bit like me, Captain. You are most efficient and do a job thoroughly."

"Thank you, my lord." Miles glowed at the compliment.

"Keep doing the same throughout your life," the older man advised. "If others cannot do something right, tell them to get out of your way and see it done correctly yourself."

"I will remember to do so," he promised.

"I have enjoyed seeing you grow as a leader, Captain Notley. I wish you the best."

The words struck him as odd. Almost as if Wellesley might never see him again. He wondered if he was being transferred to another command and wanted to ask but the words stuck in his throat.

"Good day, Captain."

The dismissive tone told Miles the briefing had ended. He saluted the lieutenant-general and exited the tent, where he found not only Hart but also Donovan waiting for him. Hart handed over a tin plate and the three men moved away from the tent.

"How was Wyatt?" Donovan asked. "Hart said you saw him."

"I did. For part of an afternoon." Miles lifted a biscuit, filled with meat, and downed it in two bites.

"Is he in danger?" Donovan persisted.

"Yes," Miles mumbled, chewing and then swallowing.

Donovan handed him a tankard filled with ale and he drank some of it before gobbling down a second biscuit filled with meat and eggs, washing it down with the rest of the ale.

Miles described the work Wyatt was doing and what he hoped to accomplish.

"I hate that he's out there on his own," Hart said. "While we three see each other when we can at camp."

"Wyatt is the daring one of all of us," he pointed out, "while you, Donovan, can be a bit reckless. It's Hart and I who are more in control. More driven. Wyatt is doing the work he wants to do. It suits him. I know we are all worried about him but the same could be said of us when we go into battle."

"You're right," Hart said. "I am simply used to having us all together." He sighed. "I miss Finch."

Finch, the fifth man of their tightknit group, had surprised them all after their graduation from Cambridge and had become a vicar, accepting the living near their mentor, Lord Marksby. Both Lord and Lady Marksby wrote each of them once a month, as did various tutors from Turner Academy.

"I received a letter from Finch yesterday," Donovan shared. "A new young miss has been flirting outrageously with him. And he sold another painting."

"At least he is out of harm's way," Miles said quietly.

Of all the Turner Terrors, Finch was the only one who had never revealed why he had been sent to the academy. Miles sensed that an inferno of rage boiled within Finch—and that one day it would erupt. God help anyone around him when it did.

Hart claimed the tin plate from him and he thanked his friend for the breakfast.

"I'm off," Hart said. "I have a bayonet practice to supervise."

"I have things to do, as well," Donovan said, a sly smile on his face.

"It must mean you are going into town to see one of your lovers," he said.

"Why, Miles, I am going to purchase provisions," Donovan said, his face now one of innocence. "And if I happen to visit with a lady friend while these supplies are being collected and loaded onto the wagons? Then I am using my allotted time wisely."

Of the five of them, Donovan was the womanizer. He had been very close to his mother, who had died in an accident when Donovan was ten. Sometimes, Miles wondered if Donovan deliberately chose not to get close to any woman because he had lost the one he loved the most. Of course, being in the military did not mix well with marriage. Though some officers were husbands and even brought their wives to war with them, none of the Terrors would most likely ever wed, being career officers.

"I will see you both later," he said. "I need to get back into uniform."

He returned to the tent he shared with Wyatt. Because of his friend's frequent sojourns, he had gotten used to the privacy.

Miles shed the clothes he had worn during his mission in order to blend in with the local population and washed as best he could with water from a bucket a young private brought him. He took the time to shave and comb his hair, knowing he now needed to report to Colonel Monroe. He needed to let his superior officer know of his return and see what duties would next be assigned to him.

Arriving at Monroe's tent, he gained admission. The colonel sat at a desk, quill in hand.

Miles saluted and Monroe asked him to take a seat.

"Did you meet with success, Captain Notley?"

"Yes, Colonel. I have come from making my report to Lieutenant-General Wellesley."

A look of disdain crossed Monroe's face. He was one of the few that did not sing Wellesley's praises. Miles figured it was a case of jealousy. Men such as Wellesley came along once in a generation. Monroe couldn't hold a candle to the viscount.

The colonel sighed and searched a stack on his desk, withdrawing a letter. He passed it to Miles.

"This came for you. I received one, as well. Are you familiar with a Mr. Fillmore?"

He thought a moment. "I don't believe so. The name is not familiar to me."

Read it," Monroe commanded.

Though Miles preferred to read his correspondence in private, he broke the seal. It seemed odd that his name wasn't written on the outside. Glancing at the letter, he saw his name did not appear in the salutation but the letter was signed by the Mr. Fillmore that had been mentioned. Miles returned to the top and began reading.

> *This correspondence is to inform you of the death of your father, the Duke of Winslow. His Grace lived a long and productive life and will be sorely missed by all who knew him.*
>
> *Unfortunately, his heir only held the title for a week, losing his life in a tragic riding accident at Wildwood. Since the new*

Duke of Winslow had not yet married and sired a son, the dukedom now falls to you.

I have discovered who your commanding officer is, a Colonel Monroe, and written to him of these unique circumstances. He is aware that as Duke of Winslow, you have obligations at home and will no longer have the pleasure of serving in His Majesty's army. I have made arrangements to see that your commission is sold. Please leave your post immediately and return to London. My office address is listed below. I will bring you up to date on matters of the estate and then you will return to Wildwood at once to take up your duties.

Respectfully,
Mr. L. Fillmore

Miles folded the letter, a kaleidoscope of emotions racing through him. It had been more than a dozen years since Winslow had banished him from Wildwood. Miles had chosen never to look back, knowing he couldn't change the past. Couldn't bring Tony back to life. He had no need to recall Ralph's role in killing Tony and laying the blame at Miles' feet. He had never been close with his father and put all thoughts of Winslow from his mind, as he had his mother, who had favored Tony and had little to do with her middle child.

Yet now, all these years later, he was being summoned home. To a place he had missed but refused to think about because it hurt too much.

He was the Duke of Winslow.

Regret rippled through him, knowing he was being made to give up his military career. He lived for his men and would miss them terribly. It also pained him knowing he would no longer see his fellow Terrors. Though Wyatt came and went like the wind, Miles tried to visit with Hart and Donovan whenever possible. Now, they would all stay and continue to fight in this unending war against Bonaparte without him.

He understood duty, though. His responsibilities now lay

with all his many tenants. The Duke of Winslow's country seat was at Wildwood, where more than one hundred families farmed, not to mention the other estates and their workers. Miles now had a new group of people to protect. Not his soldiers in red coats but the men and women who toiled upon his lands.

His gaze met that of Colonel Monroe's. "Mr. Fillmore informed you that I am now a duke?"

"Yes," the colonel confirmed. "I took the liberty of sharing this news with Lieutenant-General Wellesley."

No wonder Wellesley had behaved as he had. It had, indeed, been a farewell between the two men.

Monroe reached for some papers and gave them to Miles. "These are to be presented to the War Office in London. Mr. Fillmore will help you in selling your commission. He stated that he had been your father's solicitor for many years."

The colonel rose and Miles followed suit.

"You have been an excellent officer, Captain Notley. Loyal and steadfast. You will be hard to replace."

"Thank you, Colonel." Miles saluted the officer.

Monroe told him to pack and directed him to where he could seek transport back to England.

As Miles left the commander's tent, he went to find Donovan and Hart. He would leave a letter for Wyatt, informing his friend of the circumstances leading to his departure.

For the first time in many years, Miles felt adrift.

CHAPTER SIX

Wildwood

MILES GAZED OUT the window at the passing landscape, not recognizing any of it as the unmarked carriage took him from London to Wildwood. This would be the last time he would be anonymous as he traveled, knowing in the future he would journey from place to place in the Winslow ducal carriage, with its imposing crest on the doors. Even if he rode on horseback, he would be dressed far differently than he was at the present moment.

He glanced to the trunk on the floor of the vehicle. Mr. Fillmore had seen that Miles was fitted for an entire new wardrobe during his brief stay in London. The exclusive tailor's shop had catered to everything he needed and finished three coats and waistcoats, along with four sets of trousers. They would create the rest of his wardrobe and deliver it soon. The trunk also contained a dozen lawn shirts and cravats from London's best shirt maker, as well as a silk banyan and an extra pair of boots. More of the same would be coming, as well. It seems a duke was expected to have an expansive, lavish wardrobe.

Still, he had donned his captain's uniform for the last time before leaving London, wanting to arrive at Wildwood wearing it. He didn't know if he would recognize any of the servants since he had been away from the estate for fourteen years. If any remained from his childhood, he wanted them to know that he had made something of himself in the years of his exile.

Miles chuckled. He was probably the only duke in Great Britain who would think to care about a servant's opinion. In fact, he would wager he was the only duke in the land reluctant to claim his dukedom. Dukes didn't grow on trees. They were few and far between and most men in England would give their right arm to become one of those few. He only wished he weren't one and still back in the army, preparing for the next assault on Bonaparte's men.

The carriage slowed slightly and he saw they entered a village. Something about it seemed familiar and he realized it must be Woodmorrow, which lay approximately three miles from Wildwood. He used to walk to the village when he was a boy and wondered if the bakery still sold the sticky buns he enjoyed.

Then the coach passed the local church. Next to it stood the graveyard.

Where Tony was buried.

Miles turned away, not ready to think about his younger brother lying in the ground there all these years. He promised himself that once he settled in at Wildwood, he would make the journey to Tony's gravesite and mourn in private for the boy.

It struck him that both his father and Ralph would now be buried alongside Tony in the Notley family plot.

And that his mother might still be at Wildwood.

She had spent very little time with her three boys, though she had favored Tony of the three since he looked the most like her. Miles recalled she was very vain and seemed to criticize everything around her. Had she remained at Wildwood after Ralph's death? She usually spent most of the year in London, or least she had when he was a boy. Naturally, she would have come back for the funeral of her husband, only to be followed by that of her eldest son. Would she have fled the country and returned to the city? Or would she have remained in mourning? Either way, he would have to see her at some point.

The thought sickened him.

Somewhere still buried within him was that little boy who had wanted her to act as a true mother might. To nurture and comfort him after Tony's death. To stand up to Winslow and demand that he not ship Miles off for good. That had been wishful thinking on his part. She had never paid a whit of attention to him before and had taken to her bed when Tony was killed, so bereft that she didn't even attend Tony's funeral. The same might have occurred with Ralph's sudden, accidental death. He would need to prepare himself for their eventual encounter.

Miles only hoped it would be later rather than sooner.

He began breathing deeply, something he had been taught to do at Turner Academy when he became anxious. It had served him well during his time in the military and he had encouraged the men under him to take deep, calming breaths and clear their minds before they went into battle. He missed those soldiers and the camaraderie he'd felt with his fellow officers. Most of all, he missed his fellow Terrors.

"No sense to become maudlin," he murmured to himself, believing sentimentality made a man weak. He needed to prepare himself for what was about to take place.

The carriage turned from the road and began traveling up the lane leading to Wildwood. It had the air of familiarity and yet seemed different at the same time. He supposed because the trees and shrubbery had grown over the years, slightly changing the feel of the place. Then he saw the house and servants scrambling out the door, lining up to greet the new Duke of Winslow. He now played a more important role in the family tree and would need to wed and provide an heir to the dukedom.

That thought overwhelmed him.

Miles shoved it away and inhaled deeply, filling his lungs as the carriage came to a halt. Moments later, the stairs were set in place and the footman opened the door, allowing Miles to descend. He reached the ground and stood erect, hands behind his back, as he studied the two lines of servants. He recognized

Cook and Tom, a footman who had always been kind to him.

Then Sevill stepped forward. Miles' gut twisted at the sight of the butler. This would be the first change he made, getting rid of his father's right hand. Sevill would never be loyal to Miles and he would be uncomfortable keeping the longtime butler in a position of power.

"Your Grace," the butler said.

Miles noticed Sevill didn't truly greet him. Didn't express that he was happy to see the new duke. It reassured him that getting rid of Sevill would be a wise decision.

"Good day, Sevill," he said brusquely.

"Allow me to introduce you to your servants, Your Grace."

They moved along the first line, composed of all men. It included his father's valet, who looked frail and would need to be pensioned off, as well as Ralph's valet, a man named Crowder.

Coming to Thomas, Miles smiled. "Good day to you, Thomas. It has been a while."

The footman smiled broadly. "It is very good to see you again, Your Grace. I am head footman now."

Not for long. He decided this would be the man who would replace Sevill.

They moved on and he was glad to see Harris, the head groom, still remained.

"It's right nice to see you again, Your Grace," Harris said. "I hope you will take the time to come to the stables and see the horseflesh you own."

"Count on it, Harris. I had thought to buy a mount in London and decided I would wait and see what was available at Wildwood."

The groom grinned. "I think you'll find several to your liking, Your Grace."

They came to the end of the line and Miles turned to meet his female servants.

A handsome woman with kind eyes stepped forward. "I am your housekeeper, Your Grace. Mrs. Jenson. Let me introduce you to the rest of your staff."

He felt Sevill stiffen beside him and bit back a smile. He already liked this Mrs. Jenson, asserting herself over the snobbish butler.

She led him down the line, introducing each servant by name. When they reached the end, he turned and surveyed the group.

"Thank you for coming out and greeting me," he told them. "I look forward to getting to know each of you better, just as I did the soldiers under me."

"Would you like to go to your rooms and freshen up, Your Grace?" Mrs. Jenson asked.

"Yes. Please, walk with me, if you will."

The housekeeper accompanied him inside and up the stairs, saying, "Hot water is on its way, Your Grace."

Miles felt Sevill on their heels and glanced over his shoulder, seeing both the butler and Ralph's valet there.

"How long have you been at Wildwood, Mrs. Jenson?"

"Ten years, Your Grace. If you would like, I would be happy to show you about the house and answer any questions you might have regarding how it is run. In addition, I need to ask your food preferences. I plan the weekly menus with Cook and want to make certain she is preparing things to your liking."

He laughed. "I will be happy with whatever you select, Mrs. Jenson. After years of army rations, everything has to taste better." He paused. "I will need to speak with my estate manager as soon as possible."

"My husband, Mr. Jenson, is your steward, Your Grace," she informed him. "If you would like, I can have tea prepared and you could meet with him in the drawing room as soon as you are settled."

They reached the door to his father's quarters and Miles said, "Yes. I'll be downstairs in half an hour. Please join us, Mrs. Jenson. I may have additional questions for you by then."

"Would you mind if I included our daughter in this meeting? She assists both my husband and me in our duties. She also nursed your father and might be able to share with you about His Grace's final days."

Hearing about Winslow on his deathbed was the last thing Miles wanted to listen to but he said, "Yes, please include her, Mrs. Jenson. I will see you shortly."

He opened the door and entered the sitting room. He had only been in this room a handful of times, usually when he returned from school on holiday and his father quizzed him about what he had recently learned.

Looking to the valet, he said, "Please unpack the things in my trunk."

"Yes, Your Grace." The valet went through the next door.

Sevill asked, "Might I be included in your meeting with the Jensons, Your Grace? I feel there are things you should know."

"Yes, I expect you there. And Thomas, the head footman. Have him in attendance, as well."

The butler's mouth twitched in disapproval. "Very good, Your Grace."

Miles entered the bedchamber and found the valet already at work.

"More of my wardrobe will be arriving in the next few weeks. I had nothing but my uniforms and had some clothes made up in London."

"Would you care to change from your uniform, Your Grace?"

"No. I will remain in it for now. You may press the clothes in the trunk and have them ready for tomorrow."

The hot water arrived and he did discard his uniform's jacket and roll his sleeves up in order to thoroughly wash his hands and face. After drying them, Crowder assisted him back into the jacket.

Miles decided to speak to the valet now and ascertain whether he wanted this man working for him or not.

"Were you valet to the previous Duke of Winslow for very long?"

"No, Your Grace. I was with him six weeks when he . . .

passed."

Always a good judge of character, Miles felt the valet had more to say. "What happened to the duke's previous valet?"

Crowder composed himself and succinctly replied, "He left."

"Why?" he pressed.

"His Grace was very . . . particular."

"Are you saying Winslow was difficult?"

The valet looked horrified. "No. No, I would never make such a claim, Your Grace."

"Would you have stayed on as his valet had he lived?"

Crowder's gaze fell to the ground. "It is a privilege to serve a duke. Not many men can claim that honor."

"I will assume my brother went through valets—and other servants—often?"

Crowder's cheeks pinkened. "Yes, Your Grace."

"You won't have that problem with me, Crowder. If I become difficult, I expect you to tell me so. If I treat you unkindly, speak up. I will do my best to be a decent employer to you."

The valet's jaw dropped. Then he smiled broadly. "Yes, Your Grace. If that is all, I will finish unpacking for you."

"I think we'll do well together, Crowder," Miles predicted.

He moved around the bedchamber, noting that everything that seemingly belonged to his father or brother had been disposed of. The one item he would see removed was a portrait of Ralph that hung in the room.

"Crowder, have that portrait sent to the attics."

The valet nodded and returned to his work, unsuccessful in hiding his smile.

Miles left his new rooms and made his way downstairs to the drawing room. When he entered, he saw Mrs. Jenson already present, arranging items on a teacart. Sevill and Thomas stood nearby.

Then his gaze fell to an older man and young woman in conversation near the window. The woman was uncommonly pretty, quite tall and willowy, with raven hair. She was pointing to something out the window and the man nodded. He assumed them to be the Wildwood steward and the daughter Mrs. Jenson had spoken of.

The girl slipped her arm through her father's and steered him back to the center of the room where Miles stood.

She dipped into a curtsey. "Good afternoon, Your Grace. I am Miss Jenson. This is my father, Mr. Jenson, who has managed Wildwood for the past ten years."

"It is good to meet you both," he replied, thinking Mr. Jenson looked a bit uncomfortable.

Miles would have to get used to it. Any time he was introduced and people found out he was a duke, they would most likely react as Mr. Jenson. Wary. Wondering how to behave around him.

"Shall we sit?" he suggested, waving his hand to indicate a grouping of seats near the teacart.

As the Jenson family situated themselves, he turned to Sevill.

"Your service will no longer be required at any of my estates, Sevill," he said bluntly. "I know you served my father a good number of years and I am happy to write a reference that speaks to your abilities. If you would prefer to retire from service, I can arrange a pension for you."

The butler's face darkened with rage. "You think to replace me? After all I have done for this family?"

"Yes, that is exactly what I am saying," Miles said calmly.

"How dare you—"

"I can dare all I like, Sevill," he interrupted. "I am the Duke of Winslow now."

Sevill's eyes narrowed. "If he could have, His Grace would have disinherited you," he spat out. "You ruined this family. Things between His Grace and Her Grace were never the same afterward. The marquess ran wild and did as he pleased."

"Ralph always did," Miles pointed out. "It matters not whether my father is rolling in his grave. I am the duke—and I am replacing you. With Thomas," he added.

"Then give me a pension," growled Sevill. "I don't want a cottage on this estate. If I never see your face again, it would be too soon."

"Leave your forwarding address with Mr. Jenson. I will see you receive the desired funds," he said brusquely. "You are dismissed."

Sevill stormed from the room.

Miles turned to Thomas. "You were always capable, Thomas. I am certain with Sevill gone that you can step into his shoes and perform the required duties with ease."

Thomas nodded, his eyes filled with gratitude. "I am happy to be of service, Your Grace, in whatever capacity you see fit."

He thought a moment. "What is your surname, Thomas? I don't know if I have ever heard it."

"Trottmann."

"Very well, Mr. Trottmann. See that your things are moved into Sevill's bedchamber. Make his office yours. I hope you and Mrs. Jenson will work well together." He glanced to the housekeeper, who wore an approving smile.

"Mr. Trottmann and I will do quite nicely together," she said. "Mr. Sevill and I clashed on more than one occasion. Working with Mr. Trottmann will be a pleasure, Your Grace."

"That is good to hear. You may leave, Trottmann. In the meantime, I want to hear all about Wildwood." He turned to his steward. "It has been many years since I have been home, Mr. Jenson. I am eager to hear about the estate."

"The best way to learn about the estate is to see it, Your Grace," Miss Jenson said. "I would be happy to show it to you."

CHAPTER SEVEN

E MERY HAD NO idea why she had opened her mouth and invited the new Duke of Winslow to accompany her. The last time she had ridden out with the previous duke had been a disaster. She had almost lost her virtue.

And the Duke of Winslow had lost his life.

Perhaps it had something to do with the new titleholder sacking Sevill. The butler had ruled Wildwood with a heavy hand, constantly berating servants with his superior air. Though it seemed apparent this new duke had been away from Wildwood for many years, he obviously knew of Sevill's character and was now in a position to do something about it. She also liked that Winslow had chosen to replace the butler with Thomas, who was the perfect servant. Thomas behaved professionally. He always completed his tasks and then looked to help others with theirs. He was affable and polite. The staff at Wildwood would be overjoyed when they received news of Thomas replacing Sevill.

Emery thought it might also have a bit to do with the way His Grace held himself. She had always admired the men who chose to serve in the military. Winslow's very posture and gestures marked him as a leader, capable of whatever he put his mind to. Although he might not know anything about running an estate, she believed him to be astute. He would pick up on things quickly.

That was another reason she had volunteered to guide him

about the estate. Papa simply wasn't able to do so. While once a competent rider, she would be loath to see him in the saddle. To be asked to ride and speak knowledgeably of Wildwood at the same time would be too much for him. In the weeks since the previous duke's death and the arrival of this one, Papa had become further disconnected from the world. Emery had taken up more of his obligations until she was now managing the entire business of the estate. It wouldn't do for Papa to go off with this new duke because he would see immediately that something was very wrong.

Mama looked on with dismay as Emery asked, "Might you allow me time to change into my habit, Your Grace?"

"Certainly, Miss Jenson. Thank you for your kind offer. I will go to the stables and see that horses are saddled for us." He turned to her mother. "I would like to see the house at some point, Mrs. Jenson. I feel it best, however, to get out and see what is currently happening at Wildwood and meet some of my tenants."

"Meeting your tenants is important," Papa said, sounding lucid. "It was not a priority of the previous duke." He frowned. "He wasn't Winslow for very long."

The new duke nodded. "My brother's priority was always himself."

With that, he turned and left the drawing room.

Immediately, Mama said, "Are you sure this is wise, Emery?"

She placed a hand on her father's sleeve. "Papa, why don't you go work in your office?"

He looked at her blankly a moment and then said, "Yes. Of course. I have much to do. I will see you later, my dears."

The family left the drawing room, Papa turning in one direction and she and Mama in the other.

"Come help me change," she urged her mother, knowing her father would now go and sit behind his desk and be safe. For now.

They said not a word until they reached outside and begin

hurrying to their cottage. With no one around, they could speak freely.

"I will be perfectly fine, Mama. I know not to get off my horse once I have mounted. Besides, this man seems far different from his brother."

"I still think you should leave Wildwood," her mother said. "You are well educated. You could become a governess or companion to a great lady."

"No one will discover my lie about that day," Emery assured. "I returned to help Papa. The previous duke chose to keep riding. Several people knew how drunk Winslow was and told Sir William. No one need ever know Winslow wanted to bend me to his will and that I gave him what he deserved before leaving his presence."

They reached home and hurried inside. Mama begin undressing Emery.

"Besides, who would run the estate?" she asked. "The new Winslow may say he's interested in the property but we all know the *ton* prefers to spend their time in London for the Season. This man has a brand new title that he will want to show off. He will need to find himself a duchess in order to get an heir off her. That will give us time. We can see if Papa gets better."

"You are being ridiculous, Emery," Mama said. "As much as we might wish it, your father will never be the same man we have known. His periods of disorientation grow longer. He stares into nothing for hours at a time. We won't be able to hide his condition from others for much longer."

Mama helped her into her habit and began fastening buttons.

"We have got to try," she insisted. "Perhaps we can convince His Grace that he should bring in his own man to manage the estate. Someone younger. Then Papa could be pensioned off. I know the perfect cottage on the estate that we could move to in order to make this one available for the new steward. This way, Papa could keep his sterling reputation and you could keep your position."

Picking up her bonnet, she placed it atop her head. Mama helped slide in the pins to secure it.

"We have to try," Emery said.

"Very well. Just watch yourself with this man."

"Believe me, after my last experience with a Duke of Winslow, I plan to."

She went to the stables and Mr. Harris greeted her.

"Where is His Grace?" she asked. "Are our mounts ready?"

"What?" the groom asked, obviously perplexed.

"His Grace wished to see a bit of the estate and I offered to show it to him. I will return to the house. Have horses saddled for us, please."

"Yes, Miss Jenson."

Emery hurried back to the house and decided to cut through the kitchens to save time. To her surprise, she found the duke sitting at a table with Cook.

And he was laughing.

That alone surprised her. He had been all business in the short time she had been in his presence.

"Ah, Miss Jenson," he said, spying her and rising. "I see you are ready for our ride."

"Yes, Your Grace. I went to the stables and they told me you had not yet arrived."

He glanced back to Cook, the corners of his mouth turning up. "I had to say hello to my favorite person at Wildwood."

The old woman blushed to her roots. "Oh, go on, Your Grace," she said, smiling shyly.

"You will make the cake?" he asked.

"I most certainly will. It will grace your dinner table tonight."

"Thank you."

Those two simple words shocked Emery. She didn't remember either of the previous two dukes ever using them. Both barked orders and expected the servants to dance a jig to their tune. The fact this man actually thanked a servant gave her pause.

"Come along, Miss Jenson," the duke prodded.

She glanced up and saw he was already at the back door and moved quickly in his direction.

As they headed toward the stables, he asked, "Was the horse destroyed? The one which threw the former duke?"

Emery gasped, horrified by the thought. "No. Zeus is the finest mount you will ever see."

"I'll be the judge of that," he said curtly.

She shook her head. He might have only come into his title but he was certainly haughty enough. She supposed being an officer in His Majesty's army had been good training for his new position.

"Was he drunk?"

The question startled her. "The accident occurred in the afternoon, Your Grace, long before the hour of imbibing."

The duke halted, taking her by the elbow to stop her progress. The heat of his fingers caused an odd ripple down her spine.

"I asked if he had been drinking, Miss Jenson." His sky blue eyes stood out in his tanned face. A small scar on his right cheek caught her eye. "I expect total honesty from all my staff."

"I am not a part of your staff, Your Grace," Emery said, her chin rising a notch in defiance. "I draw no compensation from the estate."

The heat of his fingers through his gloves seared her. She felt her skin grow hot at his continued touch as her head grew light.

"Your mother led me to believe that you aid her and your father in their duties."

"That is correct," she said stiffly, stepping back from him, breaking the contact between them. Still, her heart pounded wildly in her chest, confusing her.

"What is it, exactly, that you do—for no pay? Tell me a few things."

Emery began listing them. "I pay the bills for all accounts, both those in Woodmorrow and the ones in London. I meet with the tenants and record a list of their needs and grievances. I order supplies needed. I—"

"Enough."

She swallowed, wondering where this discussion might lead.

"I would like you to draw up a list of your duties and those of your parents. I need to learn everything about this estate, no matter how long it takes."

Dismayed, she said, "I thought you would be going to London for the Season."

"Why?" he asked, as if baffled by her question.

"To find a wife, of course. It is the point of the Season. You are a member of Polite Society and one of its most powerful members now, thanks to your new title. You will need an heir."

He shook his head dismissively. "I am only four and twenty, Miss Jenson. My father did not wed until he was forty and had three sons. My first and only priority is Wildwood. I plan to learn every detail about it."

Dread filled her. This was not a man who would be trifled with. He was certainly not one who might be fooled. How was she to keep Papa's condition from him?

He started up again and she hurried to catch up to his long strides. They arrived at the stables and she saw that Zeus and Ares awaited them.

"Mr. Harris," the duke said, "might one of these creatures be Zeus? I am thinking the one on the left."

"You are right, Your Grace. This is Zeus and this is Ares."

Emery fretted, seeing Zeus was his usual ornery self, snorting and puffing, jerking his head from being held by Mr. Harris.

"I think you will enjoy being atop Ares," the groom said.

"Why not Zeus?" His Grace countered.

Harris shook his head. "You are an excellent rider, Your Grace. At least you were as a boy. But Zeus has little toleration for anyone other than Miss Jenson on his back. She is the only one who exercises him now."

The duke turned and gazed at her, those blue eyes penetrating her. She felt her cheeks heat.

"Is that so?" he asked softly.

Zeus began snorting louder, stomping a hoof. Emery moved to the horse, taking the harness in one hand and running her other up and down the horse's nose.

"You must show you are a good horse, Zeus," she told the horse. "His Grace wishes to ride you and you must let him. He is an excellent rider and will allow you your head. You like that, don't you, getting to run as fast as you can."

She kept talking to the horse, scratching between his ears and stroking his throat until he calmed.

"You have a good touch, Miss Jenson," the duke said. "You might as well ride him."

Without warning, his hands encircled her waist and he lifted her into Zeus' saddle.

Her entire body seemed to light up at his touch. The scent of sandalwood surrounded her. Then just as suddenly, he released her and stepped away, mounting Ares.

Looking down at Harris, Winslow said, "Save tomorrow morning for me. I will come and meet all the horses and look over their papers."

"Of course, Your Grace," the groom replied. "I look forward to introducing you to your stables."

The duke turned to her. "Miss Jenson? Show me what Zeus has got in him."

She smiled. "Certainly, Your Grace."

Emery barely nudged the horse with her knee and he took off. She was thankful he was a handful and took every bit of her concentration to control.

Otherwise, her thoughts would be on the Duke of Winslow and how her body craved his touch again.

CHAPTER EIGHT

MILES URGED ARES on, wanting to catch up to Miss Jenson, who had taken off faster than lightning. As he chased her down across pastureland, he couldn't help but be impressed by her tremendous riding skills. She had been correct in telling him that Zeus was an incredible horse. Miles itched to ride the beast himself.

He also knew that Ralph had been insane to climb into Zeus' saddle. His brother had only been an adequate rider and had never shown any true interest in horseflesh, unlike Miles who lived for horses. He hadn't seen Ralph in many years but he couldn't imagine the boy of thirteen with little interest in horses had matured into a man who found them fascinating, much less one who could control a mount such as Zeus. No wonder he had been thrown.

He had guessed that Ralph had been drinking. It was something Miles had caught his brother doing several times during that final summer at Wildwood. Ralph, always arrogant, had proven to be unbearable with drink in him. After Ralph shot and killed Tony, Miles always wondered if his brother had been drinking that day. It would explain why he had ventured into their father's study and dared to take the pistol from the desk drawer. Ralph had been defiant, threatening his brothers. Though a good shot, if Ralph had been under the influence of strong drink, it would explain why he had acted so careless and cavalier.

Miss Jenson slowed Zeus, allowing Miles to catch up to her. She wheeled the horse to face him. Color flooded her cheeks and excitement sparkled in her unusual eyes, deep brown ones rimmed in amber. They drew him in and he wished he could sink into their depths, straight to her soul. He blinked, trying to break the spell she seemed to cast upon him. He was here to see his estate, not wax poetic about a woman's eyes.

"What do you think of Zeus?" she asked, patting the horse and bending to plant a kiss between its ears.

Damnation. He wished he was the object of her interest and wondered what it would be like to place his lips upon her rosy, plump ones.

"He is very spirited. He does have beautiful lines. Is he sixteen hands?"

"Seventeen," she replied. "Zeus is the most outstanding mount in your stables. You'll see that when you view the other horses tomorrow." She stroked the horse fondly.

"How did you come to ride him?"

"Your father purchased him shortly before he had to give up riding. He loved the horse, though, and wanted to be sure Zeus received exercise daily. His Grace knew I went out often—usually daily—upon the estate and asked me to ride Zeus when I did so."

"It takes an adept rider to handle a horse of that temperament," he noted.

"I've ridden from a young age," she explained. "Papa and Mama both thought it important. Mama was a doctor's daughter and had herself ridden from a young age. Papa's father was a viscount who taught his four sons to ride. As a steward, he knows he must be out often on the estate."

She paused a moment. "Papa is getting older now. I take his place sometimes in riding out, acting as his eyes and ears while he toils away in his office."

"I see."

Miss Jenson was proving to be a most interesting woman.

"Well, you ride like my friend, Wyatt. Which is to say you

are an expert who may take a few chances here and there."

She laughed and the sound of it warmed his blood.

"Shall we go see some of the fields?" she asked.

"Yes."

She kept Zeus to a canter and as they went from one area to another, she schooled him on crops.

"We have used a seed drill for several years now instead of haphazardly tossing seeds about. It allows for a more even distribution of the seeds and places them deep enough in the ground to firmly take root."

"What is grown here? I seem to remember rye. Or perhaps barley."

"Wheat is the largest crop. Rye was grown at Wildwood when we first arrived but it is a low-yield crop. Wheat and barley are much higher in yield and, therefore, more profitable."

She explained to him about the balance of arable and permanent pasture land and how the estate grew turnips and clover in recent years. She went into great detail about why this had been done and how the area of fallow land could be reduced. He lost track of her explanation somewhere between how to clear the land of weeds by ploughing versus how turnips sown in rows could have weeds removed by hoes while they grew. He didn't quite follow everything but understood that the turnips and clover could be used as animal fodder.

"We also have worked into getting more nitrogen into the soil. That increases the yield of grains. We've done so by not only planting clover but legumes, such as peas and beans, which help enrich the soil with nitrogen."

He laughed. "Enough, Miss Jenson. You are showing off now," he teased.

Her cheeks flushed. "I apologize, Your Grace."

"No, don't," he said. "This is all information I need to master." He smiled. "It's just too much of it at the moment because it's so unfamiliar to me. You are a good teacher, Miss Jenson. You will merely need to be patient with me as I plod along."

She studied him. "Something tells me you were an excellent student in school, Your Grace."

"I did well in my courses. Especially languages and history." He laughed. "Neither one being very helpful in managing an estate."

"It will come to you in time," she promised. "As for history, I also have an interest in it, everything from ancient to modern history. I have learned quite a bit about this area from exploring the graveyard in Woodmorrow."

His gut tightened at the mention of that. Brusquely, he said, "What else do I need to view this afternoon?"

"Would you like to see the area where your tenants live?"

"Very much so. And meet some of them if I can."

They had been out several hours and he thought she might need to get out of the saddle for a bit. Then again, if she rode frequently, she might be used to this.

Within ten minutes, they arrived at a large group of cottages. Thankfully, they weren't bunched together. Miss Jenson pointed out how most of the tenants had small gardens planted beside or behind their cottages and how they were allowed to harvest what they grew there for personal use or to sell the produce in the nearby village.

"Would you like to walk, Your Grace? I see workers who will be eager to meet you."

"Yes. I would like that very much."

He quickly dismounted and then went to aid her from Zeus' back. His hands went to her waist and he swung her to the ground. For a moment, he gazed into those luminous eyes. Neither of them said anything. Reluctantly, he released her.

Miles stepped away, hearing the cries of children nearby. He turned and saw a group running toward them. When the dozen or so arrived, they paid him no mind at all. Instead, they all wanted Miss Jenson's attention. She hugged several of them, asking questions and praising them for little things. Observing her, he thought she would one day make for a good mother, much better than his own had ever been. She seemed genuinely interested in hearing what these children had to say and he could tell they worshipped her.

Finally, she shushed them. "Children, I would like to introduce you to His Grace, the Duke of Winslow."

Immediately, they quieted, studying him with large eyes.

"Are you going to die like the last one? He wasn't duke very long," one boy of about seven asked.

Miss Jenson scolded the boy. "That was very rude, Billy. Please apologize to His Grace."

"I'm sorry, Your Grace," the boy said, his bottom lip trembling.

Miles looked across the sea of children and saw they all were afraid. He realized it was fear of him. He wanted respect from those on his land, not fear. He had known officers in the army who liked to command using fear but he had never thought it particularly effective.

Placing a hand on young Billy's shoulder, he said, "I don't plan to die anytime soon, Billy. I hope to live a long and fruitful life." Miles offered his hand. "Here, let us shake to show there are no hard feelings."

Billy thrust his hand out and placed it in Miles' hand and they shook.

"My father always says the same thing. That if you are angry with your friend, you should shake and get over it."

A thought occurred to him as he looked more carefully at this boy. "Might your father be Kit Munson?"

"You know him?" Billy asked, his eyes widening.

"Very well. Is he around? I would like to shake his hand, too."

"Come on." Billy tugged on Miles' hand. "We live over here."

Like the Pied Piper, the others followed them. They stopped at a white cottage with gray shutters.

"Wait here," the boy instructed, rushing through the open door.

Almost immediately, a tall, lanky man appeared. A smile

broke out on his face.

"Miles!" he cried, stepping forward. Then he stopped short. "I mean . . . I am sorry, Your Grace."

He threw his arms around Kit. "I have missed you," he declared, pounding his old friend on the back and then pulling away to look at him. "You haven't changed much. Billy resembles you."

"He's more his mother than me," Kit said. "So, you are back for good?"

"Yes. With Ralph's death, I am now the duke."

"I wondered," Kit said. "If that would come to pass."

He shrugged. "Ralph should have wed and had a son. I expect he and Winslow are both turning in their graves at the prospect of me becoming the family's duke." Miles turned and gestured for Miss Jenson to join them. "Miss Jenson has been taking me across the estate. I arrived earlier today."

"You were friends once?" she asked.

Miles nodded. "Kit and I were as thick as thieves when we were boys. He was two years older than I was but a fine companion." He looked to his friend. "If you have a boy, you must have a wife."

Kit looked toward the cottage and Miles saw a woman standing in the doorway. She held the hand of a little girl who was the spitting image of her mother.

"Come on, Ann. Say hello to His Grace."

She came forward slowly, her daughter accompanying her.

Again, Miles offered his hand. "I am pleased to meet you, Mrs. Munson. And sorry you are stuck with this ugly one."

Kit's wife looked thunderstruck—and then she burst out in laughter.

"I do my best to keep him in line, Your Grace. It isn't easy," she proclaimed.

"And who is this little lady?" he asked.

"Becky," the girl said and then buried her face in her mother's skirts.

"You have a fine family, Kit," he told his friend. "Perhaps you can ask me to dinner some night and we can catch up."

Kit, who had slipped an arm about his wife's waist, froze. Miles realized he had breached an invisible line drawn between them—and found he didn't care.

"I plan to be a much different Duke of Winslow than my father," he explained.

He glanced around and saw quite a crowd had gathered as he had talked with his childhood friend. Miles decided to address them now.

"I am Miles Notley, the new Duke of Winslow. Some of you know me. Or have heard of me. Whatever you know—or think you know—I hope you will put it aside. I plan to be an active landowner and wish to get to know each of my tenants and their families. I never thought to be a duke and will undoubtedly make mistakes. I promise to learn from them and be a good landlord to you."

He looked out and saw everything from puzzlement to fear on the faces in the crowd. These people weren't used to a duke speaking plainly to them.

It was time for a change.

"I have already asked myself to dinner at Kit Munson's house. I hope over the next several months that I can share a meal with each of you and your families and come to know you and your needs."

No one spoke for a moment and Miles believed he had already shot himself in the foot. What duke went about eating with farmers?

Then a cheer erupted and he saw some tide had been turned. Kit took him by the arm and led him about, introducing him to people left and right. By the time they finished, his head swirled with too many names to remember.

"I must get back," he told Kit and Ann. "If you are willing to have me to dinner, send word. I will be happy to come."

"Can Miss Jenson come, too?" Billy asked.

Miles looked to the woman who had introduced him to his land and stood to the side as he had met his people.

"Yes. Miss Jenson would be happy to come," he announced. "We will see you later."

They waved goodbye to those still gathered and returned to their horses.

As Miles lifted her into the saddle, the subtle scent of lilac drifted from her skin and he said, "I hope you don't mind that I spoke for you. You don't have to come if you don't wish to."

"No, I would be happy to accompany you," she said. "I often stop and visit with your tenants and even share a meal with them. For me, it is nothing out of the ordinary." Her gaze pinned his. "But for the Duke of Winslow to do so? That is indeed extraordinary."

Miles mounted Ares. "Perhaps I plan to be an extraordinary duke."

CHAPTER NINE

T HEY RETURNED TO the stables and handed off their horses to Harris.

"I will be expecting a tour of the stables and an introduction to my horseflesh first thing after breakfast tomorrow," Miles told the head groom.

"I am happy to oblige you, Your Grace. I think you will be pleased with what you find."

"I plan to take Zeus out tomorrow," he shared. "That is, if Miss Jenson thinks it is a good idea."

"You are an excellent horseman, Your Grace. I believe you are adept enough to handle Zeus." She gave him a conspiratorial smile. "However, if you bring an apple for him, he might take to you more quickly."

"You are saying I should bribe Zeus?" he teased.

"No. Merely reward him for future good behavior." She laughed merrily and, once more, Miles found himself drawn to her.

He hadn't been around many women in his life. His mother had made herself scarce during his childhood and he had no sisters. Turner Academy housed only male students though he had grown close to Mrs. Nehemiah Turner and Mrs. Josiah Turner. Donovan had seen that Miles was introduced to the pleasures of the flesh during university and then Miles had engaged in bed sport occasionally while in Spain and Portugal while in the military with some of the locals or camp followers.

Still, something about Miss Jenson seemed different. Perhaps because she was so much taller than any woman of his acquaintance, just a couple of inches under six feet. It might be her engaging smile or those brown eyes rimmed in amber which drew him in. She certainly knew quite a bit about Wildwood and the running of an estate. He believed he could send her to any of his other properties and she would improve it and have it running splendidly in no time.

If he did, though, he wouldn't have the pleasure of her company. For now, he was enticed by it—and all she could teach him.

"Shall we return to the house?" he asked, wanting to offer her his arm and then deciding he shouldn't. Though she was a lady in his mind, Polite Society would not think of her as such. She was a servant. No, not even that, since she had told him she drew no wages from the estate. That would be something he would rectify immediately.

They set off and he said, "You have said you assist both your parents in their work. Why have you never received a salary for doing so?"

She halted, her features thoughtful. Finally, she said, "Mama and Papa have taught me all I know. They educated me themselves, in everything from languages to mathematics. When we came to Wildwood, I was twelve. They continued my studies but began sharing with me bits and pieces of their own duties on the estate. I gravitated toward certain things and they told me about how to accomplish those tasks." She chuckled. "I would never have gone to His Grace—whether as a child or an adult—and ask to be paid."

"You do a great deal about the estate," he pointed out. "I insist you become a member of my staff. I will speak to . . ." His voice trailed off. "Whom would I speak to about putting you on my payroll?"

Miss Jenson laughed aloud. "That would be me, Your Grace. Whenever Mama hires a new household servant, I am informed and see that they receive their monthly wages."

He smiled. "Then see yourself placed on my staff, Miss Jenson. And pay yourself fairly."

She looked taken aback. "Oh, I cannot decide my worth, Your Grace. That is for you alone."

"I have no idea what I am paying anyone, Miss Jenson. My cook. The footmen. Mr. Harris."

"Then make that your first lesson, Your Grace. I will give you the ledgers and you may study what different positions pay and set my salary accordingly."

"You are very quick in your thinking, Miss Jenson."

"Thank you, Your Grace."

They continued toward the house and he insisted they cut through the kitchens, telling her he wanted to check on the cake Cook promised to bake him.

"It's right here, Your Grace," she told him when he asked, showing him the three-tiered work of art.

"It looks just as it did . . . that day," he said quietly.

"Yes, Your Grace. It was always your favorite. I have never forgotten."

He looked to Miss Jenson. "You and your parents must come to dinner and have a piece of my cake. It is large enough that it needs to be shared."

She looked at him as if his mind had fled. "That is not suitable, Your Grace."

"Why not? I am the duke. I may invite to my dinner table whomever I please."

She hesitated and then said, "I am afraid Her Grace would not approve."

Her words struck him as hard as any physical blow might.

So, his mother was at Wildwood. She must have accompanied Ralph when he returned. She had witnessed not one funeral, but two. Still, she had not bothered to come and greet him, the new Duke of Winslow, when he arrived earlier today.

He had plenty to say to his mother. All of it unpleasant. He would not subject the Jenson family to that.

"I see. Then let us have a slice of cake now. Cook, you must join us."

"Oh, no, Your Grace. I mustn't. I am overseeing dinner preparations now. Her Grace would blister my ears if the meal arrived late."

Determination filled him. "I am in charge now, Cook. Not the duchess. If I want dinner put off by a few minutes, then that is what will happen. Please, cut three slices of the cake for us and let us enjoy it together."

He escorted Miss Jenson to the table he had sat at earlier with Cook and seated her. Soon, the three of them had plates of cake before them and cups of hot tea.

Miles took a bite and sighed. "This is heavenly, Cook."

She thanked him and quickly ate her entire piece before he was able to take another bite.

"May I be excused, Your Grace? I do want to see to dinner."

Not wanting to put undue stress upon her, he said, "Of course."

Cook left and he took another bite, savoring the rich, sweet dessert.

Then he asked, "Is the duchess very irritable with the servants?"

Miss Jenson frowned. "It is not my place to judge Her Grace."

That told him all he needed to know but he pressed her. "Please, Miss Jenson. I have spoken of honesty. I need to know the situation I am stepping into. I have been gone for fourteen years."

She worried her plump, bottom lip, causing a surge of lust to ripple through him.

"Her Grace can be ill-tempered at times. Mind you, she is very rarely present at Wildwood. She spends the majority of her time in London. When here, though, she does find fault with everything around her."

"Waspish," he concluded. "It is how she was my entire childhood. Before I was sent away."

Miss Jenson nodded. "That would describe her accurately."

"Finish your cake, Miss Jenson. It is delicious, isn't it?"

"Very much so, Your Grace."

An idea came to Miles. He knew exactly what to do with his mother. He planned never to refer to her that way again. He certainly didn't plan to have her stay under his roof.

"If I might excuse myself, Your Grace," she said. "I need to see my father."

"Do so, Miss Jenson. Thank you again for the excellent tour of the estate. You are quite knowledgeable. I am sure I will come to rely upon you a great deal."

Her cheeks pinkened at his compliment. "Whatever you need, Your Grace."

She started to leave and he said, "Wait."

She turned. "Yes, Your Grace?"

"You do seem to know horses. Would you care to accompany me as I meet the animals in my stables?"

The corners of her mouth turned up. "That would be most agreeable."

"Excellent. Come in your riding habit. I might wish to ride out afterward. If Zeus throws me on my arse, you can ride for help."

Miss Jenson bit back a smile. "I will see you tomorrow morning then."

"Yes. Eight o'clock?"

"That early?" she squeaked. "Oh, please forgive me."

"You wish to go later?" he inquired.

"No, it is just that the household is not used to a duke who rises early."

"This duke is a former military man. In my world, half the day had passed by the time eight o'clock arrived."

She laughed again, the sound rich and deep, striking a chord within him.

"Eight o'clock at the stables," she promised.

MILES STRODE TOWARD the drawing room, knowing that was where he would find his mother. He knew it customary for the duke and duchess, when in residence, to gather there before dinner for a sherry. She hadn't bothered to greet him when he arrived but she would no longer be able to ignore him as she had when he was a child.

He entered the room and saw Thomas with a silver tray in hand, offering the duchess her wine.

"I don't understand why *you* are doing this," she said peevishly. "This is *Sevill's* job. And why on earth are you dressed in that manner? It was as if you were the butler."

"Mr. Trottmann *is* the butler," Miles informed her as he crossed the room and lifted the second glass from the tray, taking a small, fortifying sip.

"I will inform you when dinner is ready, Your Grace," Thomas said and exited the room.

He thought it must be the efficient Mrs. Jenson who had made sure Thomas no longer wore his footman's livery and was now attired according to his position.

His mother frowned. Still not addressing him by name, she said, "Where is Sevill?"

"He no longer is employed here."

Shock filled her face but she quickly recovered her composure. "I assume this is your doing."

"It is. As the Duke of Winslow, I wish to have servants around me that can not only perform their tasks impeccably but also ones who hold my trust. Mr. Trottmann is certainly one of those."

"Just because Sevill was Winslow's faithful servant all those years didn't mean you had to sack him," she snapped.

"That is exactly why Sevill is no longer a part of Wildwood," he stated firmly.

She waved a hand in the air. "I suppose you will be making all kinds of changes."

"I may."

"You shouldn't," she said flatly. "You have neither the knowledge nor the acumen to do so."

Miles finished the sherry and set the glass aside. "I beg to differ with you, Madam. I received a first-rate education at Turner Academy, followed by earning my university degree from Cambridge. I have spent the past several years as an army officer, achieving the rank of captain and commanding a goodly number of troops. I had the respect of Lieutenant-General Wellesley and my fellow officers. While I might not have been raised to be the heir apparent, I possess the tools to learn how to fulfill my obligations."

She sniffed and finished her drink.

"You would do well to stay on my good side, Madam," he warned her.

Her eyes narrowed. "What do you mean by that?"

"As Winslow, I am now head of the family and control the purse strings."

"If you think to cut me off—"

"If I do cut you off, it will be because of your own actions," he interrupted. "For now, I expect you to remove yourself from Wildwood and relocate to the dower house."

She gasped. "You would toss me from my own home?"

"You mean *my* home?" He stared at her until she blinked and turned away. "I will one day bring a woman home to be my duchess. I have no plans of you being here, whispering in her ear, poisoning her. Tomorrow, you will go to the dower house until your mourning period is completed."

"Mourning? But the Season is going on," she complained.

Miles cleared his throat. "I can almost understand you not mourning Winslow. I don't think the two of you ever got along and even as a boy, I understood that you lived separate lives. But your son has just passed. Surely, you wish to mourn him?"

"Ralph would not want me to bury myself in the country. He was a good, thoughtful son."

He glared at her. "Ralph was a liar."

Her mouth twitched in disgust. "You would say that."

Stepping toward her, he bent until their noses almost touched. "Ralph shot Tony. He *killed* Tony." He raised to his full height again. "I loved Tony with all my heart. I was a good brother to him. Ralph never loved anyone but himself. He was guilty of firing the bullet that ended Tony's life. You know this. You feel it in your bones. You have simply ignored it all these years."

She looked thunderstruck. "He couldn't have."

"He did. I even believe Ralph was drinking that day he led us into the study and pulled the pistol from the desk. Ralph murdered Tony."

She shook her head violently. "I can't believe that. I won't. You are slandering Ralph's good name."

"Believe what you wish," he said dismissively. "I don't care. I only know Ralph slandered my name and reputation."

"The truth will come out about what you did," she hissed. "Winslow hid it from others."

"Winslow was as blind as you are to Ralph's shortcomings." He stepped toward her again and she shrank back, intimidated by his size. "You will go to the dower house until this time next year and mourn your losses. Only then will I allow you to go to London, where you will live in a rented house."

Her jaw dropped. "I won't live in my townhouse?"

"No. It is my townhouse. Again, I do not want a viper such as you in my midst."

Thomas entered the room at that moment. Miles shook his head and the new butler remained silent.

Recalling what Miss Jenson had said about his mother's treatment of others, he added, "While you are living at the dower house, you will watch your tongue, Madam. You will treat your servants with kindness and respect. You will not complain. You will be the model of a true lady. If you can watch both your words and actions, then I will allow you to go to London next spring. Provide for your house. Pay for your gowns and servants."

He paused and then said, "But if I hear that you have spoken of Tony's death and placed the blame at my doorstep, I will cut you off completely."

Her face grew red. "You wouldn't dare!"

He laughed harshly. "I can do whatever I want, Madam. I am the Duke of Winslow."

She began wringing her hands, her agitation clear. "You would do this to your mother?" she asked meekly.

"You may have given birth to me but as far as I am concerned, I have no mother." He looked to Thomas. "Please inform Mrs. Jenson that Her Grace will be moving to the dower house tomorrow. See that it is cleaned and aired and that an adequate number of servants staff it. I will speak to those who serve there. If Her Grace acts spitefully to any of them, they are to report the incident to me at once."

"Yes, Your Grace," Thomas said.

He turned to his mother. "It would serve you well to act and speak with your future in mind. Behave properly and you may continue to live in the manner you are accustomed to. You will be polite and gracious when we meet in society. You will spread no gossip about me, my future wife, or our children. In return, I will see you are cared for."

Miles looked expectantly at Thomas, who said, "Dinner is served, Your Grace."

"Very good." He offered his arm to the woman who stood in stunned silence. "Shall we?"

Reluctantly, she placed her hand on his sleeve.

"Do you understand everything we have spoken of this evening? You have no questions?"

"None," she said stiffly.

For some reason, Miles needed her to address him correctly and said, "That would be none, Your Grace. Or none, Winslow."

Her expression grew pained but she managed to say, "None, Winslow."

"Excellent. I am glad that we had this conversation and that you are clear about your role."

He led her from the room and as they reached the dining room, she halted.

"I believe I have lost my appetite, Winslow."

"Then you may be excused to your room. Have a pleasant evening."

Alone now, Miles entered the small dining room. Thomas himself seated Miles. He saw something in the butler's face which looked like approval.

As their gazes met, he told Thomas, "Speak freely. You have something to say, perhaps?"

The butler bit back a smile. "Only that it is most apparent that things at Wildwood will be changing." After a brief pause, Thomas added, "For the better."

Miles nodded, glad that his butler approved. "That is my intention. Know that if you have anything you wish to discuss with me regarding the staff and my household, I am always more than willing to hear what you have to say. In fact, I encourage you and anyone in my employ to do the same.

"Very good, Your Grace. I will make your wishes known." Thomas beamed at Miles. "It seems good times are coming to Wildwood." The butler bowed his head in recognition and then stepped away to supervise the footmen.

One footman poured wine for him as another placed the soup course before him. He thanked them and began to eat.

He had resented his mother for so many years. A small part of him, that little boy who longed for acceptance, had hoped upon his return to Wildwood that they might actually reconcile. He understood now that would never come to pass and accepted it. The Duchess of Winslow would not be a part of his future.

In time, a new Duchess of Winslow would take her place—and Miles would build a much different kind of family from the one he came from.

CHAPTER TEN

EMERY HANDED HER father his hat and said, "We must get you up to the main house, Papa."

He placed it on his head and walked out the front door of their cottage, looking around as if in a daze. She realized he didn't know where to go and her heart grew heavy.

Slipping her hand through his arm, she said, "I will walk with you."

She escorted him to his office and made sure he was seated behind his desk. Opening a few ledgers, she said, "Your task is to look over these today. Can you do that?"

He nodded, a vague look on his face, and then asked, "Where will you be?"

"I am going to the stables with His Grace to look over his stock and then I believe we are going to ride out and see more of Wildwood today."

Papa snorted. "He is getting too old to get on a horse."

She placed a hand over his. "No, Papa, His Grace passed away recently. His son is now Winslow." She avoided mentioning the son in-between who had only been the duke for a week. No sense in confusing Papa any more than he already was.

"That one is trouble," Papa murmured.

Emery's heart skipped a beat. "You know of His Grace?" she asked carefully. "How he left here as a young boy?"

He shook his head. "He is a bad sort. You would do well to

avoid him, Emery."

"Why? What did he do to see him banished from his own home?" she asked.

But her father's gaze fell to the page before him and he turned it, perusing figures that no longer meant anything to him.

"I will see you this afternoon," she told him and slipped from the room.

Emery had never heard a word spoken about this son by any of the servants. Of course, they may have after her family first arrived and she hadn't known to pay attention to what was being said. Perhaps Mama knew something about the duke and could tell her. She doubted it, though. Mama despised gossip and wouldn't allow anyone in her presence to partake in it. Still, it would be worth the trouble of asking her. The mystery surrounding the new Duke of Winslow was too great.

She went to the kitchens and collected an apple from the storeroom, slipping it into the deep pockets of her riding skirt. Since she had time, she went to look in on her mother and found her inside her office.

"Ah, Emery, I am glad you stopped by." Her mother picked up a sheet from the desk and handed it to her. "Will you have time today to drive into the village and place this order with Mr. Jernigan?"

"I will be out riding with His Grace, Mama. When I am done, I can go into Woodmorrow and deliver this list. If it is late, I will return tomorrow with the cart to pick everything up."

She folded the list of supplies and placed it into her pocket.

"That will be fine, my darling. Will you be out long?"

"I am not certain. We are to meet with Mr. Harris in a few minutes and let His Grace see the horseflesh he owns. Afterward, we are to ride the estate again." She hesitated a moment and then said, "Mama, do you know why His Grace left Wildwood so long ago?"

Before her mother could reply, Addy entered and said, "Mrs. Jenson, you are needed at once."

"Very well, Addy."

The maid apologized for interrupting them. Emery assured Addy that she was just leaving.

"We will speak later, Emery," her mother said and left with the servant.

She wondered if her mother had any information or would simply warn her off from seeking any answers regarding His Grace.

Leaving the office, she cut through the kitchens and went out the door. Ahead of her, she saw the duke striding toward the stables. He wasn't dressed in his regimental colors today. Instead, he wore a coat of midnight blue and tan breeches. The coat emphasized the broadness of his shoulders, while the tight breeches left little to the imagination. Winslow's long, muscular legs drew her eyes, causing her heart to pound. It had done the same thing when he had placed her into the saddle yesterday and helped her from it. She had lain awake for hours last night, thinking of his touch and how much she wanted it.

Emery hurried after him, pushing the foolish thoughts from her mind. He was the Duke of Winslow, one of the most powerful men in all of England. He would wed a woman of charm and beauty, one with an immense dowry. Men such as Winslow weren't meant for the likes of her.

It saddened her because it seemed no man was destined for her. While Emery knew everyone on the estate and many of those residing in the nearby village, she had no friends and hadn't attracted any suitors. Because of her father being a gentleman, albeit an untitled one, she seemed stuck in a place between worlds. Servants and tenants were friendly to her but not her friends. None of the farmers or staff members at Wildwood would ever think to court her.

The same proved true in Woodmorrow. Everyone was kind to her but no male had ever looked at her longingly or flirted with her in the slightest. Many females of every class were already wed by Emery's age of twenty-two, often with a child or two.

Though she longed to find a husband and eagerly wanted children, she doubted that would ever occur. Even if she left Wildwood, as her mother had suggested, she would only be an upper servant in a household, once more hovering between worlds.

Sometimes it was lonely, having only Mama and Papa as her friends. Especially nowadays, with her father's mental condition deteriorating, she delved more and more into work. With the new duke being so astute, hiding Papa's weak state of mind should be her top priority—not daydreaming about a handsome peer who was far from her reach.

She reached the stables, where Winslow and Mr. Harris were in conversation. They paused and greeted her.

"I was telling His Grace that the finest horses in the stables all have the names of Greek gods," the groom said. "Though many of your other horses are also good purchases, Your Grace. For instance, you have an excellent carriage team."

"I am eager to meet them," the duke said. He revealed an apple in his palm. "I brought the necessary bribery for Zeus," he quipped. "I will wait and give it to him just before I ride out."

"Don't let any of the others see it," she warned. "They will be hurt if you did not bring them any treats."

He snorted. "I doubt horses get their feelings hurt."

"And I am certain they can and do," she said saucily. "Give it to me. I can place it in my pocket."

The trio entered the stables. As they paused before each stall, Harris told the duke the name of the mare or stallion within and a bit about its temperament and history. Winslow insisted upon entering every stall, gliding his hands over the horse's coat and checking everything from hooves to teeth to tails. Emery liked that he had a gentle hand and took his time with each one.

They arrived at Zeus' stall and the horse immediately nudged the duke's shoulder.

"He likes you," Harris said, approval in his voice. "You always had a way with horses in your youth, Your Grace."

Emery realized that Harris would most likely be able to solve the mystery of why this man had left Wildwood as a boy. She thought to ask him later when they had privacy.

Then she watched the duke as he stroked the horse, his handsome profile making her knees go weak. It was none of her business why he had been sent away. She tamped down her curiosity, deciding it was beneath her to go about digging into his private affairs.

They reached the last stall, where Athena stood. Emery entered before the two men arrived and pulled the apple she had brought from her pocket.

"Are you giving away my apple?" the duke chided, though she could tell he was teasing.

"I brought one for Athena. As you can see, she will foal soon."

Winslow stepped inside the stall. "She is a beauty." He ran his hands along her swollen sides. "Very fine lines. Who is the sire?"

"Zeus, Your Grace," Harris responded.

"Then the foal will be magnificent. Zeus and Athena are an incredible pair," Winslow declared.

Emery offered the apple to Athena, who nibbled at it daintily. "Don't expect this from Zeus," she said. "He will gobble his apple in a single bite."

"You're a good girl, Athena," the duke told the mare. "Is this her first?"

"Yes," she said. "She will soon be a dam."

He turned to the groom. "Thank you for showing off the horses, Harris. We are well situated at Wildwood regarding horseflesh." He paused. "Are there any mounts in London?"

"Some, Your Grace. A team which takes Her Grace about. A few horses for . . . that is, ones the previous duke rode. He spent a majority of his time in London and only rarely visited Wildwood."

"Did Ralph live with my mother in the townhouse there?"

"I believe he did, Your Grace." The groom looked uncomfortable being questioned about the previous duke.

"Well, have Zeus saddled for me." He turned to her. "Miss Jenson, will you accompany me again?"

"If you wish, Your Grace," she replied.

"Then saddle a mount for Miss Jenson, as well," the duke instructed.

"Will Demeter do today, Miss Jenson?" Harris asked.

"Yes, thank you."

She accompanied the duke outside to wait for their horses and said, "I have composed a list of duties that I have taken over for my parents," she informed him. "Mama and Papa will also create their own lists and we can present these to you by tomorrow morning."

"It seems the Jensons are a very efficient family," he remarked.

"We are conscious of always doing our best for the estate," she said evenly, trying to still the giddiness in her belly as she inhaled the scent of sandalwood on his skin.

Stepping away, Emery turned as if she were looking out on the day instead of trying to deliberately put space between them.

"It is a fine day."

"Any day when I cannot hear the screams of dying men or smell their blood running into the earth is a good day," he said abruptly.

She wheeled, taken aback by his words.

"I am sorry, Miss Jenson," he apologized. "It has been a long time since I was in the presence of a lady. Too many years at war have made me cynical and my manners uncouth."

"I am no lady, Your Grace," she reminded him. "Merely a servant. A paid one—if you can come up with what wages you wish to pay me."

He closed the distance between them and her heart pounded against her ribs.

"You are a lady, Miss Jenson," he told her, his gaze warm. "You are the daughter of a gentleman."

"A gentleman who was a fourth son. One who had to make

his way in the world with no help from his father. Papa worked as an assistant steward and steward on several estates before obtaining his position at Wildwood. He did not wed Mama until he was forty, wanting to be able to provide her with a decent living."

"Your mother is a handsome woman and most impressive. I look forward to touring my home with her. Perhaps you would care to join us?"

This was getting ridiculous.

"Your Grace, you are a grown man. I believe you are more than capable of walking through your own house with your housekeeper without having me accompany you. I do have things to do, you know."

"Yes, in order to earn that fabulous salary I plan to bestow upon you," he said.

Emery burst out laughing.

"I like the sound of your laugh, Miss Jenson. It has been many years since I have heard laughter. War is no laughing matter."

Before she could ask him about it, Harris and another groom brought their horses around.

"A hand, Mr. Harris?" she asked, wanting the groom to help her into the saddle.

He obliged and she took up Demeter's reins, turning to see that Winslow stood before Zeus, talking quietly to the horse. Then he came to her and held out a hand.

"The apple, Miss Jenson?" he asked politely.

"Oh, of course, Your Grace." She removed it from her pocket and handed it over. Their fingers brushed slightly against one another and Emery was grateful of the gloves they both wore.

The duke gave Zeus the apple and the horse downed it, chomping heartily and then spitting out the core.

"I told you he was greedy," she said.

Winslow laughed. "You did not exaggerate." He mounted and said, "Try and keep up, Miss Jenson. I plan to let Zeus show me what he can do."

With that, duke and horse were gone.

CHAPTER ELEVEN

EXHILARATION FILLED MILES as he finally reined in Zeus and brought the horse to a halt, wheeling to face Miss Jenson, who galloped across the meadow. She tugged on Demeter's reins slightly, bringing her mount to a stop before him. Her cheeks bloomed with color and her eyes sparkled, making her the most attractive woman he had ever seen.

"What do you think of Zeus now?" she asked.

"That he is the most splendid creature I have ever ridden," he proclaimed. "By far, the best part about becoming the Duke of Winslow."

She cocked her head. "Surely, you jest, Your Grace. I would think coming into possession of Wildwood and all your other estates, as well as a lofty title, would be what made you happy."

He shook his head. "I am a simple man, Miss Jenson. Raised with very few material possessions, though blessed with loyal friends and a fine education." He gazed about. "I never expected all of this. Land as far as the eye could see. Unimaginable wealth. In truth, I still don't want it," he admitted.

Miles sighed. "It is mine now, however, and I must do the best I can for my people."

His gaze met hers and he saw curiosity on her lovely features. She was well-mannered, though, and would never voice any personal questions. Not to a duke. For a moment, he wished that heavy title didn't lay between them. He already found her intelligent. Caring. Enthusiastic. But he felt the wide gulf that separated them. Miss Jenson might help him learn how to run Wildwood but there could never be more to their relationship.

Or could there?

"What do you wish to see of your estate this morning, Your Grace?" she asked.

Miles thought seeing Miss Jenson was the best part of Wildwood. She might not believe she was a lady but the way she carried herself told a different story. She was incredibly beautiful and seemed unaware of it. Confident and encouraging. And by God, he was a duke! Dukes were notorious for breaking the rules of the *ton* and living by their own code.

What if he could make Miss Jenson his?

She was intelligent and kind and he could tell she already had the heart of the people. Miss Jenson would be a popular choice at Wildwood if he decided to make her his bride. Country folk wouldn't care that the new Duchess of Winslow had come from within their ranks. In fact, he thought they would celebrate it.

Of course, it would be a lot for her to take in. He had only known her for a day. Miles determined to keep silent for now and ease her into the idea. How, he hadn't a clue, but he was stubborn and strong-willed, two traits that would make sure in the end that he could claim this woman as his wife. It would also keep him from having to go to London and be forced into the gaiety of the Season. He hadn't been bred to take part in Polite Society. He was a soldier from the battlefield. Wedding Miss Jenson would allow him to keep to the country and the tasks he felt important.

If she would have him.

He chided himself. Of course, she would have him. He was a bloody duke. What woman, especially one not considered a lady by the *ton*, would turn him down?

Still, he wouldn't rush her into anything. Miles could be subtle when necessary. Something told him to walk delicately instead of trampling upon Miss Jenson's feelings. She was an accomplished woman for one so young. It would take gentle persuasion in order to convince her that they could make a good life together. A thought occurred to him.

"I saw the most important portions of the estate yesterday, from the fields to the mill to my tenants' cottages. I can ride out on my own later to visit the far corners. What I would like to do instead is go into Woodmorrow and see if the most marvelous sticky buns are still baked by Mr. Fisher. Might I tempt you into joining me on this expedition, Miss Jenson?"

She laughed, the sound rich and throaty, causing something to ripple through him. "Mrs. Fisher does the baking now. Her husband passed on a few years ago. I do believe her sticky buns are the best I have ever tasted."

"Then will you join me? Perhaps you could also introduce me to some of the town's residents. I am certain you know many of them."

"I am in the village often and would be happy to make the introductions, Your Grace. I do have a list Mama gave me that needs to be picked up at Mr. Jernigan's general store."

Distaste filled him. He remembered the shopkeeper, who always wore a surly look and had gossiped furiously about everyone. Miles wasn't the small boy from long ago that the merchant chastised. He was a titled peer. If he could face down the enemy on the battlefield, Miles could enter Jernigan's store.

"I would be happy to accompany you on your errand," he said graciously.

"Shall we let you see what Zeus can do on the open road?" she asked, a teasing light in her eyes.

"No," he said. "I have ridden him hard this past half-hour. Let us walk our mounts into Woodmorrow. Perhaps on the way home, after the horses have had a bit of rest, I might push him."

What he didn't voice was that if they galloped the three miles to the village, it would mean less time in her company.

They went into town, with Miss Jenson telling him about those who resided there. A few of the names were familiar to him though many were not. He worried how he would be received after all these years. The town folk would have heard the story of Miles accidentally shooting and killing his younger brother. He wondered how many remembered it—and if anyone would have the audacity to bring up the incident now that he was the Duke of Winslow.

They entered the village and he said, "I must ask that we stop at Mrs. Fisher's first. The memory of those sticky buns takes precedence over everything else."

"It is nice to know you have a sweet tooth, Your Grace. It makes you a little more human."

"Am I not human?" he asked.

"You always wear a stern countenance," Miss Jenson told him. "Between that and your title, you are most formidable."

"I see. I have always been a serious person," he shared. "Even my friends at school teased me about that. I don't mean to be intimidating."

She chuckled. "It's quite all right. You are a duke. You are meant to be intimidating to others, be it Polite Society or otherwise."

His gaze bored into her. "Do you find me intimidating, Miss Jenson?"

Her cheeks pinkened. "It is not for me to say, Your Grace."

"I am asking. I expect an answer."

She swallowed. "Very well. A bit, I suppose."

"I don't mean to frighten you."

"Oh, you don't," she assured him. "I mean, I don't believe you would ever harm me in any way. I am merely very aware of your position. And mine."

"I need you too much, Miss Jenson," Miles proclaimed, watching the color rise in her cheeks. "Already, you have taught me so much about Wildwood. I look forward to learning more from you. And your parents, of course."

She blinked. "Of course, Your Grace. Here. We are at Mrs. Fisher's."

Quickly, he dismounted and came around to her. Reaching up, his fingers encircled her waist, and he slowly lowered her to the ground. She averted her gaze. The faint scent of lilac surrounded her and he inhaled it as he released her.

They both tied their horse's reins to a post and he told Zeus to behave himself, causing his companion to chuckle.

Entering the bakery, Miss Jenson called out, "Mrs. Fisher? Are you here?"

A rotund woman with a dusting of flour on her cheek emerged from a back room. "Miss Jenson, how good to see you." Then her eyes flicked to Miles and her brow crinkled.

"Your Grace, this is Mrs. Fisher. Mrs. Fisher, His Grace, the Duke of Winslow."

"Oh, my!" she declared, taking a step back. "I remember you. You came in as a boy. For sticky buns."

Miles offered her a smile, hoping to set the woman at ease. "And as a man, I have often thought of those sticky buns." He inhaled deeply. "The smell of your shop is heavenly, Mrs. Fisher. It brings back pleasant memories. Do you have any sticky buns available?"

She swallowed hard, her head bobbing up and down. "Yes, Your Grace. I just took a new batch from the oven a few minutes ago."

"Then bring one each for me and Miss Jenson," he instructed.

The woman disappeared and returned with two of the sweets, handing them over. Miles withdrew a coin from his pocket.

"No, Your Grace. You are just back. I won't take payment for your first visit."

He set the coin down upon the counter. "Then take this. Miss Jenson and I plan to visit the merchants in the village so that she might introduce me around. When we are ready to return to Wildwood, I would like to take half a dozen sticky buns with me."

Her eyes flicked to the coin. "That is far too much," she protested.

"I insist. It was good seeing you again, Mrs. Fisher. Good day."

Miles escorted Miss Jenson from the shop and they stopped outside. Both removed a glove and then lifted their bun from the paper it rested upon.

"Mmm," he murmured as he bit into it, the sweetness invading his mouth. "Just the right amount of cinnamon in them. I have missed these more than I realized."

"They are the best reason to come into Woodmorrow," she agreed.

When she finished, she slipped her thumb into her mouth to lick it clean, causing a frisson of desire to run through him. He longed to do the same with her thumb. His growing attraction to her was something he knew he should stamp out but he ignored the warning in his head as she licked two other fingers. If he were to win her over, he must do it calmly and rationally and not act as a rutting bull when around her.

He saw she had a bit of sugar in the corner of her mouth and ignoring what his head had just told him, brushed the sugar away with his thumb before sliding it along her full, bottom lip. He dropped his hand at her sharp intake of breath. A dark blush stained her cheeks.

"Forgive me. You had a bit of sugar there."

Her tongue darted out to the corner of her mouth, bringing a heat to him.

She lowered her gaze and slipped her hand back into its glove. He did the same, the air charged between them.

"Shall we continue to the various shops?" she asked and then set off without waiting for his reply.

Miss Jenson took him into every building in the village. Miles meet the seamstress. The innkeeper. The tavern owner. The blacksmith. They stopped by the local doctor's home, which doubled as his office, but his daughter said that he was out on a call.

Miles promised to return at a later date and then said, "Why don't you bring your father to tea this afternoon instead?"

"We would be honored, Your Grace," Miss Collier said, her eyes a bit wide at the impromptu invitation.

They set a time and then Miss Jenson led him from the cottage, saying, "Mr. Jernigan's store will be our last stop." She removed a list from her pocket. "Mama's list. Most of the items are supplies Cook needs. Here, it is this way."

She led him to a large building and he decided Jernigan must have added on to the original structure because he didn't remember it being so expansive. Then again, it had been many years since he had stepped foot in Woodmorrow.

He opened the door for her and followed her inside, steeling himself for the encounter with the proprietor. His companion called out a greeting and, to his surprise, Miles saw she spoke to a man of about thirty.

"Your Grace, may I introduce you to Mr. Jernigan? This is His Grace, the Duke of Winslow."

"You used to come in here for a piece of candy," Jernigan said, stroking his chin. "I worked here a few hours a day after I left school, sweeping up and loading supplies into customers' wagons."

"I do remember you, Mr. Jernigan. You were a few years older than I was. Have you taken over the store from your father?"

A shadow crossed the man's face. "I will eventually. My father is still around and in charge. Mother passed away almost ten years ago. It has been . . . difficult for him. *He* has become difficult." Jernigan sighed. "Enough of my family troubles. I see you have a list, Miss Jenson."

She handed it over. "His Grace and I rode into Woodmorrow by horseback. I can send a groom with a cart this afternoon or tomorrow morning to collect what Mama has requested."

Jernigan scanned the list. "I will pull everything for you now. It will be waiting for your groom when he arrives to pick it up."

"Then I will let Mr. Harris know when we return to the stables. Thank you, Mr. Jernigan."

"It is always a pleasure to wait upon you, Miss Jenson." He gave her a warm smile.

Miles saw interest in the shopkeeper's face. Interest in her.

And he didn't like it one bit.

"Shall we go?" he asked abruptly.

"Yes, of course, Your Grace. Goodbye, Mr. Jernigan."

Miles nodded. "Good day, Jernigan."

He didn't want to be rude to the man, who had been nothing but friendly. He also struggled with the jealousy which reared within him. It was an unfamiliar feeling to Miles. He had never liked being challenged by others and he preferred being the one in control in every situation. This sudden, sweeping feeling rushing through him was ridiculous.

Opening the door, he placed his hand on the small of Miss Jenson's back and nudged her outside, closing the door behind him. Before they could take a step, a figure blocked their path.

"You."

The man before them favored the one they had just dealt with, though his hair was iron-gray compared to the son's dark brown.

"Mr. Jernigan," Miles said stiffly.

"This is His Grace, the Duke of Winslow," Miss Jenson hastily said.

"I know who he is," the old man snapped. "And I know he killed his brother." Jernigan turned his head slightly and spat. "Murderer."

Miles went cold inside.

CHAPTER TWELVE

THE WORD LINGERED in the air.

Murderer . . .

Fury filled Emery.

"Apologize at once to His Grace!" she shouted at Jernigan.

The old man glared at her. "Why should I, Miss Jenson? It is the God's truth. This man shot and killed an innocent little boy. Everyone knew about it when it happened." He snorted. *"They* said it was an accident. But Winslow sent his son away. We all knew what that meant."

Horror rippled through her. The man beside her had killed the youngest boy in the portrait. No, not this man. A boy. The duke had been but a few years older than his younger brother. Though she had only met him yesterday, after spending time in his company, Emery knew this was no vindictive killer.

"It most certainly was an accident," she said, hot anger pouring through her. "You were not present at the incident, Mr. Jernigan. Neither were any of the townspeople. How dare you slander His Grace with such an accusation! Don't you think he suffered enough, losing his brother in such a manner? And for you to perpetuate lies about the circumstances—all these years later—makes you guilty of far more than an accident."

Emery narrowed her eyes. "You will apologize at once and refrain from spreading such falsehoods in the future. Is that understood?"

Jernigan's mouth tightened. He faced the duke. "I am sorry if I have offended you, Your Grace."

With that, he stormed into his store.

"I don't think that was much of an apology at all," she said with distaste. "He wasn't sorry one whit."

"Come, Miss Jenson," the duke said, taking her elbow and guiding her away from the store and down the street to Mrs. Fisher's establishment.

"Wait with the horses," he said gently, lifting her into the saddle and going inside the bakery.

Winslow returned less than a minute later, carrying a basket. He mounted Zeus.

"How can you be so calm?" she asked him. "After Mr. Jernigan made such horrid accusations?"

He shrugged. "It isn't anything I haven't heard."

She heard the dejection in his voice.

"I knew the old gossip would arise once I returned to Wildwood. Fortunately, many of the servants are new and may never have heard the stories."

"That's all they are," she said. "Stories. Why, you were but a little boy yourself. No one should blame you for . . . an accident."

The duke gazed at her sadly. "While I am grateful for your passionate defense of me, I would ask you to keep your thoughts to yourself in the future. Fighting back—whether with fists or words—will not quiet the gossip. I must simply cease to acknowledge it."

He wheeled Zeus and took off. She gave chase on Demeter. He slowed as they came to the church. She saw he gazed at the graveyard next to the building.

"Would you like to stop and see him?" she asked softly.

"I don't know if I can," Winslow admitted, his voice breaking.

Emery reached out without thinking and placed her hand on his arm. "You should. You have been gone a very long time."

"Hullo!" a voice called.

She dropped her hand and turned, seeing Reverend Raleigh

approaching.

"Good day," she responded. "Your Grace, I would like to introduce you to Reverend Raleigh. He and his wife have been in Woodmorrow for what—seven—or is it eight years?"

"Eight, Miss Jenson," the jovial, rotund man replied. "And it is a pleasure to meet you, Your Grace. Might you wish to come in?"

She glanced to the duke and he nodded. "We would be delighted," he replied, his tone solemn, and she knew he was still deeply affected by the incident at Mr. Jernigan's store.

"Bring your horses around," the clergyman said. "Miss Jenson will know where to go. I will have Mrs. Raleigh put on the kettle." Raleigh hurried away.

"We don't have to go in," she said.

"I would like to. I need . . . time."

"Very well. Follow me."

She cantered to the vicarage and guided Demeter behind it.

"We can secure our horses here."

Winslow came around and helped her from the saddle without speaking. His eyes had lost their earlier sparkle. Her heart went out to him.

Impulsively, she reached and took his hand.

"Don't let the mistakes of the past swallow you," she advised. "The past is the past. You must look to your present and future. You are in a position of great power now, Your Grace. Do good with what you have been given."

She squeezed his hand and stepped away, hurrying to the front of the vicarage. The door swung open and Reverend Raleigh ushered her inside. The duke followed. The clergyman led them to the parlor, where he introduced his wife to the duke.

They spent a calming hour with the couple, talking first about the area in general and the posts Raleigh had held before accepting the living at Woodmorrow.

"Your father brought me here," Raleigh told them. "He had a distant cousin whom my father had tutored. Somehow, it resulted in my coming to Woodmorrow."

"I have a close friend who is a vicar," Winslow said. "The Reverend William Finchley. He was offered the living by the Earl of Marksby when we finished university and took his orders shortly afterward."

"I have never meet Finchley, Your Grace," Raleigh said. "I am sure he is a fine vicar."

Emery saw a smile tug at the corners of the duke's mouth as he said, "Finch is good at whatever he does."

She assumed this was one of the loyal friends he had mentioned to her earlier.

Mrs. Raleigh asked about the duke's time at war and Emery could tell he gave her a sanitized version of events.

Finally, the duke rose and the others followed suit.

"Thank you for the tea," he said. "It was very kind of you."

"We hope to see you in church every Sunday, Your Grace," the vicar said.

"I attended the church as a boy, always sitting in the family pew with my brothers. My parents were often in London and our governess or tutor would make certain we came in order to represent the family each Sunday."

She noticed he didn't mention if he would continue this practice.

They said their goodbyes and returned to their horses.

"I think I do want to visit Tony's grave," he said quietly.

"Would you care to go alone?"

"No. Please come with me." His voice came out a whisper.

They left the horses behind and walked to the graveyard next door to the church. The duke looked about as if unsure where to go.

"It is this way," she told him. "At the far end."

As they walked toward the Notley family plot, she added, "I mentioned to you my interest in history. I am very familiar with this graveyard and the stories it tells. The untimely deaths of the young. The headstones that reveal the few who lived to a ripe old age. The prominent families with beautiful markers."

She led him to the Notley plots and then halted. "Your brother is over there. Your father and older brother lie nearby. I will wait here."

He nodded and went slowly toward the graves, passing by those who had recently died and going straight to the brother he called Tony. She knew the gravestone read *Anthony Notley, Beloved Son of the Duke and Duchess of Winslow, 1789-1796.* It had been one which had intrigued her, not only because her parents were in the duke's employ but because the boy had died so young. Emery had wondered over the years what had happened to Anthony. If he had been fragile and in ill health. If young Anthony had perished in the rush of the influenza which had taken the area by storm since several other graves were dated with that same year, some of them even listing influenza as the cause of death.

Never, though, had she thought the boy had been killed in an accident. Shot by his brother. She supposed they had come across one of the old duke's pistols and in playing with it, it somehow had gone off. Still, it didn't seem in character with the man who now knelt at his brother's grave. The Duke of Winslow was a deliberate, rational man. He himself had told her he was a serious boy, teased for his solemn manner by his friends. It seemed incongruent that he would act in such an irresponsible manner. Then it came to her.

It was the oldest brother's fault.

Ralph Notley had been careless and carefree in his manner when he had come to Wildwood upon rare occasions. Instinct told her he had been the one to pull the trigger that day.

Emery moved toward the duke, whose head was now bowed as he wept. Her heart went out to this lonely man. She understood loneliness because it was her constant companion. Though now a duke, he seemed as alone as a person could be. His only living family member was the Duchess of Winslow and Emery couldn't think of a more self-centered woman.

Moving to stand behind him as he knelt, she placed her gloved hand on his broad shoulder. He quivered beneath her touch. Then his own hand engulfed hers as he placed it atop hers as his body trembled in grief. She felt the warmth as it spread through her.

His weeping subsided but he continued to kneel on one knee, his hand still covering hers.

"I loved him, you know. He was the only one I loved. My parents were rarely at Wildwood and abandoned us to the care of servants. Ralph only thought of himself and had little to do with Tony or me. We were a pair. Always together." His voice broke.

"Your older brother—Ralph—he was the one responsible, wasn't he?"

His hand tightened around hers a moment before he released it. The duke stood but remained facing away from her, staring out across the graveyard.

"Why would you say that?" he asked, his voice distant.

"Because you loved your younger brother. You were his confidant and protector."

"You couldn't know that."

"I feel it," she told him. "And I know a bit about the previous duke. He was selfish. Irresponsible. You, on the other hand, Your Grace, are thoughtful and deliberate. You were not the kind of boy who would recklessly play with a firearm, especially around a beloved, trusting brother."

He didn't speak. Emery studied his large, broad frame, so still and waiting.

"It was exactly the kind of the thing the most recent duke would do. He was always a braggart. He treated the servants almost as poorly as your mother does. I can see where he would hold his younger brothers in little regard."

Winslow slowly turned to face her. His blue eyes were filled with anguish. The scar, white on his cheek, stood out on his tanned face, almost throbbing.

"Did he give you that scar?" she asked.

"No. My father did. He struck me when I denied shooting Tony. Ralph told him I was the one who had pulled the pistol's trigger—and Winslow was always one to believe his heir apparent."

"He is the one who sent you away?"

The duke nodded. "Shortly after the funeral. I was sent to Turner Academy, a school with a reputation for taking in boys who had done terrible things. Boys whose families didn't want them."

Tears brimmed in her eyes. "So you were sent away and never came back. Not even for holidays."

"No," he whispered.

Emery took his hands in hers. "How old were you?"

"It was my tenth birthday that day. Cook made me a cake."

The same cake they had shared yesterday.

"I kept wanting Ralph to tell the truth. For my father to believe me. For my mother to intervene and keep me from being sent away." He shook his head and looked at her with clear eyes. "I learned I was better off without them. The instructors at Turner Academy didn't just teach academics. They molded boys into the best men they could be. I made good friends, friends who to this day are closer than brothers. I survived."

She searched his face, sympathy for the unjustly accused boy he had been growing within her. Tears cascaded down her cheeks.

"I don't need your pity, Miss Jenson," he said harshly.

"It isn't pity I feel, Your Grace. It is sorrow for the injustice you suffered. Heartache for the helpless little boy who was uprooted from his home and taken from everything he had ever known."

His hands tightened on hers. "And what do you feel for the man, Miss Jenson?"

"Desire," she whispered.

His eyes darkened. "So do I."

His head bent, moving closer until his lips touched hers. A spark flashed between them. He released her hands and took her by the shoulders, drawing her to him, even as his mouth pressed firmly against hers. Her palms moved to his broad chest, feeling the hard muscles beneath his layers of clothing.

She had never been kissed. What the dead duke had tried to force upon her didn't count. Emery never guessed what it might feel like. A humming seemed to invade her body and her senses sharpened. The feel of his wool coat beneath her palms. The sandalwood soap rising from his heated skin. Hers, too, felt on fire as he continued to kiss her, making her heart slam against her ribs and her knees threaten to buckle.

Then he eased the pressure and his tongue slid along the seam of her mouth, back and forth, hypnotizing her. He teased her mouth open and his tongue swept inside, filling her. She tasted the cinnamon from the sticky bun and something else. Dark. Masculine. Heady. Slowly, she responded, becoming an active participant as her tongue mated with his playfully.

He groaned and his hands slid from her shoulders, down her back, bringing her against him. Want—or need—rippled through her as her hands moved up his chest and grasped his shoulders for support, kneading them as if she were a purring kitten. Her breasts began to ache and dampness sprouted between her thighs, in her most private of places.

This was madness.

Emery was kissing a duke. In public. A man so far above her station that it caused her head to reel. Though they were in the far corner of the church's graveyard, anyone who entered it might see them.

She clutched his shoulders and then pushed him away, breaking the kiss. At once, his heat, which had enfolded her, was absent, leaving her bereft. Her breath came in quick, short spurts, as did his. He gazed at her, those blue eyes glowing with need.

"My sincerest apologies, Your Grace," she said stiffly and she whirled, striding across the graveyard and back to Demeter.

He caught up to her, his fingers locking around her elbow, bringing her to a stop.

"What is your name?" he rasped.

She tried to shake him off but he only tightened his grasp.

"Your name, Miss Jenkins. Your Christian name."

"Emery," she managed to get out, forcing herself to keep her hands at her sides instead of bunching them in his coat and bringing him toward her again.

"That is an unusual name," he remarked, his eyes roaming her face.

"It was my mother's maiden name. She was an only child and the surname died with my grandfather's passing. Mama said it was a small tribute to the man who had raised her to be independent and hardworking."

"Your mother has instilled those traits in you, as well, Emery." His lips smiled in approval.

"It isn't proper for you to call me by my first name, Your Grace," she said stiffly.

"Mine is Miles."

Miles . . .

It suited him.

Emery shrugged off the thought. "Your Grace—"

"Miles," he urged, his fingers now massaging her shoulders.

"*Your Grace,*" she emphasized. "I apologize for getting carried away back there."

"You shouldn't," he said, his thumbs lazily rotating in circles.

She swallowed. "Still, I am asking for your forgiveness."

"We were equal participants in the kiss, Emery."

She loved the sound of her name on his sensual lips.

"Nevertheless, it cannot happen again," she said primly.

"Why?"

"Because I won't let it."

She broke away and hurried to Demeter. Though her legs were long, his were longer and he easily caught up to her.

"Allow me to help you into the saddle," he said.

"I can manage on my own," she said stubbornly.

"Can you?" He took a step back, crossing his arms and watching her in amusement.

She struggled but somehow managed to hoist herself into the saddle, thankful she hadn't been riding Zeus today. With his height, it would have been impossible to mount.

"Impressive," he said, a slow smile spreading across his face.

Emery looked down upon him. "I will not be trifled with. Your brother thought he could behave in a similar manner. He was wrong. I made certain he understood that."

She pressed her knee against Demeter's side and the horse took off. She didn't let up until she reached the Wildwood stables, where she handed her horse off to a groom and told him of the supplies to be picked up at Mr. Jernigan's store.

As she made her way back to the house, the Duke of Winslow was nowhere in sight.

CHAPTER THIRTEEN

MILES CLIMBED ATOP Zeus and simply rode as fast as he could. He did so because with a horse such as Zeus, it would take every bit of his concentration to manage the beast.

And that would prevent him from thinking.

Finally, he slowed his mount and began walking Zeus, allowing the horse to cool down. As he did, he reflected on what had happened with Emery.

He had spoken the truth to her. About Tony's death. Not in any detail, but he had wanted her to know of his innocence, especially after their encounter with the elder Jernigan. How passionately she had come to Miles' defense, dressing down the shop owner.

And how very passionately she had kissed him.

Miles knew immediately that Emery had little experience with kissing but she hadn't held back. She had kissed him with enthusiasm—and the desire she had admitted she felt for him. There were no games with Miss Emery Jenson. She was blunt in her speech and knew her own mind.

He wanted to know more of her mind—and that body.

It bothered him that she had mentioned Ralph's unwanted attention to her. Even now, anger filled him, thinking his older brother had tried to take advantage of one as good and sweet as Emery. Ralph always acted entitled because he was. Miles was delighted Emery had stood up to the bastard. Of course, if Ralph had lived, it would probably have cost her parents their positions at Wildwood. A duke—and Ralph, in particular—would not have accepted being turned down, much less in the manner Miles believed Emery would have acted.

He didn't want her to think he was cut from the same cloth as Ralph. Even if they were brothers. What he did know was she needed time to cool down. Reflect upon what had occurred between them. And then see how very right it was. Emery only thought the kisses between them had ended today. He knew better.

Miles had found his duchess.

He realized she would take some convincing. He would have to back off a bit before he began pursuing her—but pursue her he would. She was a woman of many qualities which he admired. True, he had only scratched the surface of what made her so special but, in time, he would help her realize that, together, they could build something very special at Wildwood. More than anything, he wanted a family far different from the one he had been a member of. A woman such as Emery Jenson would bring new blood to the Notley line. Their daughters would be spirited and their sons confident without abusing their power.

He had time. All the time in the world. Moreover, Miles had determination. He would win Emery over to his way of thinking. He would prove he was different than Ralph. Miles didn't want her to think he tried to take advantage of her. Too many times, titled gentlemen did that very thing with servants. He didn't regard Emery as a servant, though. He saw her as an equal. A wife who could help him become a better duke than any Winslow before him. Already, he admired her and was inspired by what he had seen on the property. He had some new ideas for the land and wanted a partner to help him achieve them.

He wanted her. No other woman would do. The Turner Terrors would probably laugh at his tenacity, having only known Emery a short while. Still, he had always been one to know his mind. His resolve to make her his duchess wouldn't change.

He returned to the stables, where Harris met him.

"What do you think of Zeus now, Your Grace?" the groom asked with a smile as Miles dismounted.

"That he was worth every farthing the duke paid for him." He stroked the horse's neck. "I am in awe of possessing such a creature."

He claimed the basket he had looped over the saddle horn and took the sticky buns straight to the kitchens.

"Cook, I have brought you a gift from Mrs. Fisher's bakery."

Miles opened the basket to show her what it contained.

"Oh, Your Grace, you spoil me," she said, her cheeks bright with color.

"You deserve it, Cook. Just remember to leave one for me. Also, Dr. Collier and his daughter are coming for tea this afternoon."

"Very good, Your Grace. I will see they have a lovely tea."

As he left the kitchens, he thought Cook and probably all his servants deserved an increase in their wages. He knew from what he had already seen that the house was sparkling and the stables well maintained. It would never have been something that would have occurred to his father, to fully compensate the servants surrounding him and reward them with yearly increases in pay. When he examined the salaries of those at Wildwood as he set Emery's wages, he would see how much all his staff received and award them a hefty boost.

He sought out Mrs. Jenson, finding the housekeeper in her office.

"I wanted to inform you that I have guests coming for tea today, Mrs. Jenson. The local doctor and his daughter."

"Thank you for letting me know, Your Grace. Did you run across them during your ride?"

"Actually, I had your daughter take me into Woodmorrow. She introduced me to various townspeople."

The woman smiled. "Emery does know everyone in these parts. I believe she has a finger in every pie."

"Miss Jenson has already taught me much—and let me know I have quite a bit more to learn."

"Oh, dear. I hope she wasn't too blunt. Her father and I have given her latitude as she has matured. She has been of great assistance to both of us, her father, in particular. He says it would be impossible to manage the estate without Emery's help."

"Yes, I have come to realize that in my short time at Wildwood. In fact, I offered to place Miss Jenson on my staff because of all the work she does about the estate." He laughed. "She could probably run Wildwood on her own with no help from anyone else from what I have seen."

Mrs. Jenson smiled. "Mr. Jenson and I are so proud of her. She has grown into a very capable young woman." She paused. "I have encouraged her to leave the estate, however."

Her words were a physical blow to him. "Why?"

"Country life is all she has ever known, Your Grace. We have provided her with a good education. She would make for an excellent governess or lady's companion."

Miles hid his dismay at this idea and said, "No, I forbid that, Mrs. Jenson. Your daughter is essential to the running of Wildwood. I won't let a good employee traipse off to tend to whiny brats or doddering old women. She would be powerless if she took a position as either a governess or companion. Here, she can make decisions and see the results of them."

"I see." The housekeeper studied him a moment. "Of course, it would be Emery's decision. If she wants to leave and pursue another occupation, her father and I won't prevent her from doing that."

Miles swore to himself to do everything in his power to keep Emery on the estate.

"Might you have time now to give me a brief tour of the house?" he asked, taking their conversation in a different direction in order to help his sudden temper cool.

"Certainly, Your Grace."

Mrs. Jenson led him through the house, pointing out items to him. Miles soaked up all she said and thought of a few changes he wished to make.

When they arrived at the duchess' rooms, the housekeeper entered without knocking, causing him to ask, "Are these rooms empty now? She has already left for the dower house?"

"Yes, Your Grace. The dower house is in good order and I personally selected the servants to accompany Her Grace there. I was with Mr. Trottmann when he spoke to them." She paused, assessing him a moment. "Frankly, I was surprised by the idea of you demanding they receive respect from Her Grace."

"Respect for everyone is integral to good behavior," he said. "Turner Academy taught me how to treat all well, not only those of my class."

She gave an approving nod.

"I suppose Her Grace won't be there long since the Season is in full swing and she never misses it. Even in mourning, she will be happier in London, I suppose."

"No, Her Grace will remain at the dower house for the entire mourning period. She knows to act in a manner I have requested—else I will cut her off."

Mrs. Jenson gasped. "You wouldn't!"

"I would, indeed. My schooling and military career have made me into the man I am, Mrs. Jenson. I am hopefully far better—and different—from previous Winslows. I will hold everyone around me to a higher standard. That includes Her Grace."

She studied him. "Then I believe the dukedom and your people are fortunate to have you as the new duke."

"The feeling is mutual, Mrs. Jenson. I know you are most efficient and I could not have a better housekeeper."

"I will have the list of my duties that you require to you by tomorrow, Your Grace."

"That won't be necessary," Miles told her. "I trust you to see to the running of the house without my interference."

She bowed her head. "Thank you, Your Grace." She paused

and then said, "If I might be so outspoken as to also say that you elevating Thomas from head footman to butler was a very wise decision. He is well liked and pays attention to the smallest of details. Mr. Trottmann will make for a superb butler."

"Thomas was kind to me as a boy. Even at my young age, I understood he always completed his job to the best of his abilities and had a ready smile for everyone."

Mrs. Jenson nodded. "That has not changed, Your Grace. He will perform his new role with grace and efficiency. We must get you downstairs now. Dr. Collier and Miss Collier will be arriving shortly."

As they left the duchess' rooms, Miles said, "Thank you for the tour today, Mrs. Jenson. It was nice to see the house again. It has been many years since I was last here."

"It is good to have you back where you belong," she said.

"I suppose it is too late in the day to meet with Mr. Jenson," he mused. "I regret not having spoken with him sooner. Perhaps I was putting it off. Much as I need to look over the ledgers and familiarize myself with them, I dread it. Numbers have never been my friend," he joked.

"Emery is excellent with balancing numbers. She can walk you through them," the housekeeper offered. "And you are correct. By the time tea is finished, my husband will have left for our cottage. I don't know if you are aware but the cottage comes with his position as steward. I hope we will be able to keep it."

"I don't see why not," he said. "As long as Mr. Jenson is my steward, it should belong to him and his family."

He saw something flicker in her eyes and couldn't put a name to it.

"Please inform Mr. Jenson that I plan to meet with him after breakfast tomorrow morning."

They reached the landing and Thomas met them.

"Your guests have arrived for tea, Your Grace. I have placed them in the drawing room.

"Thank you, Trottmann," he said, making a point to use

Thomas' surname, which would take some getting used to but was part of the way the butler should be addressed in front of both staff and visitors to Wildwood.

Miles excused himself and went to the drawing room, hoping to push aside thoughts of Emery as he entertained his guests.

EMERY SLID THE final pin into her hair, trying to calm her nerves. Her mother had informed her that His Grace wanted to meet with Papa this morning. His moods proved mercurial, with no way to control them. She only hoped that today would be one of his good days.

As she prepared her father's breakfast, she wondered how it would be to once more be in the duke's presence. Why she had admitted an affection for him was beyond her. No, it was much more than that.

Emery had said she *desired* him.

She shuddered. That word had never left her lips before. In her mind, she would have defined the word as wishing for something, as in she desired for good weather or a new frock. That was before she had met the Duke of Winslow. She had been undeniably attracted to him from the start, else why would she have volunteered to take him about the estate? It was as if she had become a different person overnight—and that woman had admitted something that no woman should ever speak of to a man. He must think her a wanton, to go about telling a man—one far above her station—how she desired him.

And then kissed him.

That had been the most foolish thing she had ever done in her life. She was known for being rational and levelheaded. She didn't go about kissing anyone, much less a duke.

He had seemed amused by it. By her. At least, afterward had seemed that way. During the time they had kissed, Winslow had been . . .

Emery sighed. She had absolutely no words to describe what he had been. What he had done. What she had done with him.

She would have to face him today, however. She needed to be present at His Grace's meeting with Papa so she could smooth the way or even intervene if necessary. Yet her cheeks heated and her blood began singing at the thought of seeing the duke again. She was torn between wanting to flee Wildwood and fearful that her ill-mannered behavior would cause the duke to toss her from the estate for not wanting to dally with him, much as the previous duke would have done—had he lived to do so.

Somehow, she managed to get Papa's egg properly poached and the tea made. She called him in to breakfast.

"Papa, we will be meeting with His Grace today."

"Oh?" His attention returned to his egg.

"If you feel confused about anything, I will be happy to step in and clarify it for His Grace."

He frowned. "Why would I be confused?" he asked testily.

Trying to smooth things over, she said, "I have been paying the bills lately. I just thought His Grace might asked you a question about those. If you don't know the answer, it's quite all right. He knows I have been helping you and Mama at Wildwood. In fact, he is going to begin awarding me wages. I will now earn a salary, just as you and Mama do."

His features relaxed. "Why, that is wonderful, Emery. I am so proud of you."

The rest of the meal went smoothly and Emery walked with him from their cottage to the main house. Papa sat behind his desk and she pulled out a few of the ledgers she thought the duke might want to peruse.

Moments later, she heard, "Good morning, Miss Jenson. And Mr. Jenson."

Turning, she saw Miles standing there. No, His Grace. She mustn't think of him in a personal way. He was her employer. A duke whose social circle was far above her own.

Dipping into a curtsey, she said, "Good morning, Your Grace. May I introduce you to my father, Mr. Jenson?"

Papa had stood and gave a stiff bow. The duke offered his hand and the two men shook.

"Please, take a seat, Miss Jenson," Winslow encouraged. "You, too, Mr. Jenson. May I say you have raised a lovely daughter, Sir. Miss Jenson has been most helpful in my brief time at Wildwood."

"You were here before," Papa said. "Before we came."

A shadow crossed the duke's face. "Yes, I spent my very early years at Wildwood."

"They say you killed your brother."

Emery winced at the blunt statement.

"They are wrong," the duke said.

"Oh? Good to know," Papa replied as he began rearranging things on the desk.

Winslow turned to look at her and she said, "I have the list I promised you, Your Grace. The duties my father fulfills as steward of Wildwood."

She located it and handed over the list, saying, "These are the tasks performed by my father and me. My mother should give you her list, as well."

"Hmm." His gaze lowered to the pages and he studied them for several minutes. Neither Emery nor her father said a word as he did so.

Finally, the duke nodded to himself and folded the pages, slipping them into his coat's inner pocket.

"Thank you, Miss Jenson. It helps me to see what the two of you have been up to." A teasing glint came into his eyes and she felt the blush spread across her cheeks.

Turning to her father, the duke said, "Tell me, Mr. Jenson, what is your favorite part of working here at Wildwood?"

Emery held her breath as her father contemplated the question.

"I like the people," Papa finally said. "They are a good lot.

Hardworking. Kind."

"I am happy to hear that," Winslow said. "I was close friends with Kit Munson when I was growing up."

Papa nodded. "Munson is a good man and diligent worker."

The duke asked a few other questions and she was thrilled that Papa seemed to know exactly where he was and that he was able to answer them.

"As to the ledgers," the duke said, glancing at the ones stacked upon the desk.

"I pulled those," she quickly said. "The ones I thought would give you the best overview of the estate. It may take you a while to look over them. Perhaps you wish to do so in your study, Your Grace," she encouraged, not knowing how long her father's current lucidity would last.

He rose and they did the same. Winslow picked up the ledgers. "I am afraid I am abysmal at numbers, unlike my school chum, Donovan. Your mother informed me you were quite skilled at them, Miss Jenson. Perhaps you might accompany me to my study and help me understand them."

Dread filled her, mingled with an overwhelming joy. A veritable recipe for insanity, in her opinion. She didn't want to be alone with him yet it was the very thing she wanted most in the world. Being alone with the duke might lead to another kiss. No. No kissing. She had to rid herself of these wild notions. If she kissed him again, he would think her of easy virtue. Dallying with a duke was not something any woman should do, especially one who was little more than a servant in the said duke's household.

"Of course, Your Grace," she said carefully.

"Shall we?"

Emery left the room and heard Winslow tell her father goodbye. At least the meeting had gone well. Papa had spoken a little hesitantly at times but rationally.

They arrived at the duke's study and he rested the ledgers on his massive desk. She stood, waiting for an invitation on where she should sit. The duke retrieved a pencil from the desk drawer and gathered the ledgers again, crossing the room and sitting upon a settee.

Emery stood there, wondering if he meant her to sit beside him. That wouldn't do at all. The settee was of normal size but Winslow was a large man, his shoulders so broad that they took up much more room than the average male's would.

"Come, Emery. I am eager to explore these ledgers."

"What did you call me?" she asked, her heart fluttering merely hearing her name come from his sensual lips.

"You know full well that I just called you Emery. I won't do so when others are around. When we are alone, though, I will address you as I please. After all, am I not a duke? Don't dukes do as they please?"

She stood there, speechless. Finding her voice, she said, "We aren't going to be alone, Your Grace."

"Then how am I ever going to understand what is in these books?"

"You seem quite intelligent to me. You will figure it out." She began moving backward toward the door.

"Emery, please stop."

She did.

"Thank you."

He studied her a long moment, causing her to tremble. She stood her ground, though.

Finally, he said, "Yes, eventually I might make heads or tails of them. It would be so much easier if you explained things to me. You have a way of clarifying things, such as how you explained crop rotation to me. I could have read books and pamphlets about it and eventually understood. It would be much easier, though, for you to tell me the essence of what I needed to know." He sighed. "I have so much to learn. Anything that can be done to facilitate that process would be helpful. Now, come sit."

Her feet moved of their own accord and she joined him on the settee. It was as she thought. He took up a good majority of it. She perched on the edge, not daring to breathe.

"Lean back. I wish to open this rather large book and need your lap to help support it."

Reluctantly, she did so and the duke set all but the top ledger onto the floor. He opened it and placed it in both his and her laps and bent his head, frowning at the page.

"Why so many columns?" he asked, sounding perplexed.

Emery began explaining the system she had set up. Though she was incredibly aware of the length of his side pressing against hers and the scent of sandalwood surrounding her, she was in her element. She turned the pages, pointing out the various things she thought he ought to become familiar with.

After an hour, they had gone through the three ledgers and he said, "I have a great appreciation for what you do. I am merely glad you—and your father—are the ones doing it. Numbers are distinctly unfriendly, in my opinion."

She couldn't help but laugh. "Numbers need no interpretation. They are straightforward. They hide nothing."

"Unlike people?" he asked. "I have known those who have hidden from the world behind an invisible mask, not letting others in. Or those who act one way in public and vastly different in private."

"You may come to appreciate columns of figures, Your Grace," she said teasingly, trying to lighten the mood. His eyes had grown distant and she believed he must be speaking of his older brother.

"Thank you for what you shared with me yesterday," she said.

"Our kiss?" he asked.

Her face flamed. "No. I meant telling me about what happened to your younger brother. I am sorry there are those who believe you were the one to accidentally shoot him and not your older brother who did so."

"It wasn't an accident."

Emery frowned. "What do you mean?"

"Ralph deliberately pulled the pistol's trigger," he revealed, looking at her steadily.

She bit her lip, her mind not comprehending his words.

"Ralph aimed at me. Tony jumped in the way. And died because of it."

She heard the bitterness in his words even as her head reeled.

"I was the one meant to protect Tony—yet he died protecting me."

The hurt in his eyes led her to cup his cheek. Her palm heated as she touched his face, smooth from his morning shave.

"I am so sorry, Miles," she said softly.

His hand took hers, removing it from his face. He turned it palm up and tenderly kissed its center, causing a rush of warmth to flood her.

"There are times I am afraid I will forget what Tony looked like. I can never bring him back."

"I can," Emery said, rising. "Wait here."

CHAPTER FOURTEEN

E MERY LEFT MILES in his study and went to an unused wing of the house. Entering the smallest bedchamber, she went to the bed and knelt, reaching under it until her fingers found what she was looking forward. Gently, she pulled the hidden painting from its hiding place.

She had brought it here upon the Duke of Winslow's death. The house had been in chaos, with Sevill leading the charge to tend to His Grace. It had been easy for her to spirit away the painting of the three Notley sons. Though bulky, she had carried it to a place few came since the duke hadn't entertained at Wildwood in many years and slid it under this bed.

Why she had hidden it would be hard to say. Perhaps it was because she knew the new duke wouldn't have cared a fig for it. More likely, instinct told Emery he would order it destroyed. While she hadn't known who Miles was at that time, her heart told her to keep the portrait safe until a time it could be brought out again. Because she now knew the truth, she wanted Miles to see it. The painting would be a small way to give him back a piece of the younger brother he had lost in such a tragic manner.

Lifting the cloth that covered it, she stared at Miles, now knowing a part of his story. Her heart ached for this little boy, one who would lose not only his brother but his entire family and way of life shortly after this was completed. It was time to help him reclaim a small part of it.

Emery hoisted the frame, awkwardly carrying it through the door and down the corridor. When she reached the stairs, she set it down, hoping to get a better grip on it.

"Miss Jenson? May I be of assistance?" Thomas hurried up the stairs.

"Oh, yes, thank you so much, Thomas. I mean, Mr. Trottmann. Forgive me."

The butler chuckled. "I am still getting used to my new position, Miss Jenson. I know others are, as well. Think nothing of it."

"This needs to be taken to His Grace's study. He is waiting for it."

"I see." The butler gazed at the covered frame and turned back to her. "Is it the portrait of the three boys?" he asked.

"Yes. You know of it?"

He nodded. "I remember when the artist came to paint it. A Mr. Leavell. He came down from London. Very arrogant and yet quite talented."

"What was His Grace like as a boy?" she asked wistfully.

Thomas smiled. "Earnest yet with a bit of mischief in him."

"I can see that in this painting."

"He was a good boy. Very conscientious about looking after his younger brother. Lord Anthony followed Lord Miles around and was his constant shadow. The two were inseparable."

"I gather the previous duke didn't have much to do with his brothers."

"Not a bit," Thomas confirmed. "That one was full of himself, always ordering both his brothers and servants about." He paused. "Forgive me. I don't mean to speak ill of the dead."

"I won't say anything to anyone," Emery promised. "I hope His Grace will be happy to see this."

"He will. It's a good thing you knew where it was located."

She kept silent, not revealing that Sevill was the one who had maintained custody of the portrait until recently.

Thomas lifted the painting and carried it downstairs, Emery accompanying him. When they reached the door to the study, she opened it for him.

"Set it against the front of His Grace's desk," she instructed.

The butler did so and nodded deferentially before exiting the room.

She looked to Miles, who wore a peculiar expression as he rose and came toward her.

"What is it?" he asked, his brow furrowing.

"I believe it is something you will treasure. In fact, your father asked for this to be brought to him on his deathbed."

Anger filled his face and he took a step back. "Then it is nothing I want anything to do with," he said dismissively. "Ring for Trottmann and have him take it away."

"No," she said boldly, her hands fisting on her hips.

"No? *No?* he echoed. "You are telling me—a duke—no."

"Yes, Your Grace. That is exactly what I said."

"You can't do that," he sputtered.

Emery crossed her arms. "I just did."

"Leave," he commanded. "Take it with you."

"I will leave *after* you have seen it," she said firmly. "And only then will I take it. If you still ask me to. Nicely."

His features hardened. "Do not push me, Emery."

"Look at it, Miles," she said sternly.

Glaring at her, he stepped to the painting and tossed back the cover. He stood frozen before it. She watched him, his back to her. Never had she seen someone so eerily still. Then his hand reached out tentatively and his fingers touched the canvas.

"Tony," he said hoarsely.

Emery joined him, glancing at the three boys in the portrait. Now that she had met the adult Miles, she easily could see this man in the boy he had once been.

His fingers sought hers, lacing together, and they both studied the painting in silence.

Finally, Miles spoke. "Winslow asked for this?"

"He did. I had spent a couple of weeks at his bedside, tending to him as he went downhill. That last day, he asked for it. Sevill had obviously hidden it away somewhere and retrieved it."

"I suppose he wanted to see Tony once more before he died."

"When was it painted?" she asked, his fingers tightening around hers.

"That summer," he said softly. "Ralph and I came home from school. Tony wasn't old enough to go away yet. The duke had brought in an artist from London, one quickly gaining a name for himself. Winslow wanted a portrait done of his heir."

Emery noticed how he never called his parents Father or Mother, much less Papa and Mama. It was as if Miles deliberately distanced himself from them.

"Ralph was full of himself, eager to sit for the portrait. The duchess, who favored Tony, insisted that the artist also capture a likeness of him, as well. Somehow, a compromise was arrived at and the three of us sat for this together."

Her gut twisted, hearing that neither the duke nor duchess had wanted Miles' portrait painted. To be only ten years old and know his parents didn't care for him must have been hard to bear.

"I somehow remember a separate one being done of Ralph," he mused. "I believe after it was finished that the duke insisted it hang in the London townhouse. I never went there as a child."

"You never went to town?" she asked, surprise filling her.

"No. They went for the Season each year. The duchess spent huge chunks of time in London. Once she had provided an heir, spare, and then a third son, she rarely was in the duke's presence."

"And what of you? Her children?"

"The most time she spent with us was when she carried us to term," he said, no emotion in his voice. "After our births, we were shuttled off to the nursery. Even when she was in residence at Wildwood, we could go weeks without laying eyes on her."

"That is so dreadfully wrong," Emery said.

He shrugged. "It is the way of Polite Society."

"You cannot tell me that most of the peerage ignores their children."

He shook his head. "You come from a different world, Emery. You have loving parents who have taught you. Spent time with you. Enjoy being around you. For most of the *ton*, it is a different story."

"That is horrible."

He released her hand and took her shoulders. "Thank you," he said.

Miles bent and pressed a soft kiss on her lips, a very different one from yesterday's, which had been filled with hunger and passion. This was gentle. A kiss of gratitude.

He broke the kiss and gave her a sad smile. "I do appreciate seeing Tony again but I cannot look upon it."

"Because of Ralph?"

"Yes. Though I would love to hang it in my bedchamber, the thought of having to see Ralph on a daily basis turns my belly sour." He smoothed her hair. "I thank you, though. Have it taken somewhere safe. I may want to see it again someday."

With that, Miles left the room.

Emery looked at the three boys. Thomas had said an artist named Leavell had painted the portrait. He might very well be painting still. Determination filled her. She was going to find this Mr. Leavell and have him paint over Ralph Notley. It would be easy. Tony sat in a chair in the middle, with Miles on one side and Ralph on the other. She was convinced a talented artist could cover the previous duke without doing any harm to the rest of the portrait. And if the artist protested in altering his previous work, she would see if he might be amenable to recreating the portrait on another canvas, leaving out Ralph Notley so that the new work could be displayed without bringing further grief to the new duke.

Of course, creating a separate portrait of the two younger Notley boys would certainly entail more work on Mr. Leavell's part. If she was fortunate to locate the artist, she did not want to overtax him. Emery would worry about the details if and when Leavell came to Wildwood.

She went to the duke's desk and withdrew parchment, composing a brief letter to Mr. Fillmore, the family's solicitor in London. Boldly, she told Fillmore that the Duke of Winslow wished to find the artist who had previously painted the portrait of the three Notley boys and commission him to paint another portrait of the mature duke. Fillmore would act quickly if he believed this was at His Grace's request. She specified that Mr. Jenson would be handling the situation once Mr. Leavell had been located and to forward information to the Wildwood steward That way, Emery could see the letter.

And Miles never would.

Using the Winslow seal, she secured the missive and let the wax dry before addressing it. Satisfied, she rang for Thomas and told him to place the portrait in his room for safekeeping.

"This is to remain between us, Mr. Trottmann," she said.

"Of course, Miss Jenson," he readily agreed.

Emery then gave her letter to a footman to be posted. She hoped Leavell would be located quickly and that he would be willing to adjust the portrait. After all, it was for a duke. She would see the artist paid from estate funds.

Only then, when it was completed, would she return it to Miles.

CHAPTER FIFTEEN

MILES RODE OUT on Zeus early the next morning, needing time to himself. Riding had always been his escape and his large estate allowed him the freedom to be out for several hours, enjoying the outdoors. He paused on top of a ridge that allowed him a bird's eye view of most of Wildwood, savoring the quiet surrounding him. Although sometimes the bullets and blood came to him in nightmares, the tranquility of this summer day made the battlefield seem far behind.

He worried about his friends who still fought for the crown. Wyatt, who took too many risks as he spied for Wellesley. Donovan, who chased every pretty skirt he could and took chances in battle that would curl the blood of most men. And Hart, the ultimate protector who only saw the world in black and white, a man who would lay down his life for his friends and his men. He owed them all a letter. Finch, too, though the most dangerous thing Finch encountered as a clergyman were young ladies taken by his good looks, hoping to bring the confirmed bachelor to heel.

Those four men were the brothers of his heart. Miles hated he had to leave three of them behind at war but it was a path they had all chosen, thanks in part to the events which had shaped their early lives. He only wished Tony had lived so he could have met these men. They would have taken Tony in as one of their own. Of course, Miles himself would never had met the four if his own circumstances had been different. Tony's murder had led Miles to Turner Academy. Without his younger brother's death occurring, he would have returned to his regular school and his path might never have crossed with the other Terrors.

They would like Emery. Donovan probably a little too much, with his eye for the ladies. Miles hoped one day he could introduce her to his loyal comrades.

As his wife.

It seemed funny to him now that he had never thought of taking a bride. Even if so inclined, it wouldn't have been fair to the woman he chose because he would have spent so much of his time away from her because of the war. The bloody, stupid, never-ending war with that madman, Bonaparte. If England wasn't careful, Miles' own sons would one day be fighting against the French emperor and general.

Still, what had once been something that had not even crossed his mind had now become an obsession—wedding Emery. Thank goodness he was a patient man because he sensed it would take heavy persuasion and abundant time to bring her around to the idea. Perhaps kissing her again might speed up the process. The thought of having her in his bed, her long legs entwined around him, caused his heart to race. He would give her time. Just not too much of it. If she thought long and deep, she would turn down his suit. At least that's what his gut told him. Yes, Miles decided kissing definitely needed to be put into play in order to win her more quickly.

He rode down from the ridge and across the fields, where workers gathered. Spying Kit, he turned the reins slightly and led Zeus in that direction, dismounting and greeting his old friend.

"Your Grace. It is good to see you," Kit said, bowing.

Though he hated hearing such formality from Kit's lips, Miles understood why they must keep some distance between them in front of others. He needed to win and then maintain the respect of his tenants. Too much familiarity or partiality on his part would destroy that goal.

"I am still awaiting my invitation to dine with you and your family," he reminded Kit.

His friend sighed. "Are you actually serious about that?"

"Of course, I am. Did you think it was talk? That I was trying to endear myself to my tenants?"

Kit grinned. "Perhaps."

"I am serious. I do want to get to know everyone."

"It's just that dukes don't go calling upon farmers and making merry at their tables."

Miles grinned. "It is the very reason I am enjoying being a duke. Dukes live by their own rules. If I want to dine with you and the rest of the families on my land, then I will."

Kit laughed. "You always were determined. Even as a young boy." Shaking his head, he added, "All right then, Your Grace. You may come for a humble supper tonight."

He motioned over his wife and she curtseyed to Miles. "Ann, His Grace will call upon us and share our dinner tonight."

Her eyes widened even as she nodded. "Very well, Your Grace. I hope you like mutton."

"I do," he assured her. "I will bring one of Cook's cakes for us to share as our dessert."

She smiled, a dimple creasing one cheek. "That would be lovely, Your Grace." She told him what time to arrive.

Miles tipped his hat to both of them. "I better ride back and let Cook know she's to bake us a sweet for tonight. Do your children have any favorite flavors?"

"Bring whatever you wish, Your Grace," Kit urged. "Billy and Becky will be thrilled with any kind of cake." He paused. "Especially if you bring Miss Jenson with you. My Billy is sweet on her. I think most men are."

Kit's words rankled Miles. Tamping down his irritation, he bid them farewell and returned Zeus to the stables. Cutting through the kitchens, he let Cook know he wouldn't be home for dinner and that he needed a cake to take to the Munsons tonight.

"Any special kind, Your Grace?" she asked.

"Surprise me," he told her. "Nothing too grand else the Munsons might think it too pretty to eat."

Miles went in search of Emery and ran across her mother first.

"Mrs. Jenson, might you know where your daughter is at the moment?"

"She is with Mr. Trottmann, Your Grace. Several footman are polishing the silver under his direction and Emery is updating the inventory," she replied, telling him which room they were located in.

"Thank you."

He located them, Emery's head bent over a page as she scribbled away. He longed to unpin her raven hair and run his fingers through the luxurious tresses.

She looked up, sensing his presence, and he lost himself a moment in those deep brown eyes, the amber rims softening the shade somewhat.

"Did you have need of me, Your Grace?" she asked.

"Yes. I am to dine with the Munsons tonight. Their invitation extends to you. It seems young Billy Munson is a bit infatuated with you."

Her throaty laugh caused a frisson of desire to speed through him. He would definitely need to kiss her again. Soon.

Tonight.

Miles told her what time they were expected and then said, "I will call for you at your parents' cottage with the carriage."

"Why do so?" she asked. "It is but a short walk. We could be there in a quarter-hour or less."

Though he had entertained thoughts of kissing her inside the darkened carriage, perhaps a longer walk as he escorted her home would provide a better opportunity for what he had in mind.

"You are right. We should walk to our supper. I will see you later."

A slight blush infused her cheeks. "I will be ready, Your Grace."

><<<

CROWDER ASSISTED MILES from his bath and helped him to dress. He insisted on a plain, dark blue coat with a buff waistcoat and breeches, though a bucketload of clothing had arrived from his London tailor and shirt maker earlier in the day.

"Keep the knot in my cravat simple," he instructed the valet.

Miles didn't want Kit to think he was putting on any airs now that he was the Duke of Winslow. He was already aware of the vast difference between their stations and wanted his old friend, as well as Kit's family, to be comfortable in his presence. It would help with Emery coming along. She had a talent for putting others at ease.

An excellent quality in a duchess.

He bit back a smile, wondering what she would make of his wanting her as his bride. She would protest—but Miles had always been up for a challenge. Convincing the lovely Miss Jenson to take him in holy matrimony might be his greatest challenge yet. Even greater than leading first-time, terrified soldiers into battle. Yes, it would be a battle of wills between the Duke of Winslow and the lovely Emery Jenson.

And when he won?

They would both become winners.

"Enough fussing, Crowder," he said testily, eager to leave the house in order to be in Emery's company. Then thinking better, he added, "You always make me very presentable, Crowder. I am most pleased with your service."

The valet beamed. "Thank you, Your Grace. I have arranged the wardrobe that arrived today. Many fine pieces were among them, as well as everyday attire. You will cut a fine figure in them, especially when you go to London."

"I have no intention of going to London anytime soon," he informed the servant. "I hope that doesn't disappoint you."

"Not at all, Your Grace," Crowder said smoothly. "I prefer to be wherever His Grace desires to be."

"I am one for the country, Crowder. Town holds no fascination for me." He paused. "If you thought you were getting a duke who would live in London a good portion of the year and that you'd be dressing him in fine clothes for society events, you are sadly mistaken."

Relief flooded the servant's face. "I am from the country myself and quite enjoy it. Especially Wildwood. It's a lovely estate. I have even made a few friends."

"Good to know." Miles started to take the hat the valet offered and then thought better of it. "I think I will leave behind the hat. I don't think it is called for at an informal supper."

"Of course, Your Grace. I hope you enjoy your meal with the Munsons."

Miles left his suite and went straight to the kitchen, where Cook greeted him.

"Strawberry cake, Your Grace," she told him. "I have already had it delivered to the Munsons at their cottage since you are walking there. I did not want you to have to carry it such a long way."

It continually surprised him—though it shouldn't have—how even the smallest of details regarding his life were known by his servants.

"And give my best to Miss Jenson," Cook added, her lips twitching in amusement.

Had his cook guessed at his feelings for Emery?

He hoped not. If Cook knew, the rest of the staff would in due course since Cook was not one to hold back information or her opinion on any topic. And that would include Mr. and Mrs. Jenson. While he didn't think the couple would protest much if their daughter wed a duke, Miles wanted Emery to know of his intentions before everyone in his household did. She had to have an inkling, based upon the kiss they had shared. Then, too, she had told him it wouldn't happen again.

Stubborn woman.

"I will indeed, Cook. I bid you good evening."

Miles left, his step full of energy as he made his way to the steward's cottage. He remembered the location from his boyhood. The cottage was the nicest one on the estate, appropriate for the position attached to it. He still marveled how much of Wildwood seemed to be under Emery's management. She was a whirlwind of activity and probably left her father with very little to do.

He arrived and knocked upon the door. Mrs. Jenson opened it and invited him inside.

"It is a lovely night, Your Grace," she said.

"Very much so. I missed spring and summer in England when I was away at war. It is nice to be home again."

By home, he meant not only England—but Wildwood. As each day passed, he found himself becoming more and more attached to the estate. He hadn't realized how much he'd truly missed it until he returned as its duke. Though he knew he had a London townhouse and various other estates scattered about the countryside that he would eventually have to visit, he was enjoying sinking roots into Wildwood. Miles knew it would only be more of a joy once he wed and his children were born in this house.

Emery appeared, having changed her gown from the pale green one she had worn earlier. She now wore one of soft pink, the color which reminded him of the inside of a seashell. It made her skin luminous and her lips even more inviting. He would definitely kiss her on the way home after dinner. Anticipation flooded him.

"You look lovely, Miss Jenson," he said, wishing he had thought to bring her flowers. Then again, that would have been deemed inappropriate by her. He still might give some to her from his gardens, just to hear her reasons for why she should reject them. Verbally sparring with her sounded like immense fun.

Almost as much fun as kissing her.

"Thank you, Your Grace." She turned to her mother. "I won't be long. It will be dinner with the Munsons and then straight home." She kissed her mother's cheek.

"Enjoy your evening," Mrs. Jenson said, opening the door for them. "Please give my best to the Munsons."

Miles held out a hand, allowing her to go first and then following as the door closed behind them. He took her hand and tucked it into the crook of his arm.

"No protests, Emery," he said as he led her away from the cottage. "The ground is uneven and I wouldn't want to disappoint Kit and Ann if you took a tumble and turned your ankle."

She snorted. "As if I would turn an ankle. I am out and about many times on the estate. I am not some sheltered miss straight out of the schoolroom needing the support of a gentleman's arm."

He laughed. "Then perhaps I am in need of the support and using you for balance."

She pursed those lips which begged him to kiss them. "I would say as an officer who used to charge across the battlefield at full speed, you are the last person who might need a helping hand, Your Grace."

"Miles," he prompted. "We are alone."

"Not for long," she reminded him. "Besides, it simply isn't proper for me to call my employer—who happens to be a duke, by the way—by his Christian name."

"Unless the said duke has asked you to," he retorted. "I am serious, Emery. We are working closely together. It seems ridiculous to maintain such formality between us."

She sniffed. "I prefer it whether you do or not."

He fell silent, letting her think she had won a small victory. He would be the victor come the walk home.

They arrived at the cottage, where Billy waited outside for them. The boy's face lit up as they approached and Miles couldn't help but grin because he felt the same way about the woman on his arm.

"Good evening, Your Grace, Miss Jenson," Billy cried. "I greeted His Grace first because Papa said a duke is more important than anyone. Except the king. That means people should always notice him first. But you look pretty, Miss Jenson."

"I agree, Billy," Miles said, laughing. "Miss Jenson looks lovely this evening. Is your mama ready for us?"

"Oh, she's been running around in circles, Your Grace," the boy confided. "Checking this and then that. She said everything had to be perfect. That's why I'm outside. Mama was afraid I might make a mess. So she told me to come and just stand. Not run around and get hot and sweaty. Not to get dirty. Just stand and greet you. Oh! I'm supposed to tell her when you get here."

He wheeled and ran to the door, opening it and shouting, "Mama! Papa! They're here."

Kit poked his head out. "Come in, Your Grace, Miss Jenson. Thank you for coming this evening."

"Even though I practically invited myself," Miles quipped.

"I believe you did invite yourself," Kit said and they both laughed.

Ann wiped her hands on her apron and came forward, offering a curtsey. "It is a pleasure to have you, Your Grace. And thank you for also coming, Miss Jenson. Billy has talked of nothing else." She winked. "I think he mentioned something about wanting to marry you," she said softly.

"Mama!" the boy cried, his face turning bright red.

"Well, Miss Jenson is a lovely lady. I hope you will wed one as kind and sweet as she is," Ann said. "But she is older than you, Billy. She cannot wait."

"Are you going to marry someone else soon, Miss Jenson?" the boy asked, looking crestfallen before Emery even replied.

"I have no plans to wed at all, Billy."

"Not even Mr. Jernigan?"

"Billy!" his father chided.

"Well, he looks at her funny," Billy said. "And I heard Mama tell you Mr. Jernigan was sweet on Miss Jenson."

Emery's fingers tightened about his arm. He glanced at her and saw her face flaming in embarrassment. She relaxed her hold on him and slipped her hand away.

Kneeling, she told Billy, "Mr. Jernigan is a nice man. He is nice to all his customers. I just happen to be a very good one because I make many purchases there on behalf of His Grace. Mr. Jernigan is happy to see me because he knows I will be spending a lot of coin in his father's store."

The boy crossed his arms. "He likes you," he said stubbornly.

"Everyone likes Miss Jenson," Kit said. "Why don't we come to the table?"

As they sat, Miles noticed Becky clinging to her mother's skirts and said, "It is good to see you again, Becky."

The girl, who sucked her thumb, regarded him with large eyes.

Ann pulled Becky's hand from her mouth. "No sucking your thumb in front of His Grace," she said gently, pulling the girl into her lap.

The fare offered was simple yet hearty and Miles found himself relaxing being in the presence of his old friend. They began reminiscing about their younger days and soon had the others laughing at their boyhood antics.

He took a final bite of his bread and said, "That was a lovely meal, Ann. You've baked bread even fresher and tastier than Cook. But don't tell her I told you so because I will deny it to my grave."

"Thank you, Your Grace. I have an extra loaf in case you wish to take it home with you. And please thank Cook for sending the cake. The children have been eagerly waiting to cut into it."

"Then I think it is about time we did so," he encouraged.

"Yes!" Billy cried.

Ann brought the cake to the table and sliced it. Miles insisted that Billy receive the first piece.

"You can act as our taster, Billy."

"What's that?" the boy asked, obviously puzzled by the

comment.

"In the days of yore, the king would have someone who took a bite of everything before the king himself did. If it tasted good, then the king would eat his fill."

He noticed Kit looking at him with grateful eyes for not revealing the true reason a king had a tester.

"I can do that," Billy said with confidence. He took a generous bite of cake, which had a slice of strawberry atop it. "It's wonderful," he proclaimed, his mouth full.

Ann passed out slices to everyone and once they finished, Becky snuggled against her mother and fell asleep.

"That is our cue to leave," Miles said. "I don't wish to disrupt your family's nightly routine." He rose and the others did, as well. "Thank you for this evening. It has been the best meal I have had since returning to England, mostly because I so enjoyed the company."

"You are welcome to return anytime, Your Grace," Kit said. "Word has gotten out of your attendance at our table tonight. You may be deluged with invitations by tomorrow."

"I hope that is the case," he replied.

He and Emery left the Munsons' cottage. This time, she didn't protest as he slipped her hand through his arm. They strolled instead of walking, both seemingly reluctant to bring the evening to a close.

"It is very good of you to want to dine with each of your tenants," she told him.

"Kit is more than a tenant. He is my friend. Just because I have become the Duke of Winslow, it doesn't change that fact."

He glanced at her as she shook her head. "You can be friendly with him, Miles, but you must learn to maintain your distance. It is what the people expect. What they actually want, whether they know it or not."

He liked the fact that she had called him Miles. They went up a slight hill and he paused underneath a large tree. No one was in sight. They were far enough away from the tenant cottages and yet still a ways from the steward's cottage and main house. Twilight approached, its glow surrounding them as the sun began to slowly dip below the horizon.

Turning toward her, he asked, "What is it you want, Emery?"

She licked her lips nervously, setting him afire.

"Do you still want me?" he asked, his voice low. "Because I still want to kiss you. Very much."

CHAPTER SIXTEEN

E MERY SHIVERED. MILES' voice had been low and tender. So very tender. It caused her resolve to dissolve, the invisible wall that she had tried to maintain around her.

And failed. Miserably.

Her gaze met his penetrating one. The small scar stood out on his cheek. She realized he was waiting for her. He wasn't going to take from her.

He allowed her the choice to give.

And that was what made her decision.

"I would like to share a kiss with you," she said hesitantly, her usual confidence fleeing.

"Are you certain?" he asked, his eyes roaming her face.

"I am." At least she was certain in this moment that if he didn't kiss her, she might perish.

"Very well."

He took a step toward the tree and she moved with him, her hand still resting in the crook of his arm. Miles turned her and his hands captured her face, his thumbs gently caressing her cheeks.

"So very, very beautiful," he whispered.

Then he lowered his lips to hers.

The instant they touched, her body remembered. Her limbs tingled with recognition. Her breath quickened. Anticipation filled her. Her palms moved to rest atop his chest. One hand felt his heart thumping against it, surprising her.

Did she affect him as much as he did her?

His lips touched hers gently at first, causing her to want more. His hands slipped to her neck, caressing it as his kiss grew more urgent. Without him prodding her, she opened to him, causing a low groan to emerge from the back of his throat. His fingers went to her shoulders, tightening, as she felt herself moved back a step. The tree pressed against her back, his body close enough to pin her against it. Miles radiated heat, which spread to her, racing through her, her blood singing and her skin heating at his touch.

His tongue swept inside her mouth, toying with hers, engaging her in an unspoken game. Her palms crept up and her fingers touched his jaw, feeling the slight end-of-day stubble beneath her fingertips. She stroked his jaw and more low sounds emerged from him. His hands moved to her waist, anchoring her.

But Emery wasn't going anywhere. She returned Miles' kiss, her heart beating wildly, her insides giddy. Heat pooled between her legs and a fierce pounding began there. His muscular chest pushed against her, causing her breasts to grow heavy and needy. It shocked her to realize they wanted his touch on them.

Though she hadn't voiced those thoughts, it seemed his body had heard hers speak. One hand moved from her waist, dragging slowly up her ribs and then cupping her breast. She gasped into his mouth as he palmed it, squeezing it slightly. Then he tweaked her nipple and a frisson of desire shot through her, causing the drumbeat between her legs to pound violently. He rolled the nipple between his thumb and finger and then raked his nail over it. Even through her gown and undergarments, she felt the heat singe her. Something made her want to shed her clothes and Emery fought for control.

Miles broke the kiss and his lips glided along her jaw and then down the long column of her neck, even as his fingers played with her breast. He found the point where her pulse beat and licked it, causing her to shudder. Then he nipped at her, a love bite that shot a bolt of lightning through her. Her arms wound around his neck and she fought to keep him close.

His other hand moved upward and now both fondled her breasts as he continued kissing her neck. Emery whimpered and clung to him, unsure of the need building within her. She wanted something from him but had no name to attach to these desires.

"Emery," he murmured against her neck, his lips rising again to meet hers, taking her in a fierce kiss which went on and on.

Tears filled her eyes from the strong emotions that ran through her. She had no name for them—and that frightened her. Reality began to set in. She was kissing the Duke of Winslow in the middle of a field. Anyone could see them.

That thought caused her to begin struggling. She tore her lips from his and unlinked her fingers from behind his neck. She pushed against him, trying to move him away.

He only tightened his grip on her.

"What's wrong?" he asked softly, his eyes dark with need.

"Let me go," she ground out.

Immediately, he released her and took a step back.

"I am not my brother," he said quietly. "I would never—"

"I know you are not," she interrupted. "Nevertheless, you are the Duke of Winslow. You are destined to wed a highborn lady, most likely the daughter of another duke. I am not a plaything, You Grace. I have worked extremely hard to prove how capable I am. I refuse to let you destroy what I have accomplished through years of work."

"You aren't a passing fancy, Emery," he said resolutely. "I wish—"

"You think you are different," she said, again interrupting him. "You want to be a different man from your father and older brother. I understand that. I think you will be. You have all the makings to be an excellent duke. You are intelligent and already care for your people. You haven't a selfish bone in your body. But you are a member of the *ton*, Miles, like it or not. They will judge you."

"I don't care for their opinions," he insisted.

"You say that—but you will. You will want your sons and daughters to be held in respect. You will want them to make good matches. For that to happen, you must wed a woman Polite Society finds suitable for you." Emery shook her head sadly. "I am not that woman. Not that you would want to wed me. But I cannot kiss you again like that. Those kisses—those caresses—are meant for the woman you will marry, Miles. The woman who will bear you children."

Emery reached out and cradled his cheek. "You are a good man. You will be an excellent husband and father and an outstanding duke. I ask you to leave me be, Your Grace. I have found my place in the world. You must now find yours."

With that, she dropped her hand. "Only speak to me regarding estate business, Your Grace. I have already taught you much. The rest you may figure out on your own or ask someone else on the estate. The time for relying on me is over."

She lifted her skirts and took off, running the rest of the way to her parents' cottage, knowing not to look back. If she did, she would lose all reason and run straight into Miles' arms again.

EMERY EXCUSED HERSELF to her father and left the steward's office. She needed a few minutes to collect herself.

Today had been a terrible day. While her father made sense, he had been querulous since breakfast, wanting to pick a fight with her over everything she said or suggested to him. She took a brief turn outside, the June afternoon air muggy from the brief rainstorm an hour earlier.

Returning to the house, she found her mother and asked, "Could you invite Papa for a cup of tea in your office?"

"Is he giving you trouble?" her mother asked, her eyes both sympathetic and worried.

"Some," Emery admitted. "I don't seem to be able to get

anything done today."

Actually, that had proven true for the last three weeks.

Ever since her declaration to Miles—no, His Grace. She must think of him only as her employer, the Duke of Winslow. He had respected her wishes. He had merely nodded to her if they passed. When he came to the office, he would ask her father a question. Thankfully, Papa was having a good spell and was able to answer his employer. Once, when Papa had hesitated, Emery had provided the answer. The duke had given her a clipped thank you and left abruptly.

She would stare at the ledgers and find it impossible to concentrate. All she wanted to do was recall his mouth on hers. The heat. The need. His touch on her breasts. His lips traveling along her throat.

"Return to him. I'll come along in a few minutes and collect him," Mama promised.

Emery went back to the office. Her father stared off into space. She slipped into her usual seat behind the second desk that they had placed in the room and returned her attention to the ledger in front of her. As expected, her mother came and convinced her husband to come take a cup of tea with her, leaving Emery alone with her thoughts.

A light knock sounded on the door and she bid the servant to enter. A footman presented her with the day's post and she thanked him.

She culled through it, glad to have a different task before her rather than studying numbers. The last piece of correspondence contained a beautiful hand and she eagerly opened it, hoping it was what she had awaited.

My dear Mr. Jenson –

Mr. Fillmore told me of the Duke of Winslow's interest in having his portrait painted. As I am between commissions and do not take up my next one for three weeks, I would be happy to come to Wildwood immediately. Mr. Fillmore is providing transportation to the estate for me and I should arrive very soon. In fact, I have papers from Mr. Fillmore for His Grace and will present them to him upon my arrival.

Yours,
Lawrence Leavell

Panic surged through Emery. This wouldn't do at all! She had specifically asked Mr. Fillmore to forward the artist's address to her father. She had wanted to write to Mr. Leavell personally and explain a bit of the situation to see if he would be interested in making adjustments to the portrait of the three Notley sons. Instead, Leavell would arrive at the estate thinking he had been commissioned to paint Miles' portrait.

She refolded the letter and slipped it inside her pocket. Her desire to act kindly had gone badly. No, it had exploded—and she might be shattered beyond repair. She didn't know how Miles would react to Leavell's arrival, much less her idea of erasing Ralph from the portrait. He most likely would refuse to sit for a current portrait, meaning the artist would have wasted a trip to Kent. If things were better between them, Emery might go to Miles and explain the situation. Instead, the past three weeks had seen a wedge placed between them, with her barely looking in his direction and Miles acting like a duke—haughty, sullen, and distant.

What was she going to do?

"Miss Jenson?" a deep voice said, one which she recognized.

Lifting her gaze, she saw Miles standing next to her and she started.

"Didn't you hear me knock?" he asked.

"No. I didn't," she managed to get out, her mind racing as she tried to think of a way to bring up Lawrence Leavell's imminent arrival.

"I have something I wish to take up with your father. Is he available?"

"He is out on the estate," she said, thinking the duke might not approve of his employee taking time to indulge in a cup of tea. "Might I help you?"

"I suppose you can," he said loftily, seeming very duke-like to her, confirming her instincts had been correct. Though not born to the role, Miles was certainly fast becoming the Duke of Winslow.

He took a seat and briefly outlined an idea he said he'd had regarding production in the mill.

"No, that won't work," she told him, explaining step-by-step why his idea, though seemingly good, wouldn't be feasible.

"I still think it could improve efficiency," he said stubbornly.

She sniffed. "And I am saying it won't. True, in the short-term it might but one must look at the long-term results. Perhaps I did not explain it thoroughly enough, Your Grace. Let me try again."

Emery took a deep breath and went over her reasoning. His mouth set stubbornly as she spoke.

"Are you even listening to a word I am saying?" she demanded.

"I am. I just think my idea is better," he snapped.

"How would you know?" she demanded. "You haven't even been through a single harvest. I have been through a decade of them."

"While I am happy to listen to your suggestions, they are only suggestions, Miss Jenson. It is my estate and I will see things run the way I wish."

She snorted. "Then you will run it into the ground, Your Grace."

He pushed to his feet. "Do you always believe you are right about everything?"

She stood, almost as tall as he was. "I usually am. And I am about this. Ask Papa. Ask your foreman. Ask Mr. Munson. They will tell you. It is one thing to try something new and quite another to be warned it won't work and attempt it anyway. If you care so much about your tenants, as you say you do, you will be a better man and listen to reason."

Miles burst out laughing.

Emery felt her face flood with color. She grasped her hands in front of her.

"I am sorry," he apologized.

"No, I am the one who should apologize," she said meekly. "You are the Duke of Winslow. It is your estate. You should do as you wish upon it."

"We both like to assert ourselves, don't we?" he asked.

Reluctantly, she nodded. "I suppose so." She fought to keep from smiling. "We are both impatient, I believe."

"I am sorry I pushed for control," he said. "I had none as a boy. I will admit that I fear the loss of it now. In fact, I relish being in control." He cleared his throat. "I should have approached that better than I did."

"I should have—"

"What? Let me have my way and fall on my face? Cause our profits to lessen? Bring harm to my tenants?" Miles shook his head. "No, you were right to stand up to me."

"I could have managed it better," she admitted. "I was prickly. It is just that you were behaving so harsh and unfeeling. As if my opinion didn't matter one whit to you."

His sky blue eyes darkened. "It is the opposite, Emery. I am not harsh and unfeeling. I feel too much. For you."

The air between them crackled. If someone had lit a match, they would both have gone up in flames.

Her body hummed, anticipating his kiss. His touch.

Miles took a step to her.

Then a loud rap sounded on the door. Immediately, she collapsed into her chair while he strode toward the door and flung it open.

"Yes?"

"A carriage has been sighted, Your Grace," Trottmann said.

Alarm filled Emery. No visitors were expected. It could only mean one thing.

Lawrence Leavell had arrived.

CHAPTER SEVENTEEN

"WHO COULD BE coming?" Miles demanded, glaring at the butler, who also held a silver tray with letters atop it. "Is that today's post?"

"Yes, Your Grace," Trottmann responded calmly. "If you would care to read it now in your study, I can see who is calling at Wildwood and place them in the drawing room."

Emery watched Miles scoop up the correspondence, his entire demeanor disgruntled now. "Yes. Have whoever it is to wait. I will see them in due time."

He marched out of the room and inwardly, she sighed. His absence would give her a chance to speak to Lawrence Leavell first. She only hoped the artist would be cooperative instead of temperamental.

"I will see to the visitor, Mr. Trottmann."

"Is His Grace all right?" the butler asked, his eyes filled with concern.

"We had . . . a brief spat. About the running of the mill." She smiled ruefully. "I am afraid His Grace and I are both a bit mulish regarding our opinions. Our discussion placed him in a foul mood—but you did not hear that from me."

The butler nodded at her explanation. "I understand. You have quite a bit of experience, whereas His Grace is still learning." He raised his brows. "Hopefully, you brought His Grace around to your way of thinking?"

"I believe so."

The butler left and Emery went to the front hall. Her mother called out to her.

"Do you know who this is?" she asked Emery.

"I do."

Quickly, she explained who Leavell was and that his work was to have been a surprise but between Fillmore's and Leavell's wish to please the duke, the artist had left London without Emery having time to send word to him.

"Oh, dear," Mama said. "I'll see that a room is prepared while you greet him. I hope this can be cleared up without consequences."

"I do, too," she said worriedly and went out the front door just as the carriage pulled up.

A footman assisted an elegantly dressed man from the carriage. He was lean and lithe, with salt and pepper hair and a matching beard.

"Mr. Leavell?" she asked.

He gave a winning smile. "One and the same. You are far too young to be a housekeeper."

"I am Miss Jenson. I assist both my mother, who is His Grace's housekeeper, and my father, who serves as Wildwood's steward. I am the one who wrote to Mr. Fillmore, trying to locate you." She glanced over her shoulder. "I must speak quickly."

His eyes lit with mischief. "This sounds interesting."

"His Grace doesn't know you are coming. He only recently came into the title when his older brother passed away in a riding accident."

"I remember that one. Full of himself," Leavell said. "I must say I am relieved. I thought I would be painting the marquess who had become the Duke of Winslow. This will be much more enjoyable. The duke was a solemn boy but a bit of an imp once I put my brush down. I will be interested to see the man he has become."

"The current Duke of Winslow cannot abide his older, deceased brother. I had hopes that you might alter the portrait you did of the three boys. As a surprise to His Grace. He dearly loved his younger brother, who died shortly after you painted the three boys."

Leavell's eyes widened in surprise. "You want me to . . . paint over him? The older one."

"That is exactly what I mean."

"Why, what a wicked, splendid idea!" the artist proclaimed. He thought a moment. "It would be quite easy, you know."

"I agree. The eldest boy is on one side of the chair where the youngest brother sat. The current duke is on the opposite side."

"It would be very easy to do though I hate altering the original work. But to please a duke, I am happy to do so. I shall erase this loathsome brother from the canvas." He paused. "So, I suppose I am not to paint the duke's portrait now?"

"No," she said, shaking her head sadly. "That wasn't in the plan."

"If I could meet Winslow, I could still paint him. He wouldn't have to sit for me. I have a keen eye. Most people insist they sit for me but once I make a sketch of them, I can easily paint them without them being present. Since you wish to surprise His Grace, that would be two times you could do so. But I will have to meet him."

Leavell held up a pouch. "Mr. Fillmore sent papers for the duke to review. Shall we say I am one of his clerks and have brought these for His Grace to sign?" He gave her a conspiratorial smile. "It would allow me to meet him and I could compose my sketch from that."

"Are there truly papers to sign?"

"Yes, Mr. Fillmore mentioned that. He said His Grace could return them at his leisure. Perhaps I could insist he read and sign them and I would return them tomorrow? I could also take the portrait you wish to be adjusted with me back to London."

"This might actually work," she said. "Please, come inside." She looked to the footman, who stood holding Leavell's luggage.

"Bring those inside."

"Yes, Miss."

She led Leavell into the house, where her mother stood in the foyer.

"Ah, Mr. Leavell. I am Mrs. Jenson, the housekeeper. A room has been prepared for you."

He glanced from her to Emery. "You favor each other. Both of you are quite beautiful, only at different stages in your life. I would enjoy painting you together."

"Hush!" Emery warned. "You are no longer an artist." To her mother, she said, "Mr. Leavell is a clerk with Mr. Fillmore. Here to deliver papers for His Grace."

"I will see to your things, Sir," Mama said, motioning for the footman to follow her up the stairs. "Why don't you bring Mr. Leavell to the drawing room and ring for tea, Emery? It is time for it. Perhaps His Grace can join you."

"Won't you come with me?"

She led Leavell upstairs and rang for the tea and then said, "I will tell His Grace you are here." She frowned. "Do you think he will recognize you?"

"I don't think so. My hair was quite dark and I was clean-shaven then. He was but a boy. I checked my records. It has been fifteen years since I came to Wildwood and I was much younger then. Why don't you call me Mr. Lawrence instead of Leavell? The name is more commonplace. Leavell might jar His Grace's memory."

She smiled gratefully. "You are being a saint, Mr. Leavell."

"Lawrence, my dear. I think I will enjoy a bit of subterfuge. And I think you are being most thoughtful in wanting to give His Grace a painting he will be happy to view. One of him and his younger brother."

"Thank you. I will return shortly. I must speak to our butler and see that everything has been arranged to your satisfaction."

Miles went to his study and fell into his chair.

He had almost kissed Emery again.

Fortunately, Trottmann had interrupted them. It would have been a disaster if Mr. Jenson had returned to his office and come upon them in an embrace. It wasn't like Miles to be so careless.

But then again, nothing had been the same since he had met Emery Jenson.

He still wanted her for his duchess. But he was having a devil of time coming up with a way to convince her that she was perfect in every way. Obviously, she understood the barrier of class between them far more than he did. He had never moved through Polite Society nor been held to their standards. He still didn't plan to do so. As a duke, he could be a recluse if he chose, answering to no one.

She had been right, though, about their children. He would want them accepted and not looked upon as oddities because of their father's behavior. True, they would have to overcome the gossip of her mother being the daughter of an untitled gentleman—but what good was it becoming a duke if he couldn't follow his heart?

His heart was leading him straight to Emery and he refused to compromise. Convincing her to wed him shouldn't be so difficult. Then again, he wouldn't wish to marry some shy miss. If he had to work to win Emery's hand, so be it. Miles was determined to wed her. Even if he had to ruin her to do so. He had heard talk of ladies found in compromising positions with gentlemen. How being alone with one or caught in a kiss led to a quick marriage.

Of course, Emery would remind him she was no lady even if he could arrange for someone to witness them in an embrace. She would state that she couldn't be ruined in the traditional sense. If that did happen, it would only upset her. She had worked hard to attain the knowledge and position she held at Wildwood and had gained the respect of servants and tenants along the way. She wouldn't want to be seen as a women of easy virtue, susceptible to the charms of a rakish duke. Not that that described him in the least.

How was he to persuade her they were meant to be together?

He glanced at the post which he had tossed upon his desk. He had stormed out like a petulant child. Regret filled him for goading her as he had. He knew what he suggested regarding the mill wasn't wise. He had merely wanted to be near her and talk to her. Verbally spar with her.

And yes, possibly kiss her.

It had been three bloody weeks since he had and his body craved hers more with each passing day. He had taken long rides. Spoken with tenants. Swung a hammer repairing a fence. Anything to keep his mind from wandering back to her and her delicious curves.

He broke the seal and read through the first letter and set it aside. The second, though, he read twice.

It was from the steward at one of his estates in Suffolk. Fillmore had encouraged Miles to tour his holdings once he had settled in at Wildwood but he had been reluctant to do so because it meant leaving Emery. Now that a slight problem had arisen in Suffolk, it was imperative that he see the estate and make a few decisions, based upon what the steward wrote to him.

Would his absence make Emery miss him more than if she couldn't see him every day? He certainly hoped so. He would leave in the morning for Suffolk.

"Blast!" he said aloud, remembering some visitor had arrived.

Rising, he left his study, where Trottmann hovered nearby.

"The guest?" he asked.

"It is a Mr. Lawrence," the butler revealed. "Miss Jenson said he is a clerk from Mr. Fillmore's office and that he has important papers for you to sign."

"Where is he?"

"In the drawing room, Your Grace. Tea should have been

delivered by now."

"Very well. I will go see him. Trottmann, have Crowder pack for me. I'm off to Suffolk tomorrow. Something at Marblewood needs my personal attention. I will leave first thing in the morning."

"Very good, Your Grace."

Miles headed to the drawing room, where he found Emery pouring a cup of tea for their guest.

"Mr. Lawrence?" he said as he crossed the room.

The man rose and bowed. "Yes, Your Grace. I am an associate with Mr. Fillmore."

Something seemed familiar about this man. His voice? His manner?

"Have we met before, Mr. Lawrence?" he asked.

"I suppose you might have caught sight of me at Mr. Fillmore's office when you were in London. I am sorry we were not introduced." He reached for a pouch at his feet. "I have brought papers from Mr. Fillmore that you are to review and sign."

Miles wave the papers away. "I will look at them after we have had tea."

He accepted a cup from Emery, who excused herself. He allowed her to go, not wanting to force her to stay. Instead, he spent a pleasant half-hour with Lawrence, who seemed to know a great deal about the theatre and art world.

"If you will excuse me, I shall look over what Fillmore has sent now. I assume you will stay until I have done so."

"If that is convenient for you, Your Grace," Lawrence replied.

"Then I will see you for dinner. Plan on staying the night. You can return to London first thing tomorrow morning."

Miles excused himself and returned to the steward's office, where Mr. Jenson and Emery were both bent over ledgers. His steward didn't acknowledge him as he pored over the page but Emery asked if he needed anything.

"Yes. Would you be so good as to join me and Mr. Lawrence for dinner this evening? I am talked out after tea and could use a hand in entertaining him. In fact, why don't you bring your parents? I would enjoy having them come, as well. I am leaving for one of my other estates in the morning. This way, if anything comes to mind, I can bring it up during our meal."

"Is there a problem, Your Grace?" she asked, her brow furrowing.

"Just a few things at Marblewood that the steward insists I see. Some decisions he believes I should have a hand in now that I am Winslow."

"Mr. Marshall is a thoughtful man. He is slow to act at times. I am sure he will enjoy being able to show you Marblewood and allow you to have a say in what needs to be addressed."

Miles wished he could take Emery to Marblewood with him. Instead, he said, "It is good to know that Wildwood will be in capable hands while I am gone. As long as I am in the area, I will stop in at the two estates in Essex since they are near Marblewood. I will probably be gone two or three weeks," he added.

Long enough to hope Miss Emery Jenson would pine for him a bit.

CHAPTER EIGHTEEN

E MERY ENTERED THE main house and turned not in the
direction of her father's office but the stairs. Ever since Miles
had been gone, she had buried herself in work, trying to keep
thoughts of him away.

It hadn't worked. The handsome duke had constantly been
on her mind.

Caught up with estate affairs, she had delved into a new project—exploring and cataloguing the attics at Wildwood. She
mentioned the idea to her mother, who had been all in favor of
seeing what might be stored upstairs since she had never
ventured into them. Addy was enlisted to help Emery clean as
they unearthed everything from junk to treasures. Three fine
pieces of furniture had been taken downstairs already and placed
in various rooms. Old linens had been turned into cleaning rags.
Trunks of clothes from past decades awaited a good airing and
wash before Mrs. Jenson would decide what would be done with
them.

As she entered the attics, she saw Addy sweeping.

"Almost done, Miss Jenson," the maid said. "It's been fun
seeing what's all up here."

"I agree."

Deciding to make a final turn around the massive space to see
if anything had been missed, Emery walked the perimeter. Addy
called goodbye and left, broom and dustbin in hand.

As she moved through the large area, she wondered when Miles might return to Wildwood. He had been gone two and half weeks. He hadn't specifically indicated what needed to be discussed at Marblewood and only mentioned in passing he would visit two other ducal estates once he left Suffolk. She hoped Mr. Leavell would finish his work soon and be gone before Miles returned. The artist had made use of the schoolroom on the top floor, noting it had excellent light. He had forbidden anyone from entering, wanting to wait until he completed his work. Emery only hoped Miles would be pleased with the final results.

She came across a large, old-fashioned desk tucked into an alcove and wondered how this had been missed. It was battered and in poor condition, which is probably why it had been relegated to the attics in the first place. Idly, she opened a drawer and found it to be empty. She opened the rest and in the final one discovered a leather-bound book. Curious as to why it had been left inside the desk, she opened it.

Scrawled across the first page in an obvious masculine hand was a name.

Garrick Notley.

Turning the page, she saw a date written under the name, one from the mid-1700s—and began to read the first entry.

> *They have said all manner of things about me. Much of it wild invention—but a sprinkling of the truth here and there. Frankly, the stories told about me do not tell half the tale. I have lived a life of my own choosing, sowing my oats from young manhood well into middle age. Debauchery has been my closest companion and yet the bane of my existence. I was never close to anyone, not even as a child. I was bred to be the Duke of Winslow and found few and then no friends. Only those who would cling to me if I provided them drink or ready whores.*
>
> *I finally wed and sired three children. The younger two girls have nothing to do with me ever since they wed many years ago. Only the oldest comes around and that is because I still hold the purse strings. He is my heir and nemesis. My pride*

and joy and yet I feel nothing but hate for him. He is much like his mother, a woman I cared nothing for. She brought fabulous wealth and beauty to our marriage but she possessed a shrewish nature. We spent very little time together. After getting my heir and two daughters off her, I found I tired of her and thought no more sons were coming. She said it was because I was old—fifty at that point. I let her go. She lived and died in London while I have spent my final years here at Wildwood.

Emery stopped reading and flipped through the pages, seeing the entire journal filled with the bold handwriting. Who knew what family history lay within these pages? Knowing that Miles had a love for history, he would be thrilled to examine her find. She set the journal atop the desk and opened the drawers once more, making sure she hadn't overlooked anything. They were all empty.

She picked up the journal again and didn't have a good grip on it. It slipped from her fingers and fell to the ground. She bent to retrieve it and then saw something lay behind the desk. Gently, she lifted the journal and set it back on the desk before taking hold of the corners of the desk and pulling as hard as she could. The piece of furniture was incredibly heavy and it took her several tries to make any headway. Finally, it was out far enough for her to remove what had been hidden behind the desk. Emery slid it along the wooden floor until it was free from the obstacle. An oil cloth covered it. From the size, she guessed it to be a painting.

Lifting the cloth away, she saw it was a portrait turned sideways. She struggled to turn it but when it was set aright, she gasped.

Miles stared back at her.

No, she told herself, not Miles. One of his ancestors. It amazed her how much the current duke favored this relative. The man in the portrait had the same skin-kissed golden brown hair. The exact brow, cheekbones, and chin. The two men's mouths favored one another as did their general frame. The only difference she could see was that this man had dark brown eyes, where Miles had his mother's sky blue ones.

Emery studied the clothes this long-ago duke wore from decades ago and decided it was a distinct possibility that he was Garrick Notley, author of the journal she had found. Why had this portrait been taken to the Wildwood attics instead of hanging with all the many other Notleys in the portrait gallery filled with previous dukes?

The answer might lie within the pages of the journal.

It wasn't her place, though, to read it. She should make sure Miles saw both the painting and the journal upon his return. It would need cleaning, though. Even in the dim light that filtered through the nearby window, she could see the colors had been dulled by time. Fortunately, Mr. Leavell was still here. She hoped her discovery would entice him to do a thorough cleaning of this dead Notley's portrait.

She replaced the oil cloth and left the attics, immediately running into a footman.

"Mr. Lawrence is asking for you, Miss Jenson," he informed her. "Says he's ready to show you what he's been up to."

"Come with me first," she said, bringing the footman back to the portrait and having him carry it down to the schoolroom.

"Place it there," she instructed and the servant did so before leaving.

Leavell came toward her. "You have brought me something?" he asked, interest lighting his fair eyes.

"I have. A portrait which I discovered in the attics just now. Have a look."

He lifted the cloth away and gave a low whistle. "It is the spitting image of His Grace."

"I thought the same."

Leavell clucked his tongue. "It is so dusty, though. The colors have faded." He knelt and then drew in a quick breath. "It's a Julian Glanville."

The name meant nothing to Emery. "Who is he?"

"Probably the most talented English portrait artist of last century," Leavell explained. "He died in his early thirties, having only painted portraits of aristocrats for about ten years. A list exists of the ones he completed. That could help in identifying which Notley this might be." He frowned. "You said this was in the attics?"

"Yes, hidden behind a desk. I found a journal inside it." She held up the book in her hands. "Garrick Notley's. He may be the man in the painting."

"I can consult the list when I return to London," Leavell offered, "and write to you of which Notley Glanville painted."

"That would be most helpful, Mr. Leavell."

He frowned at her. "Lawrence."

She chuckled. "I think the cat is out of the bag. With His Grace gone and you staying behind, not to mention the smell of your oil paints drifting into the corridor, the servants know who you are. A couple even remembered you from before."

He shrugged. "Servants seem to know more of what occurs in a household than those who actually own and reside in it."

"That is very true." Emery glanced to where two easels stood, both facing away from them. "Might I see your work now?"

"Of course."

With trepidation, she went to the first easel. Her jaw dropped.

The original portrait of the three Notley sons had the boys placed in a library. She had thought Leavell would merely paint over Ralph and replace him with the bookshelves in the background. Instead, it was an entirely new setting. While Tony still had the wide-eyed look of innocence as before, Miles' face had been slightly altered. The two boys were now pictured in a garden, standing next to a gazebo.

She turned to the artist, shaking her head in disbelief.

"Do you like it?"

"Very much but . . ." Her voice trailed off.

"Speechless. I like it." Leavell smiled. "This is not the original." He indicated a canvas placed against the wall. "I decided I couldn't mar my previous work. If His Grace doesn't wish to see it, perhaps future generations might." His lips twitched. "I suppose you could place it in the attic."

As Emery studied the new portrait, she told Leavell, "I had actually thought of asking you to paint a second one of just the younger boys but I was afraid it would make too much work for you."

He smiled. "Though I paint for a living, I have never considered it work. My art is my livelihood but also my pleasure and passion. This allowed me to do what I was originally commissioned to create."

He came to stand beside her. "You see, the duchess wanted the boys painted in the garden. The duke refused, saying it wasn't a masculine setting. I decided to honor her wishes this time around. I merely copied the youngest boy from the original and placed him on a step so he would be more level with his brother."

"But Mi—His Grace's face? It is different."

"Yes, the difference is subtle yet noticeable to those who know him well. This version is more the boy I saw come to the sitting each day. The one who would then change his countenance and become quite serious, as if he thought that expression would please his father. I believe this second version captures more of the boy he truly was."

Tears brimmed in her eyes. "Thank you, Mr. Leavell. You have given quite a gift to His Grace. His brother died shortly after the original portrait was completed. You have given Tony back to him, in a new setting, one which will keep from reminding him of his older brother."

Emery brushed away a tear as it fell and then stepped to the second easel. Once again, Leavell had surprised her, capturing Miles as he was now. He portrayed the air of authority. The determination. The casual elegance. The good looks and charm.

"I cannot believe you were able to do this from memory," she proclaimed.

Leavell went to the table where generations of Notley children had sat and picked up a stack of papers, handing them to her.

"I made several sketches of His Grace before I started work on either of these portraits."

She flipped through them. Miles entering the drawing room. Sitting at tea. At dinner that night. Sitting at his desk, frowning over the papers to be signed.

And then one which startled her.

It was a drawing that captured his essence yet it revealed a tenderness in his eyes. It showed off his good looks and physique but she was drawn to his face and the look in his eyes.

"Do you like it? I did this one for you. The others His Grace can keep or toss away."

"For me?" she asked, her throat tight with emotion. "Why?"

"Because it is how he looks at you, Miss Jenson. When he doesn't think anyone sees. I saw him observe you at dinner that night when you came with your parents."

She shook her head several times. "No, you are—"

"Wrong? I think not. I believe Winslow has a tendre for you, whether you know it or not." He paused. "I believe you do. Are there feelings on your part, as well?"

A single tear rolled down her cheek and Emery hastily wiped it away.

"I am not of his world, Mr. Leavell. Surely, you understand that."

Sadness flickered in his eyes. "Unfortunately, I know exactly what you mean. I paint the members of Polite Society but I will never move freely among them. They clamor for me yet would pass me by on the street without a hint of recognition."

She saw a faraway look come into his eyes.

"Once, many years ago, I painted a young, beautiful girl on the eve of her come-out. Our feelings grew for one another. They were unspoken, even when we were alone and she was sitting for me—but I could see in her eyes the depth of her love. I know, too, she saw the same reflected in my eyes. Yet I knew nothing could come of it. She was the daughter of a marquess. Destined to wed a man of influence and wealth."

Leavell paused. "She did. And died giving birth to their first child. I still place flowers on her grave."

Emery's throat grew thick with unshed tears and she placed a hand on the artist's arm.

"Then you understand my position."

"I do." He placed his hand atop hers. "And might I give you a piece of advice? You have done something remarkable, giving the duke these two portraits. He will pursue you because of them. You can never be a part of his life, Miss Jenson. Not in the way you—or he—would wish. You should leave Wildwood. It would be for the best."

He squeezed her hand and then stepped away. "Keep the one drawing for yourself. It will hurt to look upon it, I daresay."

"But it is all I will ever have of him," she said, her chest tight.

Leavell cleared his throat. "I must leave for London tomorrow. It is time I got back and prepared for my next commission. I will spend today, though, cleaning the portrait you found."

"Thank you, Mr. Leavell."

"My pleasure, Miss Jenson."

Emery left and went to Miles' study. She placed the charcoal sketches on his desk, along with Garrick Notley's journal. Knowing it was foolish, she left with the one sketch Leavell intended for her. She couldn't take it to the cottage. It would be too easy to find there. Instead, she went to her father's office. He leaned back in his chair, softly puffing as he slept.

Opening the bottom drawer of her desk, she lifted everything inside and placed the sketch underneath the stack and then closed the drawer. Emery took out fresh parchment and dipped her quill into the inkwell.

She would write to Mr. Fillmore now and see if he could recommend an employment agency to her.

The time had come to leave Wildwood for good.

CHAPTER NINETEEN

M ILES GREW ANXIOUS as the carriage approached Wildwood. He had been gone more than three weeks and had missed the place. No, this wasn't just a place.

It was home.

It had always been home in his heart. Despite being banished from it. Wildwood was in his blood.

As was Emery.

More than missing home, he had missed her. He found himself constantly thinking about her during his time away. He could hear her laugh. Picture her brow furrow as she added columns of numbers. While being shown the gardens in one of his homes, he had passed a lilac bush, its sweet scent almost convincing him that she was merely around the corner. Her absence in his life created a massive hole, one that he had no way to patch. He needed her. Her kiss. Her taste. Her lecturing him about harvest statistics and the breeding of animals. Miles had never known how empty his life was until he felt her loss.

He couldn't help but wonder if she had missed him as much as he had her.

The carriage pulled up in front of Wildwood and a footman placed stairs down so Miles could exit. Both his butler and housekeeper waited to welcome him.

"Hello, Trottmann," he said cheerily, the sight of his butler raising his spirits.

"Good afternoon, Your Grace. Crowder arrived half an hour ago and said you would be here soon. Water is being heated for your bath."

"And greetings to you, Mrs. Jenson," he added.

"Will Your Grace need any refreshment?" the housekeeper asked.

"No, I can wait for tea. Make it a hearty one, though."

"I will speak with Cook, Your Grace."

He entered the house, the two servants following in his wake. A footman carried his trunk up the stairs.

"I think I will go to my study and see what posts have come in my absence," he informed Trottmann. "Then I will head up for my bath. I would like a cup of tea, though."

"I will see to it now, Your Grace," the butler said. "Would you prefer it here or in your bathing chamber?"

"Here, please."

Trottmann headed to the kitchens and Miles went to his study. Several neat stacks of letters awaited him, leading him to believe Emery had seen to their distribution and organization. As he seated himself, though, his eyes were drawn to a stack of pages. He lifted the first and stared.

It was a charcoal drawing—of him.

He studied it, thinking whoever sketched it was quite talented. Did he always appear so stern and severe to others?

He placed it aside and lifted the next, going through the stack one-by-one until he had viewed every sketch.

Who could have drawn these? And why?

His eyes landed on a brown leather book unfamiliar to him. He picked it up and opened the cover. The name, Garrick Notley, meant nothing to him. Turning the page, he began reading, quickly drawn into the narrative.

"Your tea, Your Grace."

Startled, he glanced up and saw Trottmann standing there. Miles closed the journal and set it on his desk.

Holding up a sketch, he demanded, "Do you know where this

came from?"

Trottmann's reserve did him justice. "I believe Your Grace should take that up with Miss Jenson."

What had Emery been up to while he was gone?

Sketches such as these often meant a picture had been commissioned. He remembered the artist who had come to Wildwood long ago. The man had drawn similar sketches of each Notley boy before they came to pose for their group portrait.

"Show me the portrait."

This time, Trottmann's eyes widened slightly. "Follow me, Your Grace."

He trailed after the footman, who still carried the cup of tea on a tray. They went up to the portrait gallery, a place he had only seen in passing when Mrs. Jenson provided him with a tour of the house when he had first arrived.

The butler came to a halt. Miles did the same and looked to the wall.

And saw two portraits of him hanging side-by-side.

His jaw fell open and he shut it quickly. "Leave."

Trottmann slipped from the gallery.

Miles stepped closer to the one on the right. This was most definitely him. The artist, whoever he might be, had done an excellent job in portraying Miles' strength and authority. This was the man he was now, one who had led men into battle and come home to lead his people as the Duke of Winslow. It would hang here for all his natural life and then for generations as new Notleys came and went.

It was the one of the left which interested him more, though. Miles stood before it, curious about who this ancestor was. All the other portraits hanging in the gallery had a small plate beside them, naming the figure portrayed. Only this one didn't.

What ancestor might this be, one whom Miles resembled so closely? It was as if someone had painted Miles as he went to a costume ball, dressed in clothes from decades ago. While Ralph and Tony had hair dark as night, as did both his parents, Miles' hair had always been much lighter. A light brown in colder weather, it would be threaded with golden highlights during warmer months, when he was frequently outside. He had always felt a little like an outsider in his own family since they all resembled one another so closely.

This portrait of a long-ago Notley—and probable duke—let him know he truly belonged.

This was all Emery's doing. Trottmann almost said as much. He wondered where she had unearthed the painting of his ancestor. It occurred to him that the journal he had begun reading might very well have belonged to this man. Excitement filled him. He looked forward to reading the entire contents and seeing what he might learn.

His bath had to be ready by now so he made his way to his suite of rooms. Once there, he headed straight to the bathing chamber, stripping off his clothes and tossing them at Crowder. The valet left him alone, the requested cup of tea now resting beside the tub. Miles downed it, the liquid having grown tepid, and then thoroughly soaped himself, removing the dust of the road. He soaked a few minutes longer and then called for Crowder, who brought the oversized bath sheet and helped him towel off.

Traipsing after the valet, he tossed off the bath sheet and sat, allowing Crowder to shave him. Once smooth to his satisfaction, Miles sat upon the bed, pulling on items of clothing and allowing Crowder to help him slip into others. He pushed his fingers through his thick hair, brushing it away from his face.

"Your boots, Your Grace."

Once the Wellingtons were in place, he stood and allowed Crowder to help him into his coat. Miles intended to seek out Emery now and learn the mystery behind the two portraits.

He took two steps and froze. Blinked. Surely, his eyes played tricks upon him.

He moved to a new painting hanging on the bedchamber's wall and paused, tears brimming in his eyes. It was of Tony and him. No Ralph in sight. They were no longer in the library, where they had sat for the original piece. Instead, they were in the garden. He vaguely recalled the three of them sitting for one session outside before the rest of the sittings were moved indoors.

They stood in front of a gazebo, surrounded by varying blooms. Tony stood on the top step and Miles on the ground, making them about even in height. His brother looked exactly as he had in the portrait Emery had shown Miles just before his departure. What was different was Miles himself. His pose was similar to the previous one but slight alterations to his face made him seem different. The sober, earnest boy still had a bit of the serious air about him, mixed in with a small dose of one who might be a rascal. He remembered trying his best to look solemn, hoping the duke would be proud of him.

"It is an excellent likeness, Your Grace," Crowder said. "I saw it the moment I entered your chambers. Is that a younger cousin you were painted with?"

"No. My brother. He passed away when we were quite young."

The valet's face sobered. "I am sorry to hear that, Your Grace. This is a lovely reminder of him, I suppose."

"It is," he answered, his throat thick with unshed tears.

Miles left the bedchamber, more than eager to find Emery and learn what else she had been up to during his time away from Wildwood.

EMERY RETURNED TO the stables after spending the afternoon visiting tenants. She had also stopped by to see Mrs. Harris, who had been ailing for a few days. As she left the cottage, Mr. Harris arrived and she spoke with him about his wife's fever, telling him if it didn't break by morning that Doctor Collier should be summoned.

As she approached, the first thing she noticed was the grand ducal carriage, which had been absent. Its return meant Miles was back at Wildwood. Hopefully, he would be weary from his travels and not want to talk estate business today with her or Papa. She wanted to avoid him as much as possible until she heard from Mr. Fillmore regarding his recommendation for an employment agency she might possibly use.

She had talked with Mama after she wrote to the solicitor, telling her mother why she had written to Mr. Fillmore. They had discussed the kind of positions she might be suited to do. While Emery thought the only thing she would be qualified for was a governess or lady's companion, Mama had urged her to consider other occupations, as well, including an assistant housekeeper. Mama said many of the large households' housekeepers had an assistant and that Emery would certainly be able to step into such a position with ease after her years of experience at Wildwood.

She told Mama she would consider that possibility and after some thought, believed it would be a better match for her skills. She had no experience with teaching children. She thought the idea of having to act as a companion to a woman in Polite Society foolish. Mama had explained that companions acted as friends and sometimes confidants to women who were lonely or often elderly. Emery couldn't understand why a woman's family wouldn't take on those roles, which proved her point about her distaste for those of the *ton* and why she would never want to be a part of that ridiculous world.

Even if Miles belonged to it.

She handed her reins to a groom and he helped her from the saddle.

"His Grace has returned, Miss Jenson. A few hours ago," he informed her.

"That is good to know," she replied evenly, though just the thought of Miles being nearby had heart beating rapidly. "How is Athena doing today?"

"A bit restless. Mr. Harris thinks the mare's time is drawing near."

"I think I will go stay with her a while. Would you send word to my mother? I don't want her to worry about me."

"Yes, of course. I'll go to the house myself," he promised. "Right after I see to Demeter."

Emery patted the horse. "Be good."

The groom led Demeter away and she went to Athena's stall.

"How are you, Athena?" she asked.

The mare swished her tail in irritation and nickered.

"No, I don't have any treat for you. I have been out riding all afternoon."

She opened the stall door and entered, wanting to examine the mare's teats. Sure enough, they were waxing. Emery squeezed one gently to see what the secretion would look like and then rubbed a light hand along Athena's side.

"It looks as if you will have your foal soon, my sweet. Why don't I stay with you and see what happens?"

Emery moved her hands lightly along the mother-to-be, speaking to her in soothing tones. Then Athena's head went up and stilled. Emery did the same, noting the air seemed different.

"Is she close to foaling?" a familiar voice asked as the stall door opened.

She dipped into a curtsey, her eyes downcast, and then turned back to the horse, her hand gliding gently along the mare's swollen sides.

"Yes. It could be within the hour. Certainly within the next few hours."

"How do you know?" Miles asked. "I have never seen a mare give birth."

He moved to Athena's other side and began touching the horse lightly. She watched his hands, not willing to meet his eyes yet.

"It is her teats. They begin to wax close to birth. I checked her mammary secretion a few minutes ago. Instead of being clear and watery, it has already turned opaque. As it grows thicker and more sticky, Athena will be close to delivery."

"Ah. I notice you aren't brushing her. Wouldn't she find that soothing?"

"No. She is very sensitive right now. She prefers a bare hand to bristles."

The horse snorted, her tail again swishing.

"She is telling us she is annoyed," he said. "We must be disturbing her."

Emery let her hand fall. "I will stay with her." She finally raised her eyes.

Miles' gaze bore into her, so deep that she was afraid he could see into her soul.

"Then I will keep you company."

CHAPTER TWENTY

MILES HAD LEARNED from Emery's father that she was out and about on the estate. He tried to press his steward as to the direction Emery might have gone but received no reply. It was as if Jenson drifted away, lost in a world known only to him. Miles spoke sharply, trying to gain the man's attention, and had no luck.

Puzzled by such bizarre behavior, he returned to his study, knowing it might be hours before Emery returned to the house. He rang for Crowder and had the valet bring him the journal of Garrick Notley, hoping to pass the time reading it. What he found within its pages proved to be fascinating.

It seemed Garrick was his great-grandfather. A scoundrel through and through. He was a second son who wenched his way through university and had refused to go into the army, defying his father and leaving England to travel abroad. The journal was an autobiography of sorts, written with candor and humor. Garrick detailed his adventures in detail, especially his sexual escapades. Miles couldn't help but think of the color flooding Emery's cheeks if she had read his ancestor's journal.

He stopped reading after the passage where Garrick found his brother, the heir apparent, had died and the Duke of Winslow summoned him home. Miles would take up the journal again.

After he spoke with Emery.

Instinct told him that the portrait of the ancestor he favored so much was this rogue of a duke. He wanted to learn what Emery knew and then share some of the journal with her. He chuckled to himself, picturing them sitting together as he read it aloud, her face flaming in embarrassment. No, he couldn't do that to her. But he would like to do several of the things to her that the duke mentioned in the many affairs he detailed. Only it wouldn't be an affair. Time spent away from Emery only solidified to Miles that she was made for him. Not that he'd had any doubts before, but her absence in his life let him know he would always need her by his side. Now, he must coax her into agreeing with him. Either their time apart had made her desire grow or cool. Whichever, he would make certain she understood they had a future together.

He rang for Trottmann, who seemed to know everything that went on at Wildwood, and when the butler arrived, Miles asked, "Do you know if Miss Jenson has returned from her ride about the estate?"

"Yes, Your Grace. A groom came to tell Mrs. Jenson that Miss Jenson would be spending time in the stables with Athena. The mare is close to giving birth." Trottmann paused. "Very thoughtful of her, I'd say. Miss Jenson not wanting to worry her mother. She is a lovely young woman," he praised.

Miles wondered if the all-knowing Trottmann had an inkling of his employer's feelings for the help, much as Cook seemed to suspect.

"Yes, she is very capable," he said. Rising from his seat, he added, "I think I will go and check on Athena myself."

"And dinner, Your Grace?"

"Tell Cook to hold off. I may be a while. Better yet, I will take a basket of food to the stables since I may be there for some time."

"Let me see to that, Your Grace," Trottmann offered. "I will bring it to you."

That freed up Miles to head immediately to the stables. He arrived and went to the last stall where Athena resided and stood just out of view for a few minutes, listening to Emery's soothing voice before making his presence known.

The moment he saw her, something stirred within him. A mixture of desire, joy, and longing. He thought of the times he would come home after some trip and Emery would be waiting for him. They would talk and perhaps enjoy a meal together. Then he would take her upstairs and keep her in his bed for a week. Maybe longer.

He yearned for that time to be now.

"I suppose we should sit," she suggested, moving to a corner and sitting upon the ground, her back braced against the wall.

"Your Grace? I have brought the basket."

He glanced over his shoulder and saw Trottmann had brought the food to the stables.

As the butler handed it over, he said, "Cook packed enough for two. In case Miss Jenson joins your vigil at Athena's side." Trottmann smiled at Emery. "How is Athena doing, Miss Jenson?"

"All the signs are present, Mr. Trottmann. She should begin foaling soon."

"Then you should partake of some sustenance before that occurs," the butler advised. "Shall I check back with you later, Your Grace?"

"No," Miles said sharply, not wanting any intrusions during his time with Emery.

"Then I will bid you both a good evening." The butler nodded and left.

Miles brought the basket from Cook and joined Emery on the ground.

"I am sure you haven't eaten in quite some time. We should take Trottmann's advice and have something now before the excitement begins."

He pulled out a few pieces of cold chicken, a small round of cheese, a loaf of bread that smelled heavenly, and then smiled.

"Cake," he proclaimed. "Perhaps we should start with it."

She laughed, a sound he had gone far too long without hearing. "No. Only a young boy would suggest something so foolish. Cake is the reward for finishing your meal."

Emery took charge, lifting the two plates Cook had thoughtfully packed and placing items on them. Miles discovered a carafe and two pewter mugs at the bottom and poured a ruby red wine into them.

"A toast," he said, lifting his glass.

"To what?"

He wanted to say *"To us"* but refrained from doing so. Instead, he said, "To a swift birth and a healthy foal."

He tapped his cup against hers and then drank deeply.

As they ate, he told her a little about his visit to Marblewood and the other two estates. She had never been to any of them but was familiar with all three stewards and much of what he mentioned.

"You—and your father—have been in close contact with the managers of my other estates?" he asked.

She nodded. "Papa thought it best. He says you can always learn from others and so he wrote to each of His Grace's stewards shortly after our arrival. Over the years, many letters have flown back and forth between the group."

"Do you write those letters now?" he asked, thinking of how vacant Jenson's eyes had been earlier.

A defensive look came into her eyes. "For the most part. My handwriting is better than Papa's. Much more legible. Sometimes, he dictates to me. Other times, he merely tells me what he wishes to discuss with the others and gives me the freedom to word things as I choose."

"He puts a great deal of trust in you. You seem to have an inordinate amount of responsibilities, both under him and your mother."

"I like being busy," she said guardedly. "I find it passes the time."

"And once time has passed, where do you see yourself, Emery? In five years? Ten? Even twenty?"

She blinked rapidly. "I . . . don't know. I haven't planned that far ahead."

But her gaze quickly dropped, as if she were hiding something. Before he could ask what, she pushed to her feet.

"I better check on Athena."

She went to the horse and rested her cheek against the mare's neck. Her eyes closed, contentment on her beautiful face. Inhaling deeply, she opened her eyes and said, "I adore the aroma of horses."

Kissing Athena's neck, she then stroked it. "It becomes stronger when they sweat, you know. There is nothing like the smell of these stables. Horse. Hay. Leather."

Miles almost said the smell of lilac trumped all those scents but kept from verbalizing his thoughts.

Emery bent and reached for Athena's teat. Squeezing it, she held another finger under it and then brought it up to examine.

"Just as I thought."

"Let me see."

Miles joined her, taking her wrist and bringing her hand toward him. He could see the thick, opaque beads and touched it. His fingers tightened on her wrist.

"It is sticky," he noted, brushing it between his thumb and forefinger.

Emery tugged, breaking the contact between them. Only because he allowed her to do so.

Athena snorted and began moving restlessly.

"Is there something we should do? Find Harris?" he asked. "As I mentioned, I have never been at the birth of a foal."

"Mr. Harris' wife has been ill for the past few days. I called upon her this afternoon, taking her some soup. Mr. Harris is at home with her now. I don't mind staying with Athena, Your Grace. It may still be several hours before the foal appears. Why don't you retire to the house? I can tell you in the morning what the gender of the foal is."

"You want me to miss out on all the fun?"

Her lips twitched with amusement. "I daresay Athena wouldn't term this fun."

"I'm staying."

The horse stomped and made a low noise.

"We should retreat to the corner," Emery said. "Allow her to have some space."

She sat on the ground again and he joined her, sitting close enough that the sides of their bodies touched. She smelled inviting but he knew all her concentration now was on the dam.

A short time later, Athena's foal arrived. Emery walked him through the process as it unfolded, noting how both forelimbs arrived, one slightly ahead of the other, with the head emerging next. She explained that the placenta had ruptured when a huge amount of fluids flowed from Athena.

The entire birth took a little less than three-quarters of an hour.

"It is nothing short of a miracle," he declared once the foal had fully emerged.

Emery smiled. "I have been fortunate to witness it several times. It never grows old."

"What do we do for Athena now?" he asked. "And her babe?"

"I will remain several more hours. The foal should stand within the next hour and begin to nurse by the second hour. Athena must expel her placenta. If she doesn't, I'll need to summon Mr. Harris for help in removing it."

She seemed unflappable in that moment, as if she could do anything. His admiration grew for her yet again.

"I have nowhere else to be. Except here."

With that, Miles slipped his hand around hers, lacing their fingers together.

They sat with their backs against the stable wall, no conversation necessary, as they watched the foal struggle and then finally stand on its own. After several attempts at nursing, the foal finally understood what to do and hungrily drank from its mother.

Finally, he broke the silence.

"Who would have thought something only a few hours old could stand on its own?" he marveled. "I wonder if it is male or female."

"I can check once the placenta fully emerges. I don't want to go close until then. Athena is in a delicate state. She has learned what birthing a babe is like and her mothering instinct is kicking in. She will be quite protective of her new offspring."

"I suppose females are born with that instinct," he remarked, though he assumed his mother was an exception to that rule.

It surprised him that Emery hadn't pulled away in all these hours spent side by side. Miles relished their closeness. Since he didn't know when they would next be alone, he decided to ask about the portraits.

"Trottmann took me to the picture gallery," he began. "And I saw the new additions hanging there, as well as the new art in my bedchamber."

He felt her tense and added, "I was quite surprised. And pleased."

Emery relaxed. "I know I overstepped my bounds but I wanted to please you. Wildwood is yours now. I wanted you to have more than visceral evidence. I wanted something tangible to show you that you belong. What better way than to have your portrait hanging among so many other Dukes of Winslows and generations of various Notleys?"

"How did you pull off such a task? I wouldn't know where to start. I also thought subjects had to sit for an artist in order to have their picture painted."

"Normally, that is the case."

She told him of her idea to paint over Ralph so that the picture of the two brothers could hang in the ducal bedchambers and how that snowballed.

"Mr. Leavell couldn't bring himself to paint over his original work so he created a new one. He had wanted to paint you three boys in the gardens to begin with but was overruled by the duke."

"It was Fillmore's man!" he exclaimed. "What did he call himself?"

"Mr. Lawrence. He is actually Lawrence Leavell."

"I knew there was something familiar about him. He has changed quite a bit, though. The years haven't been as kind to him as to others."

"He lost the great love of his life," she revealed. "I think that has worn on him."

Miles wondered how she knew something so deeply personal about the artist.

"And the sketches on my desk?"

"Mr. Leavell made those shortly after you left. He worked from them in creating your ducal portrait."

"Who is the other man—the one I favor so much? And where on earth was that painting? I have never seen it before."

Emery explained about her project to catalog the contents of the attics and how she had stumbled onto the portrait there, along with a journal.

"Mr. Leavell said the artist, Julian Glanville, was well known but died at a young age. He left behind a list of those whom he had painted. When Mr. Leavell returned to London, he consulted the list and wrote to me regarding his findings. The only Notley on it was Garrick Notley, Duke of Winslow."

"So, it is his portrait and journal. I started reading it as I waited to speak to you. So far, it is fascinating though it doesn't explain why he was shuttered away in the attic."

"I will admit that I read the first few pages before I realized it was a private affair that only family should read. He seemed quite alienated from his wife and children. If his heir felt strongly enough, he might have been the one who banished the portrait to the attics. Who knows how long it has been since anyone went up there?"

Miles squeezed her fingers. "I am grateful you did so and found this man whom I favor so much. I hope I can be a much better duke than he was."

"He might have been an excellent duke," she countered. "Just not a good husband or father."

"I plan to be good at both of those, as well."

He lifted his free hand and took her chin. "You have brought Tony back to me, Emery. You constantly surprise me with your candor and cleverness." He paused, knowing he needed to tread lightly. "I know you sense the attraction growing between us."

Her mouth trembled, her lips calling out to his. "Be that as it may, I am a realist, Your Grace. Any attraction should be squashed as one would a pesky fly."

"I disagree, Emery. I think the flames should be fed."

Tears glistened in her eyes. "Don't you see? You aren't of my world and I could never be a part of yours. I am practical to my bones, Miles. I understand that it could never work between us. That is why I must discourage your attentions to me."

"And I must convince you that we do not have to be part of the world of Polite Society. We can create our own world. Here. Now. Together."

CHAPTER TWENTY-ONE

E MERY DESPERATELY WISHED what Miles said could be true. Her feelings had grown for this man during his absence from Wildwood. Though she knew she should reject him outright, her heart demanded that she give in.

At least for a little while.

They might never have an opportunity such as this again. She expected to hear from Mr. Fillmore any day now and when she did, she would leave the place that had been home for so long— and with it, leave Miles and her heart behind.

She gazed up at him, into those sky blue eyes that were as clear as a summer's day. Her hand reached out, her thumb caressing the small scar on his cheek, a lasting, bitter memory for him of the day his father had disowned him. Deep inside this good man was still a lost little boy. One who deserved attention and affection. It would have to be another woman who gave that to him in marriage, healing his wounded heart.

For now, however, she could give him respite from his lonely world tonight.

"Emery," he said, his voice low, sending shivers along her spine.

His lips touched hers. One hand came and cupped her nape. She wanted to tell him she wasn't going anywhere. Not now. They had this moment. For her, it would be all she would ever have of him. She didn't know how much she would give of herself. What was important was to give him comfort.

And make a memory for herself which would last her a lifetime.

She opened to him, welcoming the sweep of his tongue, tasting the wine they had sipped and even the sweetness of the cake he enjoyed indulging in so much. His scent, that familiar sandalwood along with something utterly male, engulfed her. Her fingers pushed into his thick hair, pulling him closer. He growled, deepening the kiss, causing her pulse to flutter wildly. A low thrum of desire pooled in her belly.

In that moment, Emery decided she wanted all of him. Whatever he would give, she would greedily take.

Their passionate kisses caused her body to heat, her blood flowing like liquid fire through her veins. He gathered her into his lap, the feel of him comforting and wildly exciting at the same time. His demanding kisses bruised her lips but she eagerly sought more, stroking his hard, muscular chest.

Miles broke the kiss, his lips trailing across her cheek, his breath warm. They moved to her ear, where his teeth toyed with her lobe, tugging and then nipping it. A jolt swept through her, desire hot and potent. She wrapped her arms about his neck and brought his mouth back to hers greedily, reveling in his taste and scent. They kissed endlessly, her breasts growing more sensitive as she pushed against him.

Once again, he broke the kiss, his lips going to her throat, nipping and licking, enflaming her. Then he eased her from his lap, pushing her back onto the hay, hovering over her, his beautiful face smiling down upon her.

"You are breathtaking," he gasped before his mouth went to her throat again.

His hands covered her breasts, finally hearing her call, kneading and squeezing as they seemed to grow fuller. His fingers teased her nipples, tweaking them, lighting the fire within her until it blazed brightly. A deep longing filled her. She had this man for this one night and would make the most of it.

Her hands reached up to cradle his face, stroking it lovingly. Then she locked her hands behind his neck and brought him to her breast. Miles understood what she needed. He pulled her gown from her shoulders, lowering it to her elbows, and then pushed the front down. Only her chemise remained. His mouth took in her breast, licking her through the thin material, sucking and grazing his teeth along the nipple.

Emery cried out, her back arching. He continued worshiping her breast as his hands began roaming the rest of her body. She became dizzy with heat and need. His fingers danced beneath her hem, running up her calves and along the insides of her thighs. She craved his touch. His kiss.

Then his fingers reached their final destination. She had known all along that was the place she needed him to touch her. He stroked a finger along the seam of her sex, causing her to whimper.

"I am going to touch you, Emery. Touch you until you scream my name. I will be the last man who does this."

"I know," she murmured, knowing she would never allow any man to take such liberties.

Because she loved him. She, Emery Jenson, loved Miles Notley, the Duke of Winslow. And she would never love another.

He paused a moment, hiking her skirts up to her waist. Then he gazed at her intently as his fingers began working a spell upon her. They caressed her. Teased her. Filled her.

Her eyes never left his, even when the storm clouds gathered within her. A dam broke, her passion spilling over as she did cry out his name, bucking against his hand, riding a wave of incredible spasms that left her spent.

"Do you know how I loved seeing you come?" he asked softly. "How the amber of your eyes grew? I want to see that every night, Emery. Every day. I want to fill you. Bury myself within you. Leave my seed so that a child—many children—will grow within you. I want to raise that family with you, my darling. I want them to know the love I never did.

"Until now."

As he gazed at her so tenderly, tears leaked from her eyes.

"Don't cry, my love," he said, kissing the tears away.

"Do it," she said, determination in her voice. "Fill me."

Surprise flickered across his face. "Now? We are not yet wed."

They never would be—but he did not have to know that.

"All I know is that I want—need—you inside me," she said honestly. If there were consequences of this rash action, she would deal with them. In fact, she hoped a child would result from their coming together. It would give her a piece of him.

Miles smiled. "I need you, too, my love. More than I could ever say."

He kissed her deeply, a kiss of reverence and wonder. He unbuttoned his fall and Emery saw his manhood jut out, large and pulsing. She touched it lightly, hearing his groan, knowing she affected him as much as he did her. As she stroked it, his fingers found her again, teasing and caressing, driving her into a frenzy.

"This will hurt some the first time we couple," he warned her. "It never does after that."

"Go ahead," she said, her breathing shallow and rapid.

He pushed into her. It was uncomfortable for a moment and then the stinging subsided. She had the urge to move and did so, her hips rising to meet him as he thrust into her. She reveled in each stroke, watching and memorizing his face. When he cried out and shuddered, she did the same.

Miles collapsed atop her and she clung to him, savoring his weight and scent. Then he rolled to his side, bringing her along, and they looked into one another's eyes. Emery knew she was changed forever. She would never forget this man. This moment. This feeling of utter contentment.

He kissed her softly and then pulled her head to his chest, his hand stroking her back. They lay together for a long time, the sweet scent of hay surrounding them.

Emery finally pushed up. "We must see to Athena."

She saw the foal was still nursing. The placenta seemed to have expelled itself. She lowered her skirts and went to the mare, who seemed to be blanketed in contentment.

Stroking the horse's neck, she said, "You have much to be proud of, Athena. You have birthed your foal tonight."

By now, Miles had repaired his fall. Using hay which he gathered in his hands, he scooped up the placenta.

"I'll be back," he said, exiting the stall with it.

Emery went to the foal and checked it carefully. Its limbs seemed to be strong and, overall, the newborn appeared healthy. She found it was a female and told Miles this when he returned.

"Then we need a good Greek name for her. What do you suggest?"

She thought a moment. "Most of the major goddesses are already represented in your stables. How about Tyche? She was the goddess of prosperity and fortune."

"What do you think, Tyche?" he asked, petting the foal who now stood more firmly than an hour ago. "Do you like that name? I think it suits you." He smiled at Emery. "For tonight *was* a night of good fortune."

Sadness filled her but she smiled brightly at him. There would time for sorrow later.

"Since mother and daughter are doing well, I suppose I should return home," she said.

"I will walk you to your parents' cottage."

She nodded, knowing she couldn't refuse him anything. Saying goodnight to the pair of horses, they left the stables. Though it had grown dark, the strong light of the moon allowed them to find their way easily.

They reached the cottage, where a light glowed from within. Her mother must have left a lamp burning for her. Miles took her hands in his. He brought them to his lips, kissing them tenderly.

"I will see you in the morning," he promised and then gave her a sweet, slow kiss.

The last she would receive from him.

"Goodnight, Emery."

"Goodnight," she echoed and entered the cottage, closing the door behind her and going to douse the lantern.

Her mother sat at the table.

"You didn't have to wait up for me, Mama," she said.

"I didn't mind. How is Athena?"

Emery smiled. "She did very well. She is now the proud dam of Tyche."

"You named the foal?"

She heard the unspoken question in her mother's voice.

"His Grace was present at the birth," she said. "He approved the choice of name."

Her mother shook her head sadly. "My Emery."

She went to her mother, who rose and enfolded Emery in her arms. The tears came and she clung to her mother.

"Do you love him?"

"He makes me feel things I shouldn't feel and want things I can never have," she replied.

"Has he compromised you?"

"No." She couldn't tell her mother the truth. That she had wanted Miles so much that she had been the one to beg him to take her virginity.

"You will need to go soon," Mama urged. "I know you have been waiting to hear from Mr. Fillmore. The stage only comes twice a week through Woodmorrow. The next one leaves the day after tomorrow." Mama's gaze penetrated her. "I think you should be on it."

"But what about Papa? How can I leave when he is taking a turn for the worse?"

"You do what you must to keep your body and heart intact," Mama replied. "I have been saving for this day. You know that the Hamilton cottage has been empty for some time. I will speak with His Grace tomorrow and ask if we can rent it. Give this one up for the new steward. We cannot hide your father's condition from His Grace any longer, Emery. I am surprised we have gotten away with it this long. His Grace is a very astute man."

Emery's heart whispered to her that Mama was right.

"Very well. I will be on Friday's stage. I will go into Wood-morrow tomorrow and purchase my ticket so that I will already have it. Hopefully, I will hear from Mr. Fillmore before I leave. If not, I will find an employment agency on my own. What about references, Mama?"

"In many cases, the household's butler or housekeeper write them and the employer merely signs the reference." She studied Emery. "I am not certain His Grace will do so. He will think you too valuable to release from service."

"It wouldn't look right if you wrote one for me, Mama. Perhaps Mr. Trottmann could do so?"

"I will see that he does. A reference from the Duke of Winslow's butler would almost be as good as one from the duke himself." Mama hugged her. "Oh, I am sorry it has come to this, my sweet girl. It is for the best, though."

She nodded. "I am tired, Mama."

Her mother kissed her brow. "It is late. Go to sleep. Don't go to the main house in the morning. I plan to speak to His Grace about your father. In fact, I will have you go into town. After you purchase your ticket, you may stop at Jernigan's for some supplies. I will leave a list on the table for you."

"I don't know if I can avoid him, Mama."

"I won't tell him you are planning to leave. I will concentrate on discussing your father's condition and our future at Wild-wood. If His Grace approves and allows me to lease the Hamilton cottage, I can say you are supervising our move there. That could buy us some time until you leave for good."

Emery embraced her mother. "I love you, Mama. I hate that I have to go."

"We thought it was a possibility because of the previous duke. Although I believe His Grace is a much better man than his brother, he still might push you to do things you shouldn't do.

Men in power and position often do that to women. I want to protect you."

Her mother kissed her again and bid Emery goodnight. She went to her room and changed from her wrinkled gown, washing the small bit of blood from her thighs, the sign her maidenhead had been breached.

Climbing into bed, she allowed the tears to flow freely, determined it would be the final time she would cry over walking away from the man she would forever love.

CHAPTER TWENTY-TWO

MILES AWOKE EARLY, filled with energy.
Filled with love.

He wouldn't pretend to himself it was anything otherwise. He had found a woman he admired. Respected. One who was suitable in every way to be his partner in life and marriage. Thank God, Emery had finally come around to his way of thinking.

The time spent with her last night assured him that they were well matched in every way. He looked forward to making love to her in a proper bed—but all kinds of ideas flitted through his head. Making her his on top of his desk. In the library before a fire. On a blanket spread beside the lake. He wanted this woman every way, every day, in every place imaginable. They had only touched the tip of the iceberg last night. Miles planned to spend hours worshipping her body and giving his to her.

That meant, though, that he needed to speak to her father. Mr. Jenson needed to be made aware of Miles' intentions toward his daughter. He planned to seek the steward's permission for Emery's hand today.

Crowder entered and found Miles whistling. He greeted his valet with enthusiasm.

"You are in excellent spirits, Your Grace."

"I am indeed, Crowder."

As the valet dressed him, Miles thought of where to take Emery on their honeymoon. London would certainly be a stop.

She had never been and would be delighted by the city. He had enjoyed it for the short time he was in town after he returned to England upon his father's and brother's deaths. He had stayed in the ducal townhouse but slept in a guest bedchamber since his father's things were still present in the one belonging to the duke. By now, the staff should have cleared away those items. Perhaps Emery would want to make over much of the London residence. They could go there upon occasion but he believed they would both be happiest in the country.

He would also see that she ordered as many gowns as she liked while they were in town. He wasn't going to leave the dressing of his wife to the Woodmorrow seamstress. Nothing but the best would do for his Emery.

His Emery.

Miles hoped she wouldn't want a long engagement. Even the reading of the banns would take almost a month. Perhaps he could convince her into wedding him with a special license. He would need to ride to London to purchase it but it would be well worth the time. He only wished his fellow Terrors could attend the ceremony.

An idea occurred to him.

Finch could marry them.

It would be a lovely excuse to see his old friend and have one of his brothers-in-arms present as Miles wed Emery. He would settle a date with her today and then write to Finch. His friend would be surprised at the speed with which Miles wished to wed. Especially since he had only written once to each of the Terrors, while he had been away at Marblewood. He had mentioned Emery briefly in these letters but the Terrors would have no idea how serious Miles was about her based upon what he had written.

It didn't matter. She was to be his. They would be husband and wife, hopefully sooner than later, and he would introduce her to each Turner Terror with pride.

Miles entered the breakfast room and ate a hearty meal, fortifying himself for the upcoming discussion with Mr. Jenson. He still felt a little unsettled in the steward's presence. Jenson wasn't a talkative man. Perhaps he was shy and that is why Emery often stepped in to answer for her father. Well, he would have to listen to Miles today and respond accordingly.

He finished with breakfast and perused both the newspaper and the post Trottmann brought. His only interest in the news was what was said of the war. More than anything, he longed for it to end and his friends to come home. Though the three in the army would remain career officers once the war ended, they would be granted leave at various points during their service. Since none of them had homes to go to, he wanted them to always feel welcome at Wildwood.

He couldn't put it off any longer. It was time to visit with Jenson and claim Emery's hand. Miles left the breakfast room, surprised at the nerves he felt. Of course, marriage was a huge step. He didn't see any way that Jenson would turn down his request, though. After all, Miles was the Duke of Winslow.

Arriving at the door, he took a deep breath and knocked. He waited a moment but his steward didn't call for him to enter. Curious, Miles knocked again. Once more, no response, so he pushed open the door.

Jenson sat behind his desk, staring dreamily into space. Miles entered and closed the door for privacy.

"Mr. Jenson, it is imperative that I have a word with you."

The steward didn't acknowledge his presence.

"Jenson," he said sharply, "I wish to speak with you."

His estate manager's head turned. Miles saw nothing but emptiness in the eyes. No recognition. Nothing.

He stepped closer. "Jenson, are you all right, man?"

The estate manager blinked slowly. He frowned. "May I help you?" he asked.

"Very much so," he said, irritation filling him.

Then he saw a lost look appear in Jenson's eyes. One of panic. The steward's eyes began to dart about the room.

"Jenson?" he asked, keeping his tone soothing. "Is something wrong?"

"Who *are* you?"

"I am the Duke of Winslow. You are at Wildwood."

"Who? Why am I here?"

"You are my steward."

Jenson frowned. "No. His Grace is old. You are young. I want Emery. I want my wife." He began to weep and placed his head upon folded arms atop his desk.

Miles stood there a moment, baffled by the man's behavior. It was as if Jenson knew nothing. Who he was. Where he was. What he did for a living.

How long had this been going on?

His gut told him for some time. And that Emery knew and had hidden this from him.

Miles placed a hand on the sobbing man's shoulder. "It's all right, Mr. Jenson. You just sit here. I will go find Mrs. Jenson and she will bring you a cup of tea. Tea always makes everything better, doesn't it?"

The older man lifted his head. "Yes. Tea. That would be lovely."

Then as abruptly as he'd burst into tears, the steward calmed. He opened a ledger in front of him and ran his finger down the page as if perusing it.

"What are you doing, Mr. Jenson?" he asked.

"Looking over these figures, Your Grace. Emery usually takes care of this. I just want to make sure she's done a good job."

"Emery always does a thorough job, no matter what the task," Miles said.

He didn't know if Jenson heard him because, once more, the steward turned and gazed out into space. Miles slipped from the room.

It was time to have a talk with Mrs. Jenson.

Then Emery.

Miles left the office, closing the door. He paused, collecting his thoughts before he approached Mrs. Jenson. He had a thousand questions of the woman and hopefully would get satisfactory answers from her.

He started in the direction of the housekeeper's office when Trottmann stopped him.

"If you are available, Your Grace, Mrs. Jenson would like to have a word with you."

This was interesting.

"Of course. Send her to my study."

Miles went there and sat in the chair behind the massive desk. For a moment, he wondered if Garrick Notley, the ancestor he favored, had also used the same desk. He needed to get back to Garrick's journal, to see if he could unravel the mystery of why the former duke's portrait had been removed from the picture gallery and left in an attic corner for several decades.

A rap sounded on the door and Miles bid Mrs. Jenson to enter. If he wanted to see how Emery would age, he didn't have to look further than her mother. The two women favored each other tremendously, though Mrs. Jenson was much shorter. Emery's height had come from her father.

"Thank you for seeing me, Your Grace."

"Not at all, Mrs. Jenson. Please, have a seat."

The housekeeper took the chair in front of the desk and immediately said, "I have a request to make of you, Your Grace. My husband's health is poor. He needs to retire as soon as possible. Since the cottage we reside in comes with his position, I was hoping you might consider leasing the Hamilton cottage to us."

He knew the one she spoke of. "It's rather small for the three of you, isn't it?"

"Size doesn't matter," she said, dismissing his comment. "I know this doesn't give you much notice in regard to Wildwood needing a new estate manager. Emery has mentioned a few of the stewards she has corresponded with at your other estates. Perhaps one of them might fill Mr. Jenson's shoes."

"How long has Emery been running Wildwood on her own?"

he asked bluntly.

The housekeeper considered his question, her composure intact. "Several months now. Why do you ask?"

"I just came from trying to hold a conversation with Mr. Jenson. It was impossible."

Her eyes brightened with unshed tears. "Yes, it is getting worse. It started slowly. We barely noticed. Emery has always been eager to take on more responsibility and she began doing so. Then she told me she did so because her father couldn't think properly anymore."

She paused. "My husband had become quieter over the last year, Your Grace. Sometimes, he rarely spoke when we reached home at night. We both put in long hours at Wildwood. I thought it was enough to have his companionship as I read by the fire. Then I, too, started noticing little things. He would seem to forget how to do a simple, ordinary task. Or he couldn't recall commonplace words. The problem has grown."

"I should have been informed of it the moment I arrived," Miles said sternly.

"You are correct, Your Grace. I am sorry both Emery and I kept this from you. It's just that your brother had no interest in the estate. He was going to head back to London soon with your mother. Emery is a very clever woman. She could have kept things running on her own until . . . until my husband could no longer work at all . . . or he passed away. We both worried if Mr. Jenson lost his position that I, too, would be forced to go. We assumed, incorrectly, that you would be like your brother and that you would be off to London for the remainder of the Season." She shrugged. "After all, a duke needs a duchess to provide him with an heir."

"I don't need a London Season to find a bride. I already have the perfect candidate."

Her mouth hardened. "Surely, you cannot mean Emery."

"I do. She is the reason I went to visit with Mr. Jenson. I wished to ask him for permission to wed his daughter." Miles shook his head. "He didn't even know who I was or where he was."

She bit her lip. "Then it has truly gotten bad." Mrs. Jenson rose. "I am sorry to have troubled you, Your Grace. I apologize for any deceit and take full responsibility. I will go and write out my resignation and bring it to you."

"And why would you do that, Mrs. Jenson?" he asked.

She looked taken aback, her composure finally cracking. "I don't think you are the type of man who would lease a cottage to someone who has lied to you."

"I am not fond of lies or liars, Mrs. Jenson. What I am fond of is your daughter. I love Emery."

There. He'd voiced it aloud. Miles knew it was true and wanted Emery's mother to understand, as well, else she would never turn her daughter over to him.

"You love her, you say?" Sadly, she shook her head. "Love is rare among the *ton*. Are you not merely infatuated with my girl? She is a great beauty."

"Emery is more than the sum of her looks," he said testily. "She is kind. Decent. Intelligent. And most likely the best estate manager I could hire."

Now, the housekeeper looked taken aback. "You would place her in that position?"

"I would have her run Wildwood with help. As my duchess, she would have other responsibilities which would take time away from estate management. Such as bearing our children."

Wonder now filled her eyes. "You really do mean to wed her?"

He rose. "I am not my brother, Mrs. Jenson. I know he made some play for Emery. She vaguely referred to this. I am a man of honor. And by God, I plan to make Emery my wife. I'll either have your blessing—or I won't. Regardless, my destiny lies with her."

Mrs. Jenson smiled. Relief flooded her face. "Then you very much have mine and Mr. Jenson's blessing, Your Grace. I am only sorry that he will most likely be unaware of the situation. Know this—he would approve of the match. You are a good man. I know things were laid at your doorstep from when you were a child and—"

"I have spoken to Emery about them. She knows I am blameless. It was Ralph who pulled the trigger and killed Tony. Not me. Never me."

"I see."

"Do you know where I might find her? I'd like her to know we have spoken. I'm usually a patient man, Mrs. Jenson. But not when it comes to Emery. The sooner we wed, the better."

She smiled. "I sent Emery into town to pick up some supplies. She was also going to call at the dower house and see if they needed anything."

He shuddered. "I hope she did not see the duchess while she was there. That woman is a viper." He thought a moment. "On second thought, I believe I shall call there now and let her know there is to be a wedding. She won't want to come—and she will not be invited. I think it's time to pack her off to London. I will see that it takes place by the end of the week. Inform the servants there that they will be returning to the main house because the duchess will move to London."

"Yes, Your Grace." She turned to leave and he stopped her.

"Mrs. Jenson, the cottage will not be necessary. As my in-laws, you and Mr. Jenson will live here. You may choose to nurse him or remain as my housekeeper. The choice is yours."

"I am grateful to you, Your Grace. I enjoy being busy. I would prefer to keep my position. I can have the maids or a few footmen rotate throughout the day to keep an eye on my husband."

"Very well. And when we are with family, please call me Miles."

Her eyes widened. "I don't think I will be capable of doing so."

"Winslow?" he asked.

She grinned. "That is a possibility."

After she left, Miles decided he would go now to speak to the duchess. The almost dowager duchess.

Then he would find Emery and make sure they set a date for their wedding.

CHAPTER TWENTY-THREE

E MERY ROSE LATER than usual. She had finally fallen asleep for a few hours. Her eyes still felt gritty, though. She put water on to boil for tea. The cottage was empty. Mama must have taken Papa with her when she went to Wildwood this morning. Cook would see that he got his usual egg and tea before sending him to his office.

She hated that she was leaving right as Papa grew worse. It seemed unfair to leave her mother with such a heavy burden but Emery also knew it was time to leave Wildwood—and Miles— behind. At least she'd had a taste of what love was like. Last night would be the memory she would cling to. It would be the light during her darkest days. She only hoped Miles would forgive her. Or forget about her, as he forged a new life for himself and the woman who would become his duchess. He didn't suffer fools so his bride would need to be intelligent as well as beautiful. She only hoped he would find someone who would understand him and give him the children he so desperately wanted.

As she sipped her tea, Emery glanced at the list her mother had left for her, with many of the usual items on it. Mama had also left a separate note, asking Emery to stop at the dower house to see if they needed any additional supplies. It would be convenient since it was on her way to the village.

She went to the stables and visited with Mr. Harris a few minutes.

"You should've come to get me or one of the grooms, Miss Jenson," he chided, referring to Athena foaling last night.

"I would have if Athena had experienced any difficulties. As it was, she sailed through the experience." Hesitating a moment, she added, "His Grace was with me. He had never witnessed a mare give birth before. I think he has a greater appreciation for the process now."

"That boy always did have a way with horses. It's a good thing he was there. So, no troubles?"

"None. Tyche stood within an hour and was nursing in less than two. The placenta came and His Grace disposed of it."

"Tyche. Hmm. Another god?" the groom asked.

"A goddess, actually. One of fortune and prosperity."

"Good to know."

"May I have a cart prepared for me, Mr. Harris? Mama wants me to go into the village for a few supplies."

"I'll see to it myself." Harris gave her a wink and went inside the stables.

Minutes later, Emery was seated on the driver's bench. She turned on the lane that led her to the dower's house, wondering how the duchess had managed since she'd been placed here by her son.

Climbing from the cart, she went and knocked on the front door.

"Good day, Miss Jenson," the maid who answered the door said. "What brings you here?"

"I am going into Woodmorrow to Mr. Jernigan's establishment and Mama asked me to call and see if you needed anything."

"I don't think so but let me check with the others. I'll be right back."

Emery remained in the foyer, walking to a landscape hanging on the wall and admiring it.

"What are you doing here?" a voice asked, irritation obvious.

Turning, she saw the Duchess of Winslow glaring at her.

Immediately, Emery dropped a curtsey. "Good morning, Your Grace. My mother sent me to see if your household needed any supplies. I will be gone shortly."

The duchess sneered. "You think you can move up in the world—but you are sadly mistaken."

Heat filled her cheeks. "I have no idea what you mean, Your Grace. If you will excuse me, I will wait outside. I am sorry to have bothered you."

The older woman blocked Emery's way. "I hear the talk. Servants always know everything, even the ones here where I have been exiled. They say you spend a good amount of time with Winslow. That he eyes you with appreciation. Well, he might lift your skirts, Missy, but it doesn't mean a thing. You aren't meant for the likes of him."

Heat now flooded her face. "You are mistaken, Your Grace."

The old woman eyed her. "No, I am not. He is a man. They always have an eye out for a pretty thing. I know my Ralph wanted a piece of you."

Emery gasped.

"You are baseborn, though, just as Winslow is."

Confusion filled her. "What do you mean? His Grace is the son of a duke."

The duchess' eyes narrowed. "I am not certain that he is."

The maid returned and stammered, "A new rolling pin, Miss Jenson. That's what's needed."

"Very well. I will see that your cook gets it," she said. "Good day, Your Grace."

Emery escaped the house and hurried to the cart. Hoisting herself up, she took the reins and clucked her tongue, wanting to get as far from the dower house as fast as she could.

The Duchess of Winslow had always been a hateful woman. Emery had never had much to do with her. She wondered why the duchess would say such slanderous things about her own son.

Unless she had been unfaithful to her husband.

She wondered if Miles had ever been subjected to these rumors. That's all they could be. After all, she had been the one to discover the portrait of the previous duke, Miles' great-grandfather. The two men were close to being identical though born almost one hundred years apart. If the duchess ever had doubt who Miles' father was, she wouldn't if shown the ancestor's portrait.

Emery decided not to tell Miles of this encounter and what claim his own mother had made. No good could from of it. After all, Miles had the title. He had been born during the duchess' marriage to Winslow. Even if he were another man's child, Miles was legally the Duke of Winslow and a Notley in every sense. Things were already so strained between the pair that it made no sense to share the duchess' outrageous claim and drive a permanent wedge between mother and son. Though she doubted it, perhaps one day the two would reconcile. That would never happen if Miles knew what his mother had said about him.

She continued on the road into Woodmorrow. As she passed Mrs. Fisher's bakery and caught the aroma of yeast, she thought of sharing a sticky bun with Miles. How that simple pleasure had meant so much to him. Her throat grew thick with unshed tears. She doubted she could ever eat a sticky bun again without thinking of him.

Emery arrived at her destination and climbed from the cart, looping the horse's reins around a post. She removed the list she carried from her reticule, remembering she needed to add the rolling pin for the cook at the dower house. With a deep breath, she entered the store.

The younger Mr. Jernigan was fussing over a display. When he saw her, he smiled broadly.

"It is always good to see you, Miss Jenson." He rose to his feet. "How might I help you today? It looks as though you have a list. Prepared as always." His eyes sparkled at her.

She thought he might be flirting with her, especially after what Billy Munson had said. How only a short time ago she would have relished the thought that a man close to her age did want to flirt with her. Though she disliked the older Jernigan, his son had always been kind and friendly to her. After having met Miles, though, and giving her heart to him, Emery knew she could never do this man a disservice and act interested in him when she could never give herself to him or any other suitor.

"Yes," she said, handing over Mama's list and following him to the counter. He went behind it and scrutinized the list and she said, "Please add a rolling pin to it. A new one is needed at the dower house."

She heard the door open and then said more quietly, "I will also need to purchase a ticket on Friday's coach to London."

"Are you going to visit a relative or friend?" he asked as he took a pencil and scribbled at the bottom of her list.

"No. I will be moving there permanently."

"What?" Jernigan cried. "You can't leave, Miss Jenson."

"Why not? What is it to you?" a voice asked.

She turned and saw Baron Haddoway standing there. She had always given him a wide berth the few times their paths had crossed because she had heard disturbing rumors about Haddoway. None of them pleasant.

Especially where women were involved.

Turning her back on the baron and wanting to leave quickly, Emery said, "If you'll see to the things on the list, Mr. Jernigan, I will send a groom to pick them up. Could I please get my ticket for the stage, though?"

He nodded and said, "We will be sorry to see you go, Miss Jenson. You have been an asset to Wildwood all these years."

Jernigan bent and retrieved a ticket from under the counter and quoted her the price. Emery counted out the coins for him.

"I hope you will stop in again and say farewell tomorrow."

She nodded, uncomfortable with the baron listening to their conversation. Nodding brusquely, she said, "Good day, Mr. Jernigan."

Emery turned and swept by Baron Haddoway, pausing a moment outside to calm herself as she placed her ticket inside her reticule.

Then the door opened and the baron stepped out. His fingers latched on to her elbow, taking her by surprise.

"You are a fine one, going about ordering people such as that young man, leaving him dangling as he falls all over you. I have heard stories about you, Miss Jenson. How you ride about Wildwood as if you own it. How you snap your fingers and expect others to do your bidding. Women such as you need to be taught a lesson. Put in their place. And I am just the man to do so."

She pulled on her elbow but he only tightened his grip. "Unhand me," she commanded, steel in her voice.

"I don't think so."

❧

MILES HAD A groom saddle Zeus and he rode to the dower house. He was actually looking forward to his encounter with the duchess. He hadn't seen her since she had relocated to the dower house and had had no intention of coming into contact with her until she served what he thought of as her year of penance. Now, though, he wanted her gone from Wildwood. The estate was for Emery and him alone. He wanted them to begin their new life without the possibility of running into her. In town might be a different story. They would most likely be obligated to attend a handful of social events each year. He actually looked forward to those, introducing Emery as his duchess and seeing her sparkle amidst the dull women of the *ton*.

He dismounted and attached his horse's reins to a low branch on a bush since no stables were nearby. Knocking upon the door, a surprised maid answered it.

"Your Grace! Oh! Please, come in."

She curtseyed and stepped aside to allow him entrance.

"I am here to see Her Grace," he told the servant. "Please

have her brought to the drawing room. And take me to it now. I have never been here before."

The maid's head bobbed up and down, no words coming from her. She turned and quickly left the foyer. Miles followed her to a large, pleasant room done in shades of gold and brown.

"Thank you. Please tell Her Grace I don't wish to be kept waiting. If she balks, remind her that it is the Duke of Winslow asking for an audience with her."

"Y-y-yes, Your Grace," the servant stammered. She fled the room, closing the doors behind her.

Miles wandered about, picking up objects and books to examine. He wondered idly what the duchess did with her time, without her London friends and all the many amusements she was used to.

The door opened and she entered, her cheeks flushed with color. She closed the door and came straight to him.

"Have a seat," he ordered, taking one himself.

She perched upon the edge of her chair. "I suppose that little whore ran straight to you. She hasn't even been gone ten minutes."

Confusion filled him. "What are you talking about?"

Then it hit him.

Emery had called at the dower house.

He sprang to his feet and strode three paces to close the gap between them. His fingers gripped her elbow and raised her to her feet.

"What are you talking about?" he repeated, this time as a growl.

She yanked her arm from his grasp and took a few steps away. "You know whom I mean. That girl. The housekeeper's daughter."

"You mean Miss Jenson?" he asked, watching as her eyes nervously darted about the room.

"Yes," she hissed. "The one you wish to dip your wick in."

He sucked in a quick breath. "You go too far, Madam."

"I don't go far enough," she spit out. "I have nothing to do here all day. I am bored out of my mind. So I listen at doors to servants gossiping. Me—a duchess! And do you know what they say? That the duke is taken with this girl. That he looks at her with—"

"Enough!" he roared. "What did you say to Emery? I know she was here."

"*Emery*? Is that the chit's name? Oh, Winslow, why would you want to go after someone such as she? She is a housekeeper's daughter, for goodness' sake! You mustn't attach yourself to such a woman. You need to come with me. To London. I will introduce you to the cream of Polite Society. You will put aside your infatuation with this creature when you meet diamonds of the first water."

His temper soaring, Miles let it burn hot while he calmly stated, "Mrs. Jenson was a doctor's daughter. And Mr. Jenson is the son of a viscount. Emery's pedigree is a fine one, though it doesn't make up who she is. You are blind, Woman, if you think I would take your advice on whom to wed."

"Wed?" Her features contorted in horror. "Wed? You plan to *marry* this woman?"

He smiled. "I most certainly do. And I plan to be very happy with Emery. She is the best woman I will ever know. She will love me and our children beyond measure. As for you? You are not invited to our wedding. You are to leave for London tomorrow. I will send word to Fillmore and he will rent you a house. Forget your mourning period for Ralph. You never really loved him. You only love yourself."

When she started to speak, he waved her into silence. "You will agree. Be glad I don't turn you out on the streets for whatever evil you spoke to Emery. Our bargain still stands, Madam. You will not utter a single disparaging word about me— or my duchess. You will be pleasant and polite the few times our paths cross at events. I will know what you do. What you say. What you even think, for your servants will be ones I pay for.

Servants know everything, Madam. They will tell me what you have been up to. Whom you have spoken with. What was said. You aren't the only one who listens at keyholes."

She began trembling. "You will let me return to London?" she asked meekly.

"Isn't that what I just said?" He let out a deep sigh. "I don't want you here at Wildwood ever again. Make sure you take all your things. Send for anything you have left at the London ducal townhouse. That will be mine and Emery's. I want nothing of yours to taint it." Miles looked at her steadily. "Break our bargain and you will go from a life lived in luxury to one where you die in poverty.

"Do you understand?"

The duchess lifted her chin high. "Of course, Winslow. I understand perfectly. You have nothing to fear. I will never utter a word about you or your precious slut of a duchess. I will keep my feelings and opinions to myself. I will still go to my grave knowing you killed my beloved boy."

She paused. "I only have one thing to say to you. Be glad you were born during my marriage to Winslow because that is what makes you legitimate. It's the only reason you became a duke."

Immediately, Miles understood what she spoke of. "You had an affair," he said flatly.

"No," she said firmly. Suddenly, pain filled her eyes. "I was . . . ravished." Her voice broke and her hand came up to her mouth. Her eyes glittered with unshed tears.

Her words were as a fierce blow. "Who assaulted you?" he asked quietly.

She shrugged. "Does it matter now, so many years later?" She blinked rapidly, her hands twisting in front of her. "I never knew all those months when I carried you whether or not you were his child or Winslow's. When you were born, you had my eyes—but you looked nothing like Winslow or me." She cleared her throat. "I have always assumed you were his."

"That is why you never wanted me around," he said dully.

"Because of . . ." His voice trailed off.

"Exactly. When Anthony arrived, I knew he was mine and Winslow's child because he favored Ralph so much. You were the odd man out."

"I am a Notley," he declared stoically.

Her eyebrows arched as she regained her composure. "Legally, yes."

"No, I am. I look exactly like my great-grandfather, Garrick Notley."

"Him? Why, Winslow told me a few stories of his grandfather. He was a terrible man. Hated his entire family and the feeling was mutual. Winslow's father removed all traces of him from the house once he became the duke."

"Not all," Miles said. "His portrait was found in the attics. The resemblance between Great-grandfather and me is quite remarkable. So you see, Madam—I am a Notley—whether you like it or not." He shook his head. "You are the one who missed out on me and what I could offer you. The joy I could have brought to your life. You are a bitter, unfeeling woman, Madam. I plan for Wildwood to be a place of love. I don't want you here ruining anything."

"Oh!" She grew unsteady on her feet and, for a moment, he felt a small bit of sympathy toward her and took her arm, guiding her to a chair and seating her. It must have been awful for her, living all those years with the knowledge she had been raped and thinking a child resulted from the attack.

"I am sorry for what you suffered," he said, trying to amend the harsh words he had hurled at her. "Did Winslow ever know?"

She shook her head violently. "No. I would never have told him. He would have beaten me or had me locked away because he was close friends with Haddoway. They both had a certain . . . reputation."

"Haddoway? Baron Haddoway?"

Tears streamed down her cheeks now. "Yes," she whispered. "Your father and Haddoway were as thick as thieves. They were horrible men, performing despicable acts upon women. Why do you think once I gave Winslow enough sons that I escaped this place?" She shuddered.

"See that the maids pack your things," Miles said quietly. "I hope you will enjoy being back in London."

He moved across the room, ready to escape but her voice stopped him.

"Miles?"

He turned. "Yes?"

"For what it is worth, I am sorry for the way I treated you. Then. And now."

"Thank you."

He left the room, emotions rumbling within him. Her apology was unexpected. It didn't change everything that had happened between them but he felt he understood her a little better.

Miles collected Zeus and then headed for Woodmorrow. He was eager to see Emery and would share with her what he had learned. He needed her strength and kindness now.

And most of all, her love.

CHAPTER TWENTY-FOUR

M ILES RODE INTO Woodmorrow, passing Mrs. Fisher's establishment. The smell of cinnamon and nutmeg wafted through the air. He almost stopped to purchase sticky buns for Emery and him to eat but was too eager to see her and headed straight for Jernigan's store instead.

When he rode up, he saw Emery standing on the porch.

With Baron Haddoway.

Anger seared through him as he recognized the baron from the many times he had visited Wildwood during Miles' youth. Knowing what this man had done to Miles' mother and now seeing him engaged in conversation with Emery caused rage to roar within him.

Then he saw Haddoway's hand on Emery's arm as she tried to pull away.

He leaped from Zeus' back and raced to where they stood, shoving the man hard. Haddoway stumbled back and Miles moved in, his fist slamming into the baron's face. Blood spurted immediately but he didn't let up. He pummeled the older man until he collapsed, dropping to the ground and curling into a ball.

Only then did he feel Emery's arm on him, tugging him away. Hear words coming from her though they held no meaning for him. Miles only saw red.

Then she slapped him.

"Miles!" she said sharply.

He surfaced from the depths of his fury.

"Miles, do you hear me?"

He nodded. "I do," he responded, glancing down at the bloodied man on the ground.

Haddoway grimaced and said, "You have gone too far, Winslow. All for this little trollop. No gentleman—much less a duke—would so viciously attack another gentleman over a strumpet."

Hate burned within him but Miles reined it in. "*You* are no gentleman, Haddoway." His gaze bored into the other man. "I know what you did to my mother."

Fear sprang into the baron's eyes.

"I would have you apologize to Emery but it would only be empty words, without meaning." He took a few steps to the older man and looked down at him. "She is to be my wife. Never speak to her again. Never be in the same room or place she graces. If you are, I will do more than thrash you. You have my word."

Miles stepped back and slipped an arm about Emery's waist. He felt her trembling.

He saw the younger Jernigan had emerged from the store and stood with his mouth gaping. Others had gathered, as well.

Miles told Jernigan, "Have the supplies for Wildwood loaded into the wagon and bring it to the house."

"Yes, Your Grace," Jernigan said, swallowing.

He turned to Emery. "Come, love."

He guided her to Zeus and lifted her into the saddle, swinging up behind her, his arm going protectively about her waist. He saw Haddoway push to his feet from the corners of his eyes.

"You won't get away with this, Winslow," the baron shouted.

Miles gave the older man a withering look. "Threaten all you like. You know what you have done. You will answer for your actions in Hell."

With that, he flicked the reins and Zeus took off, thundering down the lane and away from the village. He steered the horse toward Wildwood but knew he wanted to talk with Emery before they arrived there. Veering off, he directed the horse to the

216

cottage where she lived with her parents and brought his mount to a halt.

He dismounted and looped Zeus' reins around a post near the front door before reaching up and taking Emery's waist. He brought her to the ground but held fast because she shook so. Pulling her to him, Miles enfolded her in his arms. They stood silently, drawing comfort from one another for many minutes. He stroked her hair, wishing he could make the ugly encounter with Haddoway fade away.

Emery lifted her head, revealing tearstained cheeks. He kissed both cheeks.

"Don't cry over such a piece of filth, love. Come, let us go inside. You need a cup of tea."

He led her into the cottage and to the settee. She gripped his arm, pulling him down next to her. Miles sat, waiting for Emery to speak first.

When she didn't, he said, "I came to find you so we could choose our wedding date."

She looked at him as if he'd gone mad. "What?"

Taking her hands in his, he said, "I realize I haven't even formally asked you to marry me." He brought her hands to his lips and tenderly kissed them. "I merely assumed we would after our time together. I have spoken to your mother, however, and she approves of the match."

Emery gasped. "You spoke of this with Mama?"

"I tried to talk with your father and ask him for your hand. He wasn't quite able to follow our conversation." He squeezed her hands. "Your mother told me that he has been ill for some time and that you have managed everything on his behalf."

"Miles, I—"

"I am not angry, Emery. Far from it. I was disappointed why you or your mother didn't inform me of his health issues before but I can understand why. You have nothing to fear. Your mother has decided to remain as my housekeeper. She has also agreed to move to the main house with your father. We will have servants watch over and care for him."

Her mouth trembled. "You would do that?"

He smiled gently. "Of course. They are to be my family. Just as you are."

Tears rolled down her cheeks. "I was so worried."

"You have no reason to worry. You father will be taken care of. Your mother will keep her position. She suggested bringing in another steward from one of my other estates." He grinned. "I told her you could run Wildwood."

"What?"

"Well, at least for a little while. Eventually, we will need a full-time steward. A man of your choice, one you will train. I fully anticipate you will have as much a hand in overseeing Wildwood as I do. You will not only be my wife but my partner in all things. Of course, you will have responsibilities as the Duchess of Winslow." He smiled. "Including being the mother of our children. I hope you plan to spend a good deal of your time with them. And me."

She freed her hands and placed her palms against his cheeks. "You are such a good man, Miles. More than I deserve." Then a shadow crossed her face and her hands fell away.

He captured her wrists. "What's wrong, Emery?"

"I cannot marry you," she told him. "I . . . I was responsible for your brother's death."

"But Ralph fell from his horse. That had nothing to do with you."

"I was with him. Not when he fell from Zeus but earlier. He insisted that I take him out and show him something of the estate since he was never here."

Emery stood and began pacing as she spoke.

"He had already looked at me in ways which made me un-comfortable. I was afraid to be alone with him, especially since it was obvious he had been drinking."

She went to the window and pushed the curtain aside, peering out.

"He demanded to ride Zeus. I knew it was a huge mistake."

Miles could picture it all. Ralph blustering, deep in his cups. Attracted to Emery and wanting to show off in front of her.

"I did as he asked. Took him to see the fields and his tenants' cottages. Then he told me that we were going to have fun. That . . . I was his property, the same as Wildwood." She paused, swallowing hard. "He . . . said he would take me right here, out in the open."

He shot to his feet and went to her, wrapping his arms about her, holding her snugly against him as she continued to gaze out the window.

"He forced a kiss upon me. I had never been kissed before. It was so vile." She shuddered. "I was terrified of what came next. So, I attacked him."

He rested his cheek against her hair, inhaling the lilac scent he so loved.

"I slammed my knee into his groin," she continued in a monotone. "Pushed him to the ground. I rode away as he cursed me."

"You did nothing wrong, Emery. Ralph was the one who wronged you."

She wriggled away from him, turning to face him. "Don't you see, Miles? I *killed* him. I attacked him. I angered him. Once he climbed atop Zeus again, he must have been hell-bent on catching up to me. I had embarrassed him. I was guilty of assaulting a peer. He would have had me arrested. Fired my parents without references. I caused his death."

"Emery. No."

He pulled her into his arms again, holding her tightly as she struggled to free herself.

"Ralph was a lecherous rake who tried to use his power and position to bend you to his will. *He* was responsible for his actions. Not you. He was drunk and never a good horseman. In his heart, he knew he should never have ridden out on Zeus. You can't accept the blame for what was his fault. Look at me," he commanded.

She stilled and raised her gaze to his.

"I do not blame you for his death. You are honorable and good, where Ralph was dishonorable and evil."

"He didn't deserve to die," she said stubbornly.

"No, perhaps not. But he did and we cannot change that. It was an accident as the magistrate ruled. The Duke of Winslow had too much to drink and rode a horse far beyond his skill level, one even a sober man would have trouble controlling."

Miles kissed her tenderly. "You are blameless, love. Of this, I am certain. Now, I need an answer from you. Will you be my duchess? Will you make me the happiest man in England and be my wife? I love you, Emery. It is foolish to resist me."

He saw she wavered and began kissing her, over and over, until they both were breathless.

"You are my world, Emery Jenson. My entire life. Life is not worth living if you are not by my side. You have the people's respect. You are talented and intelligent. You are my own true love. I want you to help me create the family I never had. Build a strong foundation for generations to come. I want us to live in love. To allow our children and their children and their children to know of our love story."

Love for this woman poured through him. He only hoped that their children would marry for love.

As their parents did.

He kissed her again, hard and swift, and then said, "You must wed me. I insist. You don't want to be responsible for me becoming a lifelong bachelor, lonely and living alone, with no one to carry on the Notley name. I need sons and daughters with your spirit and determination."

Emery laughed. "You have convinced me." Mischief lit her enticing eyes. "Kiss me."

"I will do more than kiss you, my love."

Miles swept her off her feet and carried her into her bed-chamber, where he made sweet, slow love to her, worshipping every inch of her creamy flesh.

When he finished, he drew her close. "When will you marry me, Emery?"

Her fingers gently stroked his bare chest. "I would tomorrow but it will take over three weeks for the banns to be read."

He brushed the strands of hair from her face, his fingers gliding along the silky locks.

"Then I will ride to London for a special license first thing tomorrow morning. We can wed the day after. No, I must write to Finch. No, better yet, I will go see him."

"Finch?"

"One of the Turner Terrors. My closest friends, whom I view as family, are from Turner Academy. Three Terrors fight for England, while Finch is a man of the cloth. Since the others are at war, it would mean a great deal to me to have Finch present for our wedding—and perform the ceremony."

She bestowed a beautiful smile upon him. "That sounds lovely, Miles."

"I'll obtain the special license first and then travel to see Finch and bring him back with me. His parish is but an hour from Turner Academy. I may call upon the Earl and Countess of Marksby, where Finch holds the living. They were quite good to me."

"Perhaps they, too, could come to the wedding. What of anyone at Turner Academy? Would you like them to attend our wedding?" Emery asked.

He grinned. "As a matter of fact, I would. I will stop and talk with the Turner brothers, the co-founders of the school." Enthusiasm filled him. "Let's plan for the wedding to occur a week from tomorrow. That will give me time to invite those I wish to be there in person and for them to travel to Wildwood."

Miles kissed Emery, his joy spilling over. "I cannot wait for you to meet Finch and the others."

Her hand glided down his body and found his manhood. "And what do you plan to do until you leave tomorrow morning, Your Grace?"

"Why, I thought I might make love again to my fiancée," he proclaimed.

"She is very much in favor of that."

So Miles did.

CHAPTER TWENTY-FIVE

MILES THREADED HIS fingers through Emery's as they walked out the front door. His carriage awaited him. Trottmann and Mrs. Jenson followed them outside, keeping their distance in order to allow the pair a more private goodbye.

Facing Emery, he took both her hands in his and said, "While I am gone, see that your parents' things are moved from the cottage and that yours are placed in the duchess' rooms."

"I will feel so odd sleeping in Her Grace's bed," she said.

"First, you are soon to be Her Grace. Second, I hope you will only sleep in that bed for the few days I am gone."

Her cheeks pinkened. "Are you saying you wish for me to be in your bed? I didn't think that was the way of the *ton*."

"I don't care what they say. I want my wife with me—in *our* bed—every night of our marriage."

Miles kissed her, despite the others around them. Emery's parents knew of their betrothal. With Trottmann and the servants at the carriage witnessing this public display of affection, the news would spread like wildfire.

"Also, I have arranged for a carriage to take my mother to London later this morning."

He hadn't called the duchess by that name in a long time, either aloud or in his head. Still, now that he had knowledge of what she had suffered at Baron Haddoway's hands, he did feel a bit of empathy for her. He had shared with Emery what his mother had revealed after they had made love at the cottage yesterday, warning her to avoid the man at all cost. She had promised not to go into Woodmorrow during Miles' absence. He was still uneasy, knowing the beating he had given the baron brought enmity between the two men. Miles didn't think Haddoway was above trying to take revenge. Legally, he could do nothing about the attack on his mother, especially after so many years. He would do his best to protect both her and Emery from such an evil man. He would speak with Trottmann and explain the threat. The butler seemed fiercely protective of Emery. If Trottmann alerted their footmen to be on guard, it would help. Miles couldn't be everywhere at once but his house was full of servants who could keep an eye on his fiancée. If he believed the danger grew, he could always send to London for a Bow Street runner to come and give her an added layer of protection.

"I will have Mama stop by the dower house to see that everything runs smoothly," Emery promised. "I don't think Her Grace particularly wants to see me at this point."

Miles had also told Emery that he had broken the news of their engagement to his mother and the bargain they had struck that would allow the duchess to live in the style she was accustomed. When Emery questioned whether another house should be rented for his mother to live in, he told her he wouldn't budge. That the London townhouse was theirs alone and they would travel to it after their wedding in order to spend part of their honeymoon in town.

"I will miss you," he said tenderly, placing a soft kiss on her lips.

"I will miss you more," she declared. "The days will drag until you come home to me."

He chuckled. "You will be busy planning our wedding. Just think—a week from today, we will marry."

They had decided to give it a full week in order for him to see his old tutors and friends and allow time for any of them to make their way to Wildwood for the ceremony.

"I wish you would have given me your ideas on what you wished served at the wedding breakfast," she told him.

"No, I leave all of that up to you and your mother. And Cook. I am certain she will have abundant ideas on what to serve. As long as there is cake, I will be happy. And champagne so that all our guests can toast my lovely bride." He kissed her again. "I must go or I won't be able to tear myself away from you."

Miles released her hands and signaled his butler to come over as he climbed into the carriage. Briefly, he told Trottmann of the possible threat to Emery and that all servants were to keep a watchful eye on her and any sightings of Baron Haddoway.

"Of course, Your Grace. Miss Jenson will be kept safe."

"Thank you, Thomas," he said softly and the butler closed the carriage door.

As the vehicle pulled away, Emery blew a kiss to him.

Once they reached London, the first stop was his townhouse. He spoke with both his butler and housekeeper about his arrival in a week's time with his bride and inspected both the duke's and duchess' suites, pleased that nothing remained in them from either of his parents. His mother's things had been packed in trunks and awaited the address of where she would reside in the future. Miles promised to send word where that would be once he spoke with Fillmore.

Doctors' Common was his next stop and he obtained the special license with ease, certain that being a duke helped expedite the process. His solicitor's office was nearby and that became the next place he called.

Fillmore came out to greet him and brought Miles back to his office.

"I had no idea you would be in London, Your Grace. How may I be of service today?

"I am getting married next week."

The solicitor beamed. "My heartiest congratulations, Your Grace. Who might your lovely bride be?"

"You have met her. Miss Emery Jenson."

Miles watched Fillmore's smile fade.

"Oh. I see. Well . . . I suppose . . . that is . . ."

"Is something wrong, Fillmore?" he asked sharply.

"No, Your Grace," the man said nervously.

"Do you not think Miss Jenson an appropriate match for me?"

The solicitor winced. "Actually, Your Grace, if the truth be told? No. Not at all. She is an ordinary miss who . . . works for a living." His nose crinkled in disgust. "Polite Society can be unforgiving."

"Even to dukes?" Miles asked evenly, tamping down his temper.

"Well, dukes *are* known to do as they wish," Fillmore hedged.

"I think Miss Jenson is perfect in every way. Beautiful. Charming. Intelligent. Compassionate. She will make for an ideal Duchess of Winslow."

Fillmore nodded solemnly, obviously knowing who buttered his bread. "Yes, Your Grace. I am certain you are correct."

"I would like to make a settlement on her. A rather hefty one. In case something happens to me before an heir arrives."

"Good thinking on your part," Fillmore complimented. "The next duke would not look favorably upon her. That is, if anything should . . . you understand that if it did . . ." Fillmore paused.

"Let's get to it, man," Miles urged.

An hour later, they had the details hammered out and all documents signed and witnessed. Miles had no intention of leaving this world anytime soon, but if he did meet an untimely death and his distant cousin, the next in line, became the new Duke of Winslow, it was important that Emery be looked after.

"I will take my leave. Thank you for your help in this matter, Fillmore."

"Does Miss Jenson know you are here today?"

"She knows I am in London to purchase the special license but she has no knowledge of the settlements I wished to see to. Why?"

The solicitor frowned. "It's odd."

"What?"

"Well, Miss Jenson wrote to me recently and I replied to her letter only yesterday."

"In what regard?" he asked. "Something to do with the estate? She has been managing it."

"No," Fillmore said, hesitating. "It was to inquire about employment agencies. I gathered that she was leaving Wildwood and would be seeking employment here in London."

Panic swept through Miles and he took a deep breath to calm himself. He had no idea that Emery had thought about leaving Wildwood. He couldn't imagine why she would want to do so. It was certainly a topic he would raise with her once he returned home.

"One last thing, Fillmore," he said. "I would like the address of Lawrence Leavell."

"Ah, the artist. How did your portrait turn out? Leavell told me that he had painted you as a boy and wondered what you were like as an adult."

"Quite well. In fact, I wish to engage him again."

"My clerk will have the address."

Fillmore escorted him to the clerk, who gave Miles Leavell's location, and he set off for the artist's quarters.

He rang the bell and a servant answered the door. "Yes, my lord?"

"It is Your Grace. I am here to see Mr. Leavell regarding a commission."

Though the servant looked in awe at speaking with a duke, she said, "Mr. Leavell is working now. No one disturbs him. If you will give me your card, Your Grace, I will see he receives it."

"No, that won't do. I am leaving town early tomorrow morning and must speak with him before I go. Where is he working?"

"On the top floor because the light is best there but . . . Your Grace! Please! Wait!"

Miles had pushed past the woman and started up the staircase. She scurried up and tried to block his way.

Sympathizing with her, he said, "You will not be in trouble for allowing me upstairs. Leavell will be pleased to see me. If for any reason he blames you for allowing the interruption—"

"He will," she interrupted. "And then what'll become of me?" she moaned.

"If you lose your position, then you may come to work at my London townhouse or one of my country estates." Miles gave her his card. "Give this to my butler in town if it comes to that. I will let him know the circumstances."

Her eyes lit with wonder. "Why . . . thank you, Your Grace."

She stepped aside and he continued up three flights of stairs. He only saw one door and chose not to knock upon it, slipping inside instead. The strong scent of oil paints permeated the air.

Leavell was at work, his back to Miles, but he must have sensed the door opening.

"I have told you no interruptions. If you value your position, leave at once."

"I forced my way past your servant, Mr. Leavell. She is not to blame."

The artist turned. "Why, good afternoon, Your Grace. You turning up here speaks either very well or terribly poor about my work for you." He set his brush down. "Which is it?"

"I was most pleased by both portraits," Miles said. "So much that I wish to hire you again."

Leavell smiled broadly. "I thought you would like them both. So did Miss Jenson. A lovely young woman. So accomplished in all she does."

Hearing praise about Emery from this man stirred a bit of jealousy within Miles. "You speak as if you know her well."

Leavell shrugged. "We did speak on several occasions. She is highly regarded by your staff. And by Your Grace?"

Possessiveness filled him. "She is. My regard is such that I have asked her to be my wife."

Amazement filled the older man's face and then he grinned.

"Well done, Your Grace. It is the rare man in your position that would recognize the gifts Miss Jenson possesses—much less act upon it and offer marriage to her."

"Emery is everything I want in my wife," he stated confidently.

Giving Miles a knowing look, Leavell said, "I suspected you had feelings for her when we dined at Wildwood the night of my arrival. I am used to studying others. I sensed you cared for her." He paused. "I suppose it is a good thing she chose not to take my advice."

His words puzzled Miles. "What do you mean?"

"I shared with Miss Jenson how I developed feelings for one of my subjects many years ago. The daughter of a wealthy aristocrat and how it was impossible for us to be together. When I confronted Miss Jenson, Your Grace, she admitted she had feelings for you. I advised her to leave Wildwood because if she didn't, those feelings might destroy her. After all, what lovely young woman would wish to see the man she loved bring home a bride from the *ton*. I had thought Miss Jenson had no chance at a lifetime with you."

So that was why Emery had decided to leave. Thank goodness Fillmore had taken his time in replying to her letter, else she might have up and left, leaving him bereft.

"I am sorry you could not be with the woman you loved, Leavell. I, on the other hand, will be blessed to wed my choice."

"It is a brave choice, Your Grace. Not all will look kindly upon it."

"Do I appear to be a man who cares for the opinions of others?" he demanded.

The artist smiled. "Not at all, Your Grace. Now, what may I do for you?"

Miles said, "I was quite surprised that you could paint me without any sittings. I saw the sketches you did of me. They were excellent. Because of that, I wanted to see if you could do it again. This time, with Emery. I would like her in a gown which will complement her raven hair and eyes. I also want to commission a second one of her parents. Mr. Jenson is in poor health, you see, and I want her to have a lasting memory of him."

"I gathered as much from my short stay at Wildwood. He seemed a bit vague at times. My father experienced something similar." Sadness crossed Leavell's face. "By the end, he didn't know any of his family."

"Would it be possible to paint these portraits without any sittings?"

Leavell considered it. "Yes, I believe I could. I will work on a few sketches, of course. Mr. Jenson will be the hardest to capture. Mrs. Jenson will be quite easy. She is a handsome woman and she and her daughter resemble one another. Miss Jenson will be the easiest of all. She made quite an impression upon me. When would you like these completed?"

"I wish them to be a wedding present. We will marry Friday next."

Leavell frowned. "That is a bit soon, Your Grace. I am afraid I cannot be hurried."

"You may take all the time you need, Mr. Leavell. I suppose I don't have to give Emery her wedding present on her wedding day." He thought a moment. "In fact, it will give me an excuse to give her jewels to wear at our wedding. She can think that is her wedding present—until you arrive with your two portraits in tow."

"I will send word when I have completed them. I believe I can be finished in two weeks. Once I complete my current commission." He indicated the painting he was working on.

"I am delighted to hear that, Leavell. Emery and I will come to London after the ceremony and spend a couple of weeks here. Why don't you bring the paintings to our townhouse once they are completed? That way she can see them as soon as you have finished. I will have them sent to Wildwood after that."

Miles offered his hand and Leavell shook it. "I wish you much happiness, Your Grace. Something tells me you and your duchess will find it in abundance."

CHAPTER TWENTY-SIX

E MERY SAT WITH her mother and Cook, going over the final details for the wedding breakfast.

"I think His Grace'll be right pleased," Cook said. "We'll be serving some of his favorite dishes."

"As long as we have cake, he will be happy," she said, thinking it endearing that Miles had such a love for cake.

"He always did have a sweet tooth," Cook told her. "He was a good little boy. I hope you have a dozen little ones just like him."

Her cheeks heated, thinking that the possibility of a new Notley might be growing in her womb even as they spoke.

"Are you certain you are happy with the ceremony being held at Wildwood?" her mother asked. "I did check and the village church is available in case you have changed your mind."

"No, I think a garden wedding will be lovely this time of year," she said. "All we need to know now is how many guests will attend the breakfast."

She knew Miles was stopping by his former school to see if any of his tutors would be available to attend the ceremony. They had decided to keep the ceremony small but open up the breakfast to his tenants and household staff, as well as people from Woodmorrow. She believed he was eager to show off the place that he now called home and at the same time share the happy occasion with the people at Wildwood. She doubted any duke in England had invited so many commoners to his wedding breakfast. It made her love him all the more.

"If that's everything, I have work to attend to," Emery said, excusing herself and heading to the steward's office.

She said hello to the footman standing outside. Her parents had moved into the main house, with Mama telling Papa that the duke wanted his estate manager to reside here from now on. Papa took the news in stride and even mentioned how he enjoyed the bed he now slept in far better than the one in the cottage. Her parents took meals with Emery in a small sitting room that was adjacent to their bedchamber since her mother felt eating with the large staff below stairs would be too overwhelming for him.

It was her mother's idea to station a footman outside the office each day. That way, if Papa got into his head to leave, the footman could follow at a discreet distance and keep him out of trouble. As of now, Papa was still physically fit. If or when the day came that he was bedridden, Mama would create a schedule of servants that could rotate and sit with Papa and tend to his needs.

Her mother pointed out how generous it was for Miles to have them live at Wildwood and still allow her to keep her position. For now, Emery managed estate affairs but when she and Miles returned from their honeymoon, they would discuss which of his stewards from the multitude of his estates they visited would be promoted to the same position at Wildwood. While she always wanted to have a hand in the estate, she knew, as the new duchess, she would be taking on additional responsibilities. She was willing to help whoever took the position, though, and would occasionally look in on things to see how they were running, knowing her husband would also do the same.

Her father scribbled on a page as she came in and didn't acknowledge her presence. Emery seated herself behind her desk and began attending to the correspondence awaiting her. She had only been at it half an hour when Trottmann entered, his smile broad.

"His Grace's carriage has been sighted, Miss Jenson."

She quickly rose to her feet, her insides exploding with butter-flies.

"Thank you, Mr. Trottmann."

She followed him from the office and he said, "You must refer to me as Trottmann."

His words puzzled her. "I am only showing you the respect that your position deserve."

"You are the future Duchess of Winslow. You need to address me as Trottmann."

Emery shook her head. "I still find it a little hard to believe. You have outranked me in the household for so long."

"And now you shall be the head of it with His Grace," the butler said. "The staff is most happy with His Grace's choice in a wife. You are universally loved."

"Don't be foolish," she said as the butler opened the door and they stepped out into the bright sunshine.

The carriage pulled up and before it came to a complete stop, the door swung open. Miles bounded from it and raced to her, catching her by the waist and swinging her about. Then he stopped and gave her a long, satisfying kiss.

"I missed you," he said.

"I missed you more," she told him, breathless. "So much that I may not let you leave again without me."

He laughed and kissed her again, only breaking it when someone cleared his throat. Emery peered over Miles' shoulder and saw a very handsome man nearby, about six feet tall and with an athletic build. His dark blond was a little longer than fashiona-ble and his bright blue eyes shone with mischief.

"Emery, may I introduce to you my good friend, the Rever-end William Finchley. Finch, this is Miss Emery Jenson, soon to be the Duchess of Winslow."

The clergyman took her hand and kissed it. "I can see now why my solemn friend lights up whenever he mentions your name. It is a pleasure to meet you, Miss Jenson."

"Likewise, Reverend Finchley. You are the first Terror I am

meeting."

A knowing smile spread across the vicar's face. "Ah, so he has told you of us?"

"Some. Not nearly enough. I expect you to spill all his secrets," she teased.

"If I am to do so, you must call me Finch. I look upon Miles as a brother and feel you will be a sister to me."

"Then I am to be Emery."

"You will soon be dead, Finch, unless you release my fiancée's hand," Miles said.

Finch kissed her hand again and whispered, "I do love antagonizing him." Then he released it.

Miles slipped it possessively through his arm and glanced to where Trottmann, Crowder, and her mother stood.

"Ah, here are my butler, Trottmann, and Emery's mother, who serves as Wildwood's housekeeper. And my sullen valet, who was upset that I did not take him with me on my quick sojourn. You can also wait on the good reverend, Crowder. He will adore the attention you bestow upon him."

"I've sent hot water to both your chambers, Your Grace," her mother said. "Perhaps once you freshen up, you would like tea."

"Yes, please. In the drawing room," Miles said.

"Let me escort you to your guest chamber, Reverend Finchley," Trottmann said.

They all entered the house and Emery walked Miles to his rooms.

"Has everything gone smoothly in my absence? No trouble from my mother or Baron Haddoway?"

"Her Grace left the day after you departed and the dower house has been cleaned and aired again. Its staff has now been absorbed back into the main house. As for the baron, I haven't been to the village, as you requested."

Emery had been shocked to hear of Haddoway's abuse of the duchess and had no problem remaining at Wildwood while Miles had been gone.

"What of your parents?" he asked. "Are they settled here?"

"Yes. Mama says they have everything they need."

"How do you find the duchess' suite?"

"Incredibly large. And terribly lonely," she added.

Miles slipped an arm around her waist. "We can remedy that tonight. I hope that you will join me each evening, Emery. I want to fall asleep with you in my arms and awake each morning and make love to you."

His words warmed her. "I doubt it's done that way but I am more than happy to spend my nights with you."

He paused in front of his door. "I love you." He kissed her, giving her a small preview of what would come later that evening.

"I love you more. Ridiculously more," she said saucily.

"We shall see about that."

"I'll see to tea. I cannot wait to get to know Finch better."

Miles frowned. "It may be hard. He isn't as open as the other Terrors. We all were sent to Turner Academy for various reasons, none of them valid. Finch, though, is the only one of us who never shared why his family abandoned him there."

"It isn't important," she assured him. "Finch is your friend. That's all I truly need to know."

He went to kiss her again and she stepped away. "Go wash, Your Grace. I will be waiting for you in the drawing room."

Half an hour later, Emery had a maid roll in the teacart and found both her fiancé and his longtime friend already present. She dismissed the maid and poured out for the two men and then herself.

Watching Finch only put two items on his plate, she clucked her tongue. "You will be on Cook's naughty list if you eat no more than that, Finch."

"I was being polite," he proclaimed.

"Cook values a hearty appetite over politeness," she said. "So, tell me all about my future husband."

The young clergyman entertained her with various stories of

Miles and the other Turner Terrors.

"I am sorry your fellow Terrors cannot be with us," she said. "You seem like family."

"We are," declared Finch. "We always will be."

"I must thank you for coming to Wildwood and agreeing to perform our wedding ceremony."

Finch looked at her blankly. "I am?"

"Miles," she chided. "Did you not ask Finch to do so?"

He looked at her sheepishly. "I meant to. I just assumed he would."

"I will do it for Emery because I believe she will keep you on the straight and narrow," Finch said.

"Is anyone else outside of Wildwood coming?" she asked.

"Yes. Knowing the school was on its summer break, I went to Lord and Lady Marksbys' estate, Markham Park, which is only an hour from Turner Academy. Lord Marksby was friends with the Turner brothers and gave them the funding to begin the academy. They also invited the school's tutors and any students remaining to visit for a few weeks during the summer. The Terrors and I went every year."

It hurt her heart to know Miles and his friends were so unwanted by their families that they even spent holidays at the school.

"The Marksbys never had children and treated the Terrors as their own," Finch explained. "Lord Marksby also offered me the living associated with Markham Park. Once I finished university, I knew the path I would take."

"Both Lord and Lady Marksby will be in attendance," Miles continued. "As will Mr. Nehemiah and Mr. Josiah and their wives. Since they were both Mr. Turner, that is how we distinguished them from one another."

"I am happy they agreed to come," Emery said.

"They'll arrive Thursday, the day before the ceremony, along with Mr. Whitby, who taught languages, and Mr. Morris, who was the mathematics tutor. And Mr. Smythe."

"Who is he?" she asked.

"Mr. Smythe was a general servant," her betrothed explained. "He did a little of everything at the academy and was someone the Terrors turned to for advice."

"I look forward to meeting all of them. I need to let Mama know who is arriving so that enough bedchambers can be prepared for them." She rose. "In the meantime, why don't you show Finch the portrait of Garrick Notley and tell him about the journal."

"Who is Garrick Notley?" Finch asked.

"An ancestor of mine whom Emery found in the attic. His portrait. Not a dead body," Miles quipped.

"Too bad. It had all the makings of a fascinating story."

"It still is. Let's go see Garrick—and my portraits, as well. I want you to see Tony," Miles said quietly.

Emery left them and went to find her mother, informing her of the guests that would be arriving on Thursday and then sharing the same information with Cook.

She returned to the office to finish up her correspondence, satisfied that Miles would have people dear to him at their wedding ceremony.

One letter was from Mr. Fillmore, apologizing for not having replied to her inquiry regarding employment agencies sooner. He and his wife had gone to visit their son's family and had been away from London for a week. She said a quick prayer, knowing if the solicitor had answered her letter sooner, she might have left Wildwood, missing out on the life she would soon share with Miles.

Opening the final letter, she began reading and gasped. She forced herself to finish it and then folded it, placing it in her pocket.

The letter was unsigned. It spewed vile things about her. Intuition told her Baron Haddoway had written it. She was afraid to show it to Miles, fearing he would immediately call for Zeus and ride straight to the baron's estate and pummel him again.

Or worse.

Instead, she slipped the letter from her pocket and opened the bottom drawer of her desk, secreting it where she had placed the sketch of Miles that Lawrence Leavell had given her. She wouldn't trouble her fiancé about the anonymous ramblings. In three days' time, she would be the Duchess of Winslow and have the protection of his name.

Emery hoped that would be enough.

CHAPTER TWENTY-SEVEN

EMERY AWOKE IN her own bed in the rooms designated for the Duchess of Winslow.

She would become that duchess this morning.

She had insisted on sleeping in her own bed—alone—for the first time since Miles had returned. Convincing him to spend the night apart had been difficult but he had accepted her request in the end.

As long as it was the last time they would be parted.

Emery readily agreed. The days he had been gone when purchasing their special license and going to invite his friends to their wedding ceremony had seemed like years. She had no intention of being separated from him again. Ever.

He had shared his plans for their honeymoon. They would leave after the wedding breakfast this morning and head to London, where she was to receive an entire new wardrobe. When she balked at the idea, Miles told her that just as she had told him the people of Wildwood had expectations regarding their duke, the same would be true of their duchess, as well as members of Polite Society. She understood and agreed, finally becoming excited about the new clothes she would wear. Though neither of them wished to spend large amounts of time in London, he did want them to attend a few events of the Season while they were in town. Miles said he was eager to introduce his wife.

After a few weeks in London, they would travel as planned to several of his holdings. Emery was actually more excited about that part of their honeymoon than seeing London for the first time. She had corresponded with so many of the estate managers in recent years and couldn't wait to see all the places Miles had inherited. They had agreed that while on this trip, they would consider which of the stewards would be most suited to move to Wildwood to replace her father.

She rose as Addy entered with a breakfast tray, followed by her mother.

"It is a glorious day for a wedding. Hot water for your bath is coming, Emery. Addy, have you pressed my daughter's dress?"

"Yes, Mrs. Jenson. I'll fetch it now."

Both Emery and her mother had worked on the gown she would wear today, a mint green muslin trimmed with ribbons in a darker green. It was much fancier than what she was used to wearing but, after all, it was for her wedding.

She ate the single piece of toast, spread with marmalade, and drank the cup of tea to fortify herself. Soon, servants brought in buckets of hot water and Emery sank into the bathtub, where her mother had poured a small amount of lilac. The fragrance wafted up. Miles had told her how much he favored the scent on her and how he wanted lilac bushes planted at each of their estates.

After her bath, Addy helped Emery to dress and then Mama did her hair. She allowed a few ringlets to artfully frame Emery's face.

"There." Her mother touched Emery's shoulders as they both gazed into the mirror. "You look lovely." Mama paused. "Except for one thing."

Reaching into a pocket of the apron she wore, Mama said, "Close your eyes."

Emery did as asked and felt something going about her neck. "Open."

She did—and saw a necklace of pearls hanging there. She gasped.

"It is from His Grace. He wanted you to have a gift for your wedding day." Mama pulled something else from her pocket and opened her palm. "Earrings to match."

"It is so generous," Emery exclaimed.

"His Grace is a generous man," Mama agreed. She smiled as Emery put on the earrings. "I think you will suit very well together."

"I know we will. We have so many things we wish to do at Wildwood once we return from our honeymoon. We will be busy with that and dining once or twice a week with the various tenants."

"His Grace is an unusual man. I know, however, that he already had the respect of his people but with his marriage, he has earned their love."

Tears brimmed in both their eyes and they embraced.

"I must go change my clothes," Mama declared. "And make certain that your father is ready, too. I will see you downstairs in half an hour."

Emery bid her mother goodbye and then sat and looked at her image in the mirror. The pearls looked creamy against her skin. She had never owned jewelry of any kind and couldn't think of a better choice. She supposed she would be expected to wear jewels when they were in London. The pearls were tasteful and would go with any gown. She couldn't wait to thank Miles for such a lovely gift.

She went to the window and saw guests already coming up the drive, most likely those from Woodmorrow. They would not attend the ceremony but be at the breakfast that followed.

A knock sounded on the door. She hoped it wasn't Miles. Addy had told her it was bad luck for the bride to see her groom before the wedding, one of the reasons Emery, though not superstitious, had decided to sleep in her own bed last night.

She went to the door. "Who is it?"

"Your escort to your wedding," a voice replied.

She opened the door and found Finch standing there.

"I don't believe I have ever seen a more handsome vicar," she told him. "Please, come in. We still have a few minutes before we need to be downstairs."

In the days before their guests arrived, Finch had been charming and witty. He had teased Emery unmercifully, just as a brother would, and she had spent a good deal of time with him. Once the others arrived, though, Finch changed. Though he was familiar with everyone, he seemed to pull into himself. He was polite but distant.

"Are you comfortable with those attending the ceremony being present?" she asked.

He studied her a moment. "You are very perceptive, Emery."

"It's just that you seemed more outgoing before the others arrived."

Finch sighed. "I am only truly comfortable in the company of the Terrors," he admitted. "We spent over a decade together. Every single day. They know me as well as I know myself."

"And yet you never shared with any of them why you came to Turner Academy," she said softly.

"No. I didn't. I couldn't at first. It was too raw. Too painful. I didn't know whom I could trust. Once we became friends, it wasn't something I wished to talk about. It was as if it happened to another person. They accepted me all the same."

"Yet you still carry this burden within you." Emery touched his arm. "I hope someday, Finch, you will find the right person you can share your story with."

"I doubt it."

"Lord and Lady Marksby seem to dote on you."

"They have been good to me over the years. The Turner brothers, too. I am glad they could all come for today's ceremony."

Emery had liked the Marksbys on the spot. She and Lady Marksby had much in common and the countess had already invited Emery and Miles to come to Markham Park whenever they wished. She also liked the Turners and their wives and even gruff Mr. Smythe, the former soldier who served as a type of father figure to the Terrors.

"I came to ask you if there is anything special you wish for me to include in today's ceremony."

"Nothing I can think of," she admitted. "You must perform marriage ceremonies all the time."

"Yes—but not for those I consider to be family."

Finch bent and kissed her cheek. "Miles couldn't have chosen a better woman to make his duchess. And I benefit by having a new sister." He smiled at her. "Shall we make our way to the garden?"

He offered his arm and she accepted it. They went downstairs and through a set of French doors to the terrace. Emery saw her parents waiting.

"I'll give you a moment," Finch said. "Signal when you are ready to begin."

He left them and she went to her mother, who embraced her.

"I am so very proud of you, Emery."

"Don't cry, Mama."

"If I do, they are tears of joy." She touched her husband's sleeve. "My darling, you are to escort Emery to where those people are." Mama pointed at the semicircle in the distance. "Can you do that?"

"Of course," Papa said, sounding like his old self for a moment.

Mama kissed her again. "I love you." She went down the stairs, leaving Emery alone with her father.

"Why are we going to see those people? Shouldn't we be working?" he asked, letting her know that he didn't realize what was about to take place.

"Not today, Papa," she said gently. "I am getting married. To His Grace."

He looked startled. "You can't wed a duke."

"Why not?" she countered.

"I don't know," her father said blankly.

"Papa, I love Miles. Very much. And he loves me."

A glint came to her father's eyes. "You do? I love your mother, you know."

"I do know." She slipped her hand through his arm. "Miles is my choice, Papa. He is a good duke and a good man."

Her father smiled. "Then I hope you shall be happy together."

"We will be. I know it."

Emery glanced to Finch and nodded. He said something to those gathered and they all turned and looked as she and Papa came toward them. Her gaze went to Miles, standing there looking ever so handsome in a white waistcoat and a double-breasted dark blue coat. He even wore a striped cravat, probably Crowder's doing. His eyes never left hers as she came toward him. Her heart slammed against her ribs in excitement as she and Papa reached her groom.

"Thank you, Mr. Jenson," Miles said. "For trusting me with your daughter."

"She will make you proud, Your Grace," Papa said.

"That she will," Miles agreed.

Finch opened the small book he held and began the ceremony. He spoke of the solemnity of marriage and yet wove in a few lighthearted stories, the perfect mix of serious and joyful. As Emery spoke her vows to Miles, she thanked the heavens for bringing this man into her life.

Finch pronounced them man and wife and said to the small gathering, "I present to you the Duke and Duchess of Winslow."

Miles kissed her and then asked, "How does it feel to be a duchess?"

"I only like it because of you being my duke."

He kissed her again and then Mama said, "Shall we make our way to the breakfast?"

As their handful of guests went to join the others who had been invited to the celebration, Mama said, "Spend a few moments alone and then make your way inside." She hurried away, catching up to her husband.

"Your mother is a wise woman," her new husband said. "She knows I need privacy with my wife."

He slipped his arms around her as she linked her fingers behind his neck.

"I rather like hearing that. Wife," she said.

"Wife." He kissed her. "Wife," he murmured and kissed her again. "Wife," he said, almost growling the word and kissing her long and deep.

Emery reveled in hearing that word and enjoying those kisses. She pressed against him, ready to make love with him again.

Miles broke the kiss. "We cannot disappoint Cook and our guests. We must make an appearance at our own wedding breakfast."

"I suppose so."

He laced his fingers through hers. "Come, Emery Notley."

"Oh, that's right. I have a new name."

"And a title," he reminded her.

She smiled blissfully. "I rather like it. Emery Notley. It sounds as if it were meant to be."

They joined their guests in the ballroom, where Trottmann had ordered tables to be placed in order to accommodate the swell of people. A violinist began to play as she and Miles entered to applause. They spoke to a few guests as they headed to a table for two at the head of the room.

Soon, the first course came out and several more after that. Once they finished eating, she and her new husband circulated about the room, at first together and then separating to cover more ground.

Then a footman appeared and handed her a slip of paper. She opened it.

Come to the library.

She glanced about and saw Miles speaking with Mr. and Mrs. Oldham. She supposed he would slip away and join her. Emery excused herself and left the ballroom, heading for the library, chuckling to herself. Her handsome duke had planned a brief tryst in the middle of their wedding breakfast.

And she was delighted he had.

She would share a few kisses with him—maybe even more than kisses—and then she would change into traveling clothes since they were to leave for London soon.

Smiling to herself, Emery entered the library and closed the door behind her, thinking of future events they would host when she and Miles might slip away for a brief respite and indulge in kissing while their guests had no idea what their hosts were up to.

Then her feet stopped and her heart began to pound ferociously.

Baron Haddoway stood there.

With a pistol pointed at her heart.

CHAPTER TWENTY-EIGHT

M ILES MOVED THROUGH the crowded ballroom, trying to speak to as many people as possible. A slap on his back had him turn to look over his shoulder.

A smiling Kit grinned at him.

"So, you're an old married man now," his friend said. "It won't be long before fatherhood follows."

He knew Kit was joking but Miles hoped Emery would turn up with child in the next few weeks. He wanted a large family and would lavish each child of theirs with love.

Finch joined them and Miles introduced his two friends, excusing himself so he could continue about the room, knowing he and Emery were scheduled to leave soon for their honeymoon.

He greeted a married couple, tenants at Wildwood. "Mr. and Mrs. Oldham. Thank you so much for coming."

As he spoke to the couple, he glanced about the ballroom and found his wife. Emery was on the move, though, and left the ballroom. He wondered if she went to change and thought perhaps he might assist her. He excused himself and started toward the doors when a footman he didn't recognize handed him a slip of paper. Miles knew Trottmann had hired a few villagers to come in and help in the kitchens during the wedding and supposed he had done the same regarding footmen.

Reading the note, he bit back a smile.

It seemed his bride wanted to rendezvous in the library.

He strode from the room, eager to see her. Even more eager to kiss her. It was just like Emery to plan a short, sweet interlude of kissing on such a busy day. He tingled with anticipation as he entered the library and threw the lock, making sure they wouldn't be interrupted.

When Miles turned, fear struck him in an instant.

Baron Haddoway stood with a gun in his hand, trained upon Emery. She walked toward the older man with trepidation and had almost reached him.

"Stop!" he cried out.

Haddoway's eyes flicked to Miles. "Ah, I see His Grace has joined us. Good of you to do so."

He took a step forward and the baron said, "No," in a commanding tone, causing Miles to halt. Then Haddoway said to Emery, "Keep moving toward me," and she did, obviously reluctant.

"Stop, Emery," Miles pleaded.

She glanced over her shoulder. "Leave. I beg you."

"What? You're mad to think I would abandon you."

Her body shook. "He told me he would kill you," she said, her voice full of anguish.

As Miles moved toward his wife, Haddoway reached out and snatched her arm, pulling her close. His arm went about her waist, pinning her to him, the pistol, pressing against her temple. Fury and frustration rippled through Miles, followed by a feeling of helplessness.

"Don't hurt her. I beg you," he pleaded.

"She needs to be put in her place," the baron said.

"She is a duchess. She knows her place—and it is far above you," he snapped.

"Haven't you learned the lesson yet that all women are worthless? Your father and I knew it and acted accordingly. Women are meant to be used up and tossed aside, whether they are a whore or a high and mighty duchess." Haddoway smiled dreamily. "Ah, the days and nights I spent with your father, debasing useless women. Winslow was a real man. He was a master of putting a woman in her place."

He tightened his grip on Emery. "He would have enjoyed having his way with this one, so smug and pretentious. In fact, I believe your brother did so. Ralph confided in me how he wanted to deflower Miss Jenson." Haddoway laughed. "Ralph would be tickled that you got his leftovers."

Miles' mind raced, trying to figure out a way to save Emery. He couldn't believe he was in this same room again, a gun in play, the life of someone he loved at stake. Using a gun had been unavoidable during his army days and Miles had sworn never to pick up one again once he left the military. Not after what had happened to Tony in this room.

But how was he to rescue Emery?

By offering himself in her stead.

Miles began walking slowly to Baron Haddoway, his arms held wide, trying to convince the man he was no threat.

"Stop!" the baron cried.

"Take me," Miles said. "Let her go."

"No!" shouted Emery, her face devoid of color. "Don't sacrifice yourself for me, Miles."

He paused and gazed at her intently. "I would gladly walk through the fires of Hell a thousand times for you, Emery."

Haddoway now pointed the gun at Miles, who began moving forward again, knowing a small bit of progress had been made with the gun no longer pointed at his wife.

"Stop, Winslow," the baron said nervously. "I mean it."

"I do, too, Haddoway. Let Emery go. You have no quarrel with her. I am the one who beat you. Embarrassed you in public. Deal with me."

He had almost reached them. Only a few more steps.

Then Emery screamed loudly, piercing the air. She stomped on the baron's foot. The nobleman staggered back. Haddoway lost his grip on her and he lowered the gun, trying to snatch her back. Miles threw himself in the air, knocking Haddoway to the ground, allowing Emery to escape his grasp.

The baron brought the pistol up as they struggled, the gun now between them. Miles clamped his fingers on Haddoway's wrist, forcing it to turn away.

Then the gun went off, the noise shattering. The pistol fell to the ground. Miles struck Haddoway hard, slamming his fist into the older man's temple, stunning him. He scampered off the baron and kicked the gun away.

Emery flew into his arms and he clung to her, telling her over and over that it was all right.

A pounding sounded at the door and he remembered he had locked it. He released his hold on Emery and took her hand, pulling her in the direction of the door, away from Haddoway, who sat up, dazed. Flinging it open, he found Trottmann standing there, along with several people behind him.

"Fetch the magistrate. As discreetly as possible," Miles said and then he closed the door.

His wife wrapped her arms about his waist. "What will happen to him?" she asked anxiously.

Miles looked across the room as Haddoway rose unsteadily to his feet.

"Whatever does, he will not trouble us again. That I will guarantee."

Trottmann returned with Sir William Grant and Dr. Collier. For a moment, Miles grew queasy, seeing the magistrate in the library again, everything that had happened years ago with Tony and Ralph flooding back. He steeled himself, knowing Emery needed him in the present and not the past.

"Baron Haddoway tried to kill my wife and me," he told Sir William. And then he added, "He also forced himself upon my mother many years ago."

Sir William's brows rose a good inch. "I see."

By now, the baron had dragged himself into a chair and sat stonily as his eyes darted from Miles back to Sir William.

Dr. Collier stepped forward. "I am not excusing Baron Haddoway's behavior but I want you to know that he is very ill."

"How ill?" Miles asked. "Enough to try to murder a duke and his duchess on their wedding day?"

"I am dying," Haddoway said succinctly.

All eyes turned to the baron.

Sir Williams asked the physician, "Is this true?"

Collier nodded. "I diagnosed Baron Haddoway myself. He had the diagnosis confirmed in London. He won't live but another two or three months."

The magistrate cleared his throat and then said, "It could get very ugly, Your Grace. Trying to bring Haddoway to justice. I doubt you want that."

He didn't, mostly because he didn't want Emery exposed to it. Though she was his duchess now, there would always be a few members of the *ton* who would speak ill of her. He refused to add fuel to any fires they might try to set.

"What do you suggest?" he asked Sir William.

"I could place him under house arrest. See that he does not leave his estate until he passes."

"Very well. See to it," Miles said. "Only keep him in this room for now." He glanced to his butler. "What does anyone know?"

"Your guests are still in the ballroom, Your Grace," Trottmann said, unflappable as always. "A noise was heard— which I came to investigate—and I reported it was nothing to worry about. I was very careful in finding Sir William and bringing him here."

"Good." He looked to Emery. "Go and change. I think it best we leave for London at once. Can you do that?"

Love for him shone in her eyes. "Of course, Your Grace," she said and left the room.

"Trottmann, send Her Grace's mother up to her to help her ready herself. Dr. Collier, we should return to the ballroom." Glancing to Sir William, he said, "Only bring him out once we and the guests have left."

"Yes, Your Grace. And I will keep the matter quiet."

Haddoway finally spoke. "Would you really treat me so unkind, Winslow? There is a possibility that I am your father."

Miles stiffened at the words. He went to stand before the man who had wronged his mother so long ago, the one who might have killed Emery. Only through sheer willpower did he keep from using Haddoway as a punching bag.

"You may have raped my mother but I am not a result of your misdeeds. I closely resemble my great-grandfather, Garrick Notley. Our portraits hang side-by-side in my picture gallery. There is no doubt—I am a Notley. I do hope, however, that you rot in Hell with the previous two Dukes of Winslow. Even then, that is probably too good for you."

He gestured to the physician and the two men left the room, returning to the ballroom. Stoic as ever, Miles pretended as if nothing had happened, going about to greet every guest he hadn't spoken to previously. Within a quarter-hour, Trottmann approached him.

"Her Grace is ready, Your Grace," the butler said.

"Thank you." Miles turned to the room. "The Duchess of Winslow and I are leaving for London now. We will honeymoon there and across England, where we will visit some of our estates. Upon our return, I hope to dine with many of you. If you would now, please accompany us outside so we might say our farewells."

He spied Mr. Jenson, looking a bit lost, and went to his new father-in-law.

"Mr. Jenson, come and say goodbye to Emery and me."

"Oh, yes, Your Grace," the older man said and Miles led his steward to the foyer.

Emery and Mrs. Jenson awaited them and he handed off the steward to his wife and then took Emery's hand in his.

"Everything all right?" he asked lightly.

She gave him a sweet smile. "It is now that I am with you

again."

Leading her from the house, they went to the waiting carriage. Once inside, they waved goodbye as their driver started up the team. Miles heard cheers as the vehicle rolled down the lane.

Once out of sight, he pulled his bride onto his lap and kissed her thoroughly.

"London awaits us," he proclaimed after breaking the kiss.

Emery stroked his cheek. "As long as we are together, it doesn't matter where this carriage goes. How long until we reached the great city?"

With a wicked grin, Miles said, "We have plenty of time to entertain ourselves." His hand slipped under her skirts and stroked her sleek calf.

"Take all the time you need, Your Grace. I am all yours."

"I think I wish to make love to my bride in our ducal carriage," he declared.

"Oh, you do, do you?" Emery paused a moment and then asked, "Then what is taking you so long?"

Miles laughed, feeling the last of the chains of his past dissipate, and kissed his duchess.

EPILOGUE

Wildwood—October 1811

M ILES GAZED DOWN at his son. "Is it wrong to say that a boy is beautiful?" he asked softly.

"Not at all," Emery said, snuggling closer to him, resting her head on his shoulder.

They sat in bed together, watching the baby sleep. He had only been in the world two weeks but they were the best two weeks of Miles' life. The love that filled him every time he looked at Ben threatened to spill out. He couldn't imagine being happier.

Emery had wanted to call their baby Anthony, after his brother. Miles had told her it was kind of her to want to honor Tony's memory but he wanted their boy to be his own person, with no remnant of the past. They had both liked the name Benjamin and so their son became Ben.

"He's already changed so much since his birth," Miles noted.

"Mama said that happens, especially during the first year. That his hair may fall out and come in a different color. Even the color of his eyes could change."

Ben's eyes were blue now, identical to his father's. In a way, Miles hoped they would stay this way.

"I think we should send for Mr. Leavell," he told her. "He could capture Ben at this age and continue to do so every few months."

Emery laughed, that deep, throaty laugh that always caused desire to ripple through him.

"If Mr. Leavell paints Ben that often, he might as well come and live at Wildwood," she told him. "The house is large but eventually we might run out of space on the walls to hang all those portraits."

Pressing a kiss against his temple, she added, "There will be other babies to consider. You wouldn't want to take up all the wall space with pictures of Ben."

Miles turned and brushed his lips against hers. "Then once a year. Leavell can paint him. And with Ben's brothers and sisters once they come along. Each year we can see how Ben changes and how we add to our brood."

She chuckled. "Whatever you want, my wonderful duke. I have found I can never say no to you."

His wife kissed him tenderly, and Miles' heart soared with love. "I can never thank you enough for having Leavell paint Papa and Mama. Even though he has passed, it brings me comfort to see him brought to life in that portrait. It will allow Ben—and any future siblings—to know what their grandfather looked like as I tell stories of him to them. It is a gift that I will forever cherish. Just as I cherish you, my love."

He cupped her cheek. "I hope Wyatt is as happy as we are."

His friend had returned to England this past February. With the unexpected death of his brother, Wyatt had become the Duke of Amesbury. It had been wonderful having Wyatt back in England.

And watching him fall in love and marry his own duchess.

Miles bent and kissed his son's brow. "Ben will be the best duke of all."

Emery stroked her husband's cheek. "That will be many years down the road. For now, my husband is the best Duke of Winslow. The man I married. The father of my child. The man I will always love."

He kissed her tenderly, happy in their present.

And eager to see what their future would bring.

About the Author

Award-winning and internationally bestselling author Alexa Aston's historical romances use history as a backdrop to place her characters in extraordinary circumstances, where their intense desire for one another grows into the treasured gift of love.

She is the author of Regency and Medieval romance, including: Dukes of Distinction; Soldiers & Soulmates; The St. Clairs; The King's Cousins; and The Knights of Honor.

A native Texan, Alexa lives with her husband in a Dallas suburb, where she eats her fair share of dark chocolate and plots out stories while she walks every morning. She enjoys a good Netflix binge; travel; seafood; and can't get enough of *Survivor* or *The Crown*.